THE FANGS OF SUET PUDDING

THE FANGS OF SUET PUDDING

ADAMS FARR

With an Introduction by

Chris Mikul

RAMBLE HOUSE

ISBN 13 978-1-60543-559-6

ISBN 10 1-60543-559-7

First published in 1944 (GB)
Published 2011 by Ramble House

Preparation: Fender Tucker, Gavin L. O'Keefe
and Chris Mikul

INTRODUCTION

You may not be able to judge a book by its cover, but you can often tell quite a lot about it by its title. And that, happily, is the case with the remarkable volume that you hold in your hands.

I first read about *The Fangs of Suet Pudding* in Russell Lake and Brian Ash's marvellous compendium of literary oddities, *Bizarre Books* (1985). Lake and Ash are book dealers who had been collecting weird, and weirdly titled, books for years, and this book brought together the best of them – *Scouts in Bondage*, *Fish Who Answer the Telephone* and *The Romance of Leprosy*, to name just a few. Since the late nineties, some of the books featured in it have been displayed in the window of Ash's shop, Jarndyce, in London. Situated across the road from the British Museum, Jarndyce specialises in nineteenth century literature, and walking into the shop, with its wood panelling and tall shelves stocked with elegant, leather-bound volumes, is a bit like travelling back in time. Whenever I am in London, I always spend a few minutes marvelling at the window display, and the book in there I most longed to own was *The Fangs of Suet Pudding*. After all, the humour in most of these books does not go much beyond the title (I mean, I have never read *Scouts in Bondage*, and for all I know it's a laugh riot from beginning to end, but somehow I suspect it's not). *The Fangs of Suet Pudding*, on the other hand, promised to be a genuinely strange reading experience. Certainly the brief passage from it quoted in *Bizarre Books* suggested as much.

When the internet came along and booksellers went online, one of the first titles I searched for was *Suet Pudding*, but as I soon discovered, it is now a very scarce item. (The copy in the window of Jarndyce, by the way, disappeared some time ago, presumably into the hands of a collector who made an offer too good to refuse.) Finally, after years of searching, I located a copy—in South Africa! I read it as soon as it arrived, eager to find out if it would fulfill the promise of its title.

Oh, it did.

The Fangs of Suet Pudding was first published by Gerald G. Swan in London in 1944. That first edition is a small hardback produced to war economy standard with cheap paper and tiny print, but with a striking and colourful dustjacket by Douglas Lovern-West depicting the pallid face of the villainous Suet Pudding, a fleet of German bombers, and the chateau in France where some of the book's action takes place.

Gerald Swan was an enterprising fellow who began his career as a bookseller in the early thirties specialising in American comics and children's papers. He started his publishing company in 1938 and, in a stroke of genius, printed a great quantity of material in its first year of operation which he stored in three London warehouses. When war broke out and other publishers faced chronic paper shortages, Swan slowly released this material onto the market. Over the next few years he issued a stream of books and magazines, mainly in the crime, science fiction, western and romance genres, as well as comics, children's annuals and the like, and his cheap and cheerful productions must have brightened the lives of many during the war. His most prolific author was William J. Elliott, who specialised in American-style crime novels with titles like *Freak Racket* and *Snatched Dame*, along with a series about a charming British vigilante named Silk. Swan treated his authors squarely, paying promptly on delivery of a manuscript, and while most of his output is not known for its literary qualities, to say the least, he did publish more than a few unusual and interesting items, including some of the early works of thriller writer Elleston Trevor, and the first historical novel by Jean Plaidy. But I doubt that anything else he published comes close to *The Fangs of Suet Pudding*.[1]

Adams Farr's book contains all the elements that might be expected in a thriller—a ruggedly handsome and resourceful hero (or two), an impossibly evil villain, car chases, shoot-outs, false identities, an underground lair, a torture chamber, plenty

---

[1] Swan continued to publish at a giddy pace until 1960. For more information about him see *The Mushroom Jungle: a History of Postwar Paperback Publishing* by Steve Holland (Zeon, 1993).

of narrow escapes and a mad scientist who has invented the most powerful bomb in the world – but it is the way that these elements are juggled together which makes it unique. From the moment that the book's narrator, Loreley Vance, wakes one morning during a storm to find a stranger lurking outside her bedroom window, the narrative unfolds in a way that is anything but formulaic or predictable. While the backdrop of the Nazi invasion of France is dramatic and deftly drawn, and the book does have its moments of seriousness, its overall tone is more like a screwball comedy with surreal touches.

And towering above it all is the figure of Suet Pudding[2] himself, Carl Vipoering, that violet-scented "jelloid Nazi", that "expert in blood and terror", that "apostle of savage intrigue". He's a remarkable creation, more hallucination than human being.

> *A distorted vision of Suet Pudding rose like a grey balloon in front of my eyes. Balloon-fashion, he seemed to stir the atmosphere around me – sluggishly, like a pond in which mud is busy settling.*

Wartime and the imperatives of propaganda invite a writer to caricature the enemy, of course, but it seems to me that passages like this go beyond caricature, creating a palpable vision of evil which is genuinely compelling.

As this suggests, while *The Fangs of Suet Pudding*'s innumerable oddities of plotting and characterisation would be enough to make it notable, what makes it work as a book—and as a thriller—is the wonderfully engaging voice of its narrator, who combines a certain wide-eyed innocence with plenty of that quality the British used to call 'pluck', and constantly surprises with her unusual turns of phrase. On seeing the body of a man stabbed to death, she declares how sickened she is at seeing "all that surplus blood out of so small a body". Describing the chaos as the Germans invade France, she notes that "On the

---

[2] For those who may not be familiar with it, suet pudding is a quintessentially English dish, usually a dessert, the chief ingredient of which is suet, the hard fat around the kidneys and loins of cattle or sheep. Mmm!

roads north, panic-rotted people were strangling everything." Loreley's way with a sentence may be a trifle odd but it is often very effective, and her enthusiasm for the wild adventure she finds herself in ("My world was widening rapidly."), mixed with occasional bouts of terror, inevitably draw the reader along with her.

Loreley's voice rings so true that I am sure that *The Fangs of Suet Pudding* was written by a woman. And this brings us to the central mystery surrounding the book—who was Adams Farr? *Suet Pudding* is the only book published under this name, by Swan or anyone else, but it's such an assured—if somewhat crazed—performance that I find it hard to believe it could have been the author's only work. Some have speculated that it was written by one of Swan's regular authors under a pseudonym, and I suppose that there is an outside possibility it was an experiment by one of his romance authors, for it plays with the conventions of that genre as it does with those of the thriller. It also seems likely that the author spent time living in France, for the background detail seems natural and unforced. But all of this is just speculation. (Needless to say, if anyone reading this has any information about Adams Farr, I'd love to hear from you.)

Anyway, enough speculation. It's time to go to France. It's 1942, the Germans are invading, and there are games of snakes-and-ladders to play!

[Thanks to Gerald G. Swan enthusiast Andrew Parry for providing information about the publisher.]

Chris Mikul
Australia 2011

THE FANGS OF SUET PUDDING

CHAPTER I

THE BURGLAR UNDER THE BED

I WAS AWAKENED EXACTLY AT MIDNIGHT. It was June, 1940, and, thanks to Aunt Sophie's stubborn refusal to leave French hospitality, we were still at Vieux Bonnat. To quiet my elastic-sided heart, I decided it was nothing more than a thunderstorm plus our English passion for fresh air that had brought me awake, and got out of bed to shut the creaking window. I put my foot into a puddle of rain-water on Aunt Sophie's new carpet—and came face to face with a strange man staring at me from the garden.

"May I come in?" he whispered in English. I heard Aunt Sophie making wakeful noises in her room across the passage.

"Who are you?" I whispered.

"A burglar!" he hissed.

"Oh!" I said.

He was quite young, with a pleasantly interesting face, and he looked half-drowned and very clean. I suppose it was tantamount to starting another war, but in the middle of Hitler's effort, a half-drowned burglar was so prosaically English that my heart warmed. With a gulp of thankfulness I remembered that the valuables had been banked at Bordeaux.

He threw a hunted look over his shoulder.

"For God's sake, let me in!" he pleaded; "it's a matter of life and death!"

Strange as it may seem, I believed him. I was either mad or *fey*—I didn't know which.

"All right," I said; "but for goodness' sake, mind the paintwork!"

His strained face broke into a grin—a nice, heartening grin that looked as if it habitually belonged to the rest of his face—and he threw a leg over the sill. At which instant, I heard Aunt Sophie coming.

I clenched my teeth. Aunt Sophie is a dear, but, outside international situations, she does fuss so. I gave one last glance at the rain streaming down outside, dragged my eyes back to the young man half inside my bedroom and apparently as paralysed as myself—and, in blind panic, pulled in the rest of him.

"Quick!" I gasped; "Under the bed! And mind the big trunk!"

He nodded casually and dived. A smothered "Damn!" told me he had found the trunk. The man was English all right.

"Good gracious, child, get that window shut!" commanded Aunt Sophie, bustling into the room. "Think of the carpet!"

Amongst other things, I was thinking of the carpet. On its virgin surface, besides the original puddle, it now flaunted a row of large, masculine footprints. I made a desperate effort to stand over them, reply adequately, shut the three of us inside, and not show the strain.

"Darling!" I yelped, with harrowing inspiration, "I believe I left the bathroom window open!"

It worked. The paintwork in the bathroom was also new. By some happy chance, too, her woollen combinations were on my chair. They were ideal moppers-up of footprints, but I feverishly prayed *le bon Dieu* that I should have time to wash them out again before the weather turned colder. They fell scraggily from my hand as I heard her coming back, and I had sufficient sense to kick them under the bed. I was forming an interesting collection under that bed.

"Don't stand there shivering in that thin nightdress, child!" said my aunt.

I sat weakly on the bed. I thought I heard a faint gulp underneath.

"All right, darling; I'm just getting in," I said. "Put out the light, there's a dear!"

She tucked me up and then brought me a dose of eucalyptus. Next came a duster and some brisk work on the wet window-sill. I closed my eyes. I was by this time in a quiet heat that, had she but known, made her eucalyptus quite superfluous.

It was a long time before I looked out again.

"Are you still there?" I gave faint whisper.

"I am," came the male whisper from underneath.

Well, it was ridiculous to lie there one on top of the other like a couple of pieces of luggage in the lost property office. I got out, wrapped a dressing gown round me, and once more put on the light.

Except for the absence of Aunt Sophie, we then seemed very much in the *status quo.* I groveled on my hands and knees on the floor and peered at him.

Clutching Aunt Sophie's combinations, he blinked out at me.

Otherwise, as far as appearances went, he looked all right. Rather like a wet dog asking to be tickled down his back. Not that he wanted his back tickled, of course.

"I say, d'you want me to get up now?" be enquired courteously and softly.

That was just the point. The possibility was that he would prove more of a problem on his feet than curled up underneath the bed. The next thing I knew, he had answered his own question: we were both up, and he had his hands on my shoulders.

It occurred to me that this was where I ought to scream for Aunt Sophie.

"You're a damn' good little scout," he said—and, quite ridiculously, I thrilled. It was an educated, pleasantly pitched voice, and somehow inspired confidence. Shrugging myself free, I tried to get back to the point at issue.

What was I going to do with him now I had got him inside? Aunt Sophie slept with her door wide open and one ear provisionally at half-cock. The only other concession she made to a warring world was a night light in the passage. It was too much to hope that this light was not functioning on this night of all nights.

"Look here," explained the burglar suddenly, "I'm in a particularly devilish hole."

Well, I knew that, perhaps even better than he did. If Aunt Sophie caught him now . . .

My knees wobbled afresh. Yet one could not turn a dog out into a night like this. I repeated to myself that he was not a dog. He was an Englishman in a hole. An Englishman, moreover, of my own class. The fact that he was young and good-looking was merely incidental. But the more I considered his predicament, the more I saw that, unless he went out into the rain again, he would have to stay in my bedroom.

"Eh?" he jerked, as I explained these alternatives. He looked so embarrassed that I felt an immediate and appreciable rise in my own confidence.

"Aunt Sophie!" I added in a brief whisper.

"Oh!" This time he nodded gravely and understandingly.

The rain was challenging us on the window. I studied him frankly. He had said it was a matter of life and death, and I believed him. But Aunt Sophie must never find out.

"You could get under the bed again," I suggested.

He nodded.

"Yes, I suppose I could."

"You could also take off that awful wet mackintosh and let it dry a bit."

"Yes," he said again, "I could do that."

"For heaven's sake," I stamped my foot in sudden irritation—and brought it hard against the bed in the process—"make up your mind!"

He gave the grin of the real enthusiast at the mishap to my toes and then became admirably serious.

"What do I do with this?" he breathed, holding out his mackintosh.

I stopped the massage of my toes and considered it. First the man, then his mackintosh. Naturally, my bedroom was not designed to cope with such irregularities. Coldly, I motioned it away. What did he think?

"Roll it up and put it on top of the trunk. Then it will be nice and handy in case Aunt Sophie comes in again,"

"Oh!" he jerked; but he did exactly as he was told.

I found we were both frowning at the accommodation I was offering him. I added a couple of blankets from the box under the window, and he had a grateful look in his eye as he disappeared with them. I turned out the light. This time, I decided, I would like the curtains drawn back as well.

His head popped out behind me, and then disappeared again.

"For the love of Mike, don't open them too far! They may be searching the garden for me!"

I waited for my heart-beats to return to normal.

"It is the police, not a mental home?" I enquired frigidly.

I felt rather than saw him wriggle.

"Well?" I pressed.

I guessed from the sound of his voice that he had wriggled again.

"Well—er—" he said. Then lay just vegetating.

He was quite right. What I didn't know, I couldn't worry about. I climbed back into bed. Besides, belated explanations might cause his voice to rise dangerously. Then Aunt Sophie would come in armed with a poker, and I should cease to feel like the original Good Samaritan, in favour of the idiot I probably was.

"Thank you," came his polite, astonishingly easy whisper from underneath me; "I'll be pushing off early in the morning."

"What time?" I asked.

"Oh—er—somewhere about dawn, don't y'know."

It did not sound too cheerful a time to me, but I suppose burglars can't be choosers. For some time I found myself listening hard for any sound that he might make. Finally, his faint, even breathing told me he was prosaically asleep. With a vague idea that if Hitler started bombing Vieux Bonnat that night, I should have to join him under the bed, I at last dropped off myself, and dreamt that Aunt Sophie was chasing a black and white striped elephant with a poker.

~ ~ ~ ~ ~

But Fate nearly brought our scheme to disaster. It was long past dawn when I awoke. Aunt Sophie was moving about in the kitchen. I felt curiously excited even before I remembered . . .

When I did, I broke out into a cold sweat. I had been mad all right! I sat up in bed and pushed the hair out of my eyes. And, with a fresh shock, I realised that—now it was safely over—I was *glad* I had zipped up my courage to it. In these days, that one night's sanctuary might have meant such a lot. Moreover, I knew quite well that I wouldn't have been able to sleep a wink, picturing a fellow-countryman like that slinking about from one rain-soaked spot to another. Completely satisfied with myself—though I suppose it was all part of the madness that I had been able to sleep at all—I smiled. If I ever met him again, of course—which was improbable—I should cut him dead. Then—

I felt myself becoming as rigid as death. Without foundation, without reasoning, I knew that my midnight visitor was still under the bed!

He was using the top part of Aunt Sophie's combinations as a pillow.

"Here, wake up!" I whispered feebly. "It's nearly 8 o'clock!"

He turned over and grunted.

I got out of bed and pulled with both hands at his blankets.

"What the hell—?" he enquired, and yawned wide to heaven.

There were times when I had been exceedingly bored with my careful upbringing, but, even in France, was it better to be found with a young man in your room at midnight, or at eight o'clock in the morning? Across the passage, Aunt Sophie sounded ominously quiet. I could picture her, horror dawning in large, comprehensive chunks . . .

With the easy vitality that seemed characteristic of all his actions, the wretch crashed his head into the wire mattress.

"Damn and blast!" he hissed.

He was now wholly awake.

Aunt Sophie opened the door.

"Good gracious, darling, fancy finding you out of bed before you're called!" Was she being subtle? I could only smile a weak smile and creep back to the bed again. Supposing the burglar underneath sneezed, or something?

"What's the News?" I begged frantically.

"Oh, jam and pickles, as usual. But it does seem to be true that they've taken Rouen." This was a disaster she had refused to believe yesterday.

Rouen! I caught my breath. That terrible red gash of the Nazis into France was deepening frighteningly. I looked up into my aunt's calm face. After all, as she said, we were a long way from the front line. The retreat must be stopped soon.

"I think I'll turn your mattress, my dear, while you're in the bathroom," she said. "It's a marvellous morning again after the storm, and the sun will get to it nicely."

I had no doubt about that.

"But, darling," I just breathed through the constriction round my throat, "surely it can wait till after breakfast, when Marie can help you?" Marie is our *cuisiniere's* niece, and periodically comes in to help Tante Theresa.

My aunt sniffed.

"If I can't manage a bit of a bed like that without Marie—!"

"Well, of course you could," I hastened to reassure her, "but you really ought to be more careful, darling. You don't want to strain anything."

It sounded weak even to me. She looked at me straightly, and I almost sobbed out the whole story. Apparently satisfied that if I were sickening for anything, I had not yet come out in spots, she pushed me towards the door.

"You run along to your bath, child, and don't worry about me."

It was the young man under the bed I was chiefly concerned about, but I couldn't tell her that. I fled.

It was a most unusual bath; profligate more in imagination than soap. My mind bubbling like a witch's cauldron, I pictured Aunt Sophie turning my bed . . . the discovery of the masculine intruder . . . I alternated between frenzies to hurry to the spot and frenzies to linger at a safe distance. Maybe I lingered too long. At last, heart in mouth, comparatively clean knees wobbling, feeling a cross between Lady Macbeth and Nell Gwyn, I went back. The burglar was dusting the seat of his trousers in front of my wardrobe glass.

"Oh!" he said.

"Oh!" I echoed. And quickly shut the door behind me.

"She's gone?" I whispered. It was an unnecessary as well as a stupid question. Aunt Sophie has not the type of figure one could miss in my bedroom.

I liked the serene, English, matter-of-fact way he moved across to me. A miracle had happened. The first, had I known it, of many. He had not yet seen more of Aunt Sophie than her feet and possibly six inches of ankle. He laid her combinations and the neatly folded blankets in my arms like a lily.

"For some ghastly minutes," he whispered dramatically, "I thought she was going to lay violent hands on the thin piece of felt that lay between me and discovery!" He had the grace to mop his forehead at the remembrance. "She contented herself with straightening the edges . . . Good God, here she is again! See you later!"

With that, he was across the room and out of the window, leaving me still clutching the blankets and looking once more as if I had been hit between the eyes with a hammer.

It was not until after breakfast that I discovered he had left his mackintosh under the bed. Aunt Sophie was not present at the time.

CHAPTER II

THE CHÂTEAU DES ROCHES

IT WAS THE FOLLOWING EVENING, and, after twelve hours of baking sunshine, raining again with midsummer madness.

"Loreley, you cannot possibly go out on a night like this!" said Aunt Sophie.

I had known, of course, that there would be trouble, but, even if it killed me, I was determined to go to Bobby Treslin's farewell party at the Château. I stopped wriggling into my new cyclamen georgette and turned as tragically angelic a countenance as I could manage. Being a natural blonde but for the misfit of two "large, soft brown eyes like a gazelle's" (Cousin Dick on a certain occasion), it was not too difficult. Aunt Sophie, although she should have been fairly hardened by now, reconsidered me.

"Well," she decided, "if you wear your mackintosh and your galoshes, and fasten up your dress with an elastic round the waist, perhaps you'll be all right. And, if you're careful with it, you can take my umbrella."

"Thank you, darling," I said.

She eyed me suspiciously. Fortunately, at that moment the door bell rang.

"That must be Bobby!" I chirped.

"Loreley!" came my aunt's voice grimly behind me.

"Yes, darling?" I was almost out of the room, clutching the door like a defensive barrier. But it was only that I had left my dress hitched up at the back like a bustle. I had to admit that it did not show the dress at any rate to advantage. Not that Bobby would mind. From the saucy glint in his eyes when I did appear, I think he heard anyway.

"Am I," he enquired in a sort of pained surprise, "seeing things? Or is the child nearly ready?"

I have known Bobby Treslin since he and Cousin Dick took it in turns to stick pins into my rag doll, so in spite of his present six feet one and a bit, I put him back into his proper place at once.

He took it with his usual equanimity, but he knew now he had at least another half-hour to wait. It was Aunt Sophie's fault that this became three-quarters. To my disgust, the wretch looked practically asleep when at last I was ready for him. Do all men drop off for forty winks when no one is looking? Perhaps their mighty brains need constant resting?

"My dear!" he sighed; and, to his everlasting credit, he managed to infer the restless energy of a horse being led from the paddock. We were both over-optimistic, however.

"Here is a pair of my woollen stockings you can put on over those stupid silk ones," declared Aunt Sophie.

I caught my escort's grin out of the corner of my eye.

"But, darling," I said indignantly, "I'm wearing galoshes!"

"These will keep your knees warm," suggested Bobby, thoroughly refreshed by his nap.

"Besides," said Aunt Sophie, "Mr. Treslin's car is almost certain to break down on one or both of the journeys."

"My dear Miss Vance!" said Bobby, properly shocked.

"But—but haven't you any but those awful check things?" I stammered, knowing I should have to come to woollen stockings sooner or later, and trying to avoid the worst.

My aunt sniffed. Bobby, the large and perfect gentleman, stepped into the breach.

"These are probably All Wool, y'know." I was aware of that. I could have gone for him with a meat chopper. Without another word, I held out my hand.

"Run along to your room and put them on, darling," crooned my aunt, beaming again.

There, chin in air, I became actively belligerent.

"If I can't put them on where I am, I'm going without them!"

"Good gracious, Bobby," said Aunt Sophie, in the sudden silence, turning uneasily to that poor, purblind male with his handkerchief to his face, "you haven't a cold, have you?"

He withdrew the handkerchief, and very wisely decided that he hadn't a cold. In fact, realising the importance of his denial, he rather youthfully overdid it. For the rest of the time, my aunt divided her anxiety equally between us.

"Dear old soul, your aunt," was Bobby's characteristic comment as he opened the gate for me.

Bobby Treslin should have lived in an age when Knights were Bold. He had the cheerful blond size for it. What he did for a contemporary living—except range, bachelor-fashion, between England and France—I was suddenly surprised to find I didn't know. It was his grandfather, the dashing young cavalry officer from England, who had married the famous and beautiful Comtesse de Treslin; hence Bobby's title to the Château des Roches.

Built by a Charles de Treslin in 1572, Bobby loved his grandmother's Château; loved every stick and stone of it. But now . . . well, even before the war, he had never been well off, and now he just couldn't afford to keep it up any longer. Looking back, I felt a certain pride in the very correct dinners he had given here from time to time. Opulent-looking guests, arriving in opulent-looking limousines, cannot be fed on bread and cheese. Not that Bobby's wide circle of friends and acquaintances were all like overweight spaniels. Far from it. Peter Westlake and the Tampler boy, for instance, his two English pals who were often at the Château: Peter had a long, pale face and the figure of a professional skater. But there, again, so far as I know, there was no caviare or special delving into the cellar for him. They may have had it on the quiet, of course. Still . . . I had to admit this for Bobby's crowd: they were a little different from the portly, lean-eyed humans who usually included Vieux Bonnat on their way to cure the malefactions of their livers at Vichy Spa.

I was still trying to clarify to myself the essential difference when Bobby's car broke down. It annoys me intensely to find that Aunt Sophie is so often right. We sat for some time expecting a tow from somebody, and then, as Bobby was the host, and it would be better if he arrived at the Château before his guests, we got out and walked. I think I was rather rude to him. He informed me that if I didn't look where I was going, I should land in a ditch. Which would, he went on to explain carefully, be *malheureux* as we were so nearly there. I thought he might have put it another way, and said so.

Through the slashing rain, I could now make out the big stone entrance to the Château, with its curious old gargoyles. Bobbing up between these came Pierre, the *cocher,* with a lantern and a wide grin of welcome. Which was typical of both Pierre and Bobby.

Then a hand seemed suddenly to close over my throat, and I stopped dead in a puddle. Silhouetted in the thundery fight against the blue-black pines on the opposite side of the gorge over which it had held sovereignty for centuries, with its wet, gleaming steps, its dim, cloister-like arches and slender turrets, the Château looked like a dream out of some misty, rather awesome fairyland. Moreover, tumultuous years, beating, intriguing against its turreted walls, had matured it into a root that had anchored a roaming Treslin breed for generations.

"Oh, Bobby!" I said impulsively, "isn't money damnable!"

He looked at me queerly for a moment, and I thought he was going to say something. Then he pulled me forward, and I saw that he had been standing in a puddle too. Close together under Aunt Sophie's umbrella, with the drippings raining down his neck, we trudged on. As was so often the case, with the queer thread of understanding that there was between us, we had no real need of words.

"Probably it will be requisitioned by the Government, and then after the war a nice fat American will take it over," he said at last. "Unless, of course, a miracle happens in between."

Unfortunately, one couldn't just order a miracle by telephone. How often in the uncomfortably near future was I to wish we could! I gave the arm in mine a good squeeze, and the drippings from the umbrella transferred themselves to my own neck.

"Bobby!"

"Yes?"

"What are you going to do when—when you get to England?" It was like a slap in the face, that question. Bobby had always been here when I wanted him . . .

"Oh, find some blinkin' field and be a lily in it, I suppose," he drawled cheerfully, searching his neck for some of the umbrella drippings; "that is, until they find some nice, sunny niche for me in the war effort."

I looked at him steadily, putting my own interpretation on his words. Bobby's age-group was not yet due to be called up, but I had a secret conviction that he had pushed himself forward with some priority notice.

"I have," I said, reverting to the safer first part of his speech (after all, if he didn't want to tell me, he didn't), "seen better lilies in our dustbin."

He seemed taken aback.

"I wish—" He stopped. "Well, we've got the ancestral hall to-night," he said, with that laughing, boyish note back in his voice. "Let's make the most of it while we can!"

I started with the best intentions in the world; but the room which had been set aside as the ladies' cloakroom was the one which Charles VII and Anne of Bretagne had once used. Moreover, I found myself staring at the great Empire bed in the corner, and thinking what a sensible space they had left underneath it for real emergencies.

With something of a shock, I inspected my party face in the cherub-fringed mirror. Where, oh where, was that sophisticated matt foundation, that careful dusting of Rachelle No. 2, that slight suspicion of *Soir de Paris* lipstick? Assiduous search discovered the powder in damp block formation under each ear. The *Soir de Paris* lipstick had fled without trace.

I put in ten minutes' hard work before I matched the georgette again. After all, though I suppose I am not such an asset to the Château as beautiful Anne and Bobby's famous ancestors, and there is not a great deal of me, I am not really bad-looking. None of the Vances were . . .

I went rather thoughtfully down the sweeping marble staircase. In spite of the delays, we had arrived before the other guests. But it was not the quietness that caught me as I opened the door, but a strange feeling of warning. Little puffs of wind set the air and the old tapestries quivering with resentment. Almost with prevision I felt in some way keyed-up to something grand and terrible. The old Château was alive. Its resentment pierced my consciousness . . . more than resentment . . . Suddenly that odd alertness left me. Something—maybe an unusual tickle—told me I was not all a beautiful guest should be.

It was just that I had forgotten to take off the Vance check woollen stockings.

I gave a thoughtful look at the marble staircase before I parked myself inelegantly in the middle of it. I was rehitching the last suspender when a young man swung round the bend and nearly trod on me.

I just sat there and stared back.

Tall, slim, dark and in immaculate evening-dress, even Aunt Sophie would have approved of my burglar this time.

CHAPTER III

THE FATE OF AUNT SOPHIE'S STOCKINGS

"Good heavens!" I at last gasped; "how did you get here?" And wondered wildly how I had ever thought of him as a nice wet dog. With complete self-possession, he helped me to my feet.

"I—er—you left your mackintosh behind!" I conversed disapprovingly. He grinned.

"I'll call for it later, and present my compliments at the same time to Aunt Sophie."

His easy, impressive materialisation against the sixteenth century Treslin marble had taken away nine-tenths of my breath; his vocal effort paralysed me.

He very kindly stooped and picked up the check stockings. Fate seemed to have singled him out for retrieving Aunt Sophie's spare woollies . . .

"Here, I'll have those!" I wailed dismally.

He handed them over and waited. Evening bags are designed to hold a multitude of small troubles, but never my aunt's lingerie. The attempt was hopeless from the start.

"Far better let me keep them for you," he suggested. There was a suggestion of fascinated superiority in the way he was eyeing my bag.

I gave him a push so that I could inspect the great hall below us. Pierre Retourmel, the *Prefet* of Vieux Bonnat, had arrived with his wife and four coy daughters. Bobby, his feet neatly together in the exact spot on the great tiled floor sacred to such ceremonies for centuries, was inclining himself over them with all the elegance at his command. All six Retourmels were obviously charmed. I simply had not the heart to march up to him and tuck ladies' woollen stockings into his pocket. Behind the Retourmels, I saw svelte Claire Latour and her new boy-friend from the Vichy *gendarmerie.* They, in turn, were backed by the tall American from the Clermont Ferrand Red Cross. The little lady clinging to him was partially obscured by her mother. It was the district's night out; the last party most of us would go to for a very long time. I dangled the Vance wet-weather hose in my hand. It meant going back to the bedroom, and even there they would be a nuisance.

"Well, if you would be so kind," I crooned, handing them back to the burglar.

"*Enchanté*" he said, with a little bow. "And now, I assume, you are ready to dance?"

"Well—er—" I said, watching the stockings disappear into his pocket like the conjuror's rabbit . . . After all, dancing with a burglar in evening dress isn't a chance that should be missed by any girl.

He bowed again.

"Is it possible that I may have the honour?"

I accepted in the same pre-Boer-war spirit, and we swept down the remainder of the marble staircase as if we were the Lord Mayor's Show.

I caught Bobby's eye on me. His glance took in the burglar, but, for some reason, his warm, healthy-looking face showed amusement rather than perturbation.

The burglar and I were, of course, the first couple in the ballroom, and old Jean Dupont, one-legged ex-sailor owner of the *Coq d'Or,* tried out his fiddle on us. I soon forgot Jean, however. Dancing with the burglar was like sweeping on the top of the clouds.

"Jove! This is great!" he breathed suddenly in my ear.

I remembered to correct this superfluous enthusiasm.

"Well," I said, "when he's had plenty of his own *vin ordinaire,* old Jean does his best, and Marcelle at the piano isn't too bad for time."

If I had expected to see the burglar wilt away from me, I was disappointed. He merely looked puzzled and a little grieved.

"Things change, of course," he said at last, "but to play dance music on that piano seems almost a sacrilege."

I was so surprised that I actually stood on his dancing toes. He apologised for their being there, and we swept on.

He had, however, set my brain whirling too. It was not a remark one expected from a burglar, but he was quite right. The piano on which Marcelle's bony fingers bounced in crisp, Gallic abandonment to rhythm was part of a dusk-shadowed room, with slowly falling rose petals, and the gently rippling notes of an old Anglo-French chanson. With a gulp, I brought myself back to the present and Marcelle and fat old Jean Dupont. After all, very soon now, the Château des Roches, with its piano, its panelling, and its tapestries, would be closed and shuttered. Or would it? . . .

~ ~ ~ ~ ~

Occasionally, like fugitives from justice, one or two of the party (now reinforced by some of Bobby's friends from Paris) sneaked out into the great hall to hear the hourly news-bulletins. Bobby had warned them that he would consider such defection from gaiety an insult to himself.

"*Toujours l'amour,*" he crooned in my ear. He was a less exciting and more painstaking dancer than the burglar, but he held me well and obviously enjoyed it. Moreover, one of his unexpected qualities was an excellent tango. Altogether, I was so hot with happiness that had I possessed wings they would have caught fire.

"If only we could go on and on like this!" I sighed.

"Why not?" chirped Bobby encouragingly.

A complete stranger whispered something in his ear, and he dropped me like a hot potato.

So much for my pipe-dream. I had been awakened even sooner than I had expected. As I watched the two men disappear out of the door, I saw easy-going Bobby's hand in his pocket, American gangster fashion, and his eyes shining like blue steel. Well, well . . .!

I quietly withdrew myself from the centre of the floor. I could think of only two reasons for this spectacular exit. One was the burglar. The other the Germans. Both were disturbing. I became certain of two other things: (1) that Bobby did not like the mysterious stranger who had summoned him, and the stranger did not like Bobby; and (2) that I was going to be in whatever Adventure promised. Unfortunately, our private code, which in some respects beat that of the Medes and Persians, prohibited me from following, and getting under his feet immediately.

Telling myself that he deserved it, however, I gathered a small crowd around me and gave them a highly-spiced (and highly appreciated) version of his desertion of my *beaux yeux.* The news brought back by one of the radio imbibers that Pontoise had fallen, and that, under cover of a smoke cloud, the Germans had crossed the Marne at Château-Thierry, terrifying and bewildering as it was, gave me a further breathing space.

I allowed myself to drink a cup of coffee which Pierre Retourmel brought me, and then, feeling more than a little virtuous, I prepared to slip out. My expression must have been more grimly determined than I realised, however.

"Ha, ha! The Vances Ride Again!" applauded Anton Villiers, a Marlene Dietrich fan and dealer in Brussels lace. I saw that his madonna-haired, very intelligent wife was talking charmingly to a long, lean Swiss who looked as if he might yodel at the slightest provocation. "Is it that I give myself the pleasure of coming with you?"

Inwardly I hesitated. He might afford me gallant protection if such became necessary. Outwardly I struck an heroic attitude.

"The Vances Ride Alone!" I squeaked, to the necessary mock applause.

"Pétain is too old for the job."

"Pétain will save France."

The argument behind me was, in Bobby's absence, reaching crescendo point.

"They shall not pass! They shall not pass!! They shall not pass!!!' " The Marshal's cliché of a quarter of a century ago hammered at my back as I reached the door, and rang in my ears long after I had closed it behind me.

Now I was alone, the arguments and the revelry apart. Not even Jean Dupont's fiddle penetrated to this wing of the Château. What was I about to discover? My head high, I hurried down the picture gallery. And from somewhere ahead, almost it seemed in the secret passage behind the picture gallery, I heard footsteps. Stealthy footsteps.

I found myself suddenly afraid.

Where was Bobby?

What had happened to him?

The footsteps came nearer . . .

"Why, hullo! May I have the next dance?" greeted my burglar cheerfully, as he rounded the bend.

Before I had collected either dignity or wits, I was retracing my steps back to the safety of the ballroom. But was it safe even there? Was I perhaps walking with Bobby's murderer?

With a shiver, I remembered the bulge which I was sure had been a gun in Bobby's pocket . . . The others congratulated me on my return with another and, on the surface, equally presentable man, and enquired what I had done with the other.

It was the burglar who answered for me, after one cool, purposeful glance around. His hair, I began to notice, was not quite so smooth as it had been, and his breathing was just a little hurried as if he had been running before I met him.

"Our host has had a bit of an accident. Tripped over a piece of the ancestral furniture and left a small portion of scalp on it. O Lord, no!" as they all looked interested, "it's nothing serious! He'll be down here, picturesque with bandage and wounded hero expression before long!"

Should I give battle straight away? Everyone, provided they were as innocent as they looked, would think I was mad, but they might back me up for the fun of the thing. On the other hand, supposing I were wrong? Supposing there had been no fight between Bobby and the burglar?

"The sight," I sniffed, *à la* Aunt Sophie, "should be extremely interesting. Where is he now?"

"Here, my angel!" said Bobby's voice.

I sprang round, wobbly with relief. Bobby and his mysterious stranger had come up behind me. Bobby had the prescribed bandage round his head. The stranger was undamaged.

"Piece of furniture be scuttled!" chuckled Anton Villiers, his round face puckering into shrewd fines. "Loreley scored an English bull's-eye for walking out on her. Three cheers for the ladies! Hip, hip— !"

The party, even the Paris section, had reached the stage when it would have cheered for far less than that.

"*Quel est* the weapon, Loreley? A hammer, *peut-être?* A saucepan?"

"A poker," interposed Bobby, winking out of a perfectly solemn face at the burglar. The cheek of the man, stuffing his embroilments on to me!

"*Vive l'Angleterre!*" shouted someone.

"*Vive la France!*" shouted Bobby and I and the burglar together.

In the excitement, the burglar slipped out. Conscious of watching eyes, I swung round to find the mysterious stranger apparently obsessed with me. For my part, with my circulation leaping, I discovered that the dark, vivacious face, with its thin, puzzled mouth, was not unpleasant. Moreover, it was sufficiently intelligent to be disturbing. He was not a man I expected to find in a corner by himself much longer. Heavens! he didn't really think I had hit Bobby on the head with a poker, did he?

I followed Bobby and offered to hold his hand. Somewhat churlishly he refused and, just to pique him, I danced for the rest of the evening with Georges Lemaine, one of the press representatives from Paris. It was not on the whole a colossal success. The burglar did not return. After generous refreshment and a whispered consultation with Bobby, the mysterious stranger disappeared likewise.

Nor had I an opportunity of cross-examining Bobby on the way home. Of—I suspected—guile aforethought, we travelled with three of his other guests. I gritted my teeth stubbornly. If he didn't want to tell me, I didn't want to know. Perhaps he didn't think it fit for my ears. If he imagined I for one moment accepted that "tripped over the ancestral furniture" story, he was crazy—that's all.

In view of the bandage he had acquired during what should have been an evening of innocent enjoyment, he very wisely left me at the gate.

"Well, I only hope you haven't caught Bobby's cold," greeted my aunt from the depths of her bed, as I tiptoed past her open door and the rows of packed emergency cases outside it.

I halted dutifully. There was nothing else for it.

"Don't be silly, darling," I said; "he hasn't a cold." Which, so far as it went, was correct.

"I put your umbrella in the left-hand comer of the hall stand," I continued cheerily.

"That's right . . . Did you enjoy yourself? . . . And—oh, what about my stockings? I suppose you weren't sensible enough to put them on to come home?" Something clicked inside my brain.

"Good gracious!" I gasped unthinkingly; "that man still has them in his pocket!"

Aunt Sophie sat bolt upright in bed, her hand-embroidered winceyette nightdress heaving tumultuously.

"A man has my stockings in his pocket?" she repeated ominously.

CHAPTER IV

THE MURDER IN AUNT SOPHIE'S PORTICO

THE NEXT MORNING MORE THAN FULFILLED my expectations.

"*S'il vous plaît, Madame,*" screamed Marie, hurtling past my door at seven minutes to seven, "there is a man dead in your portico!"

I rose up in bed as if propelled by a ghostly back-draught. There was a man dead in Aunt Sophie's portico . . . Aunt Sophie's portico was the most ridiculous place . . . The next minute I was out of bed and in full flight through the hall.

The dead man was . . . no one I knew. I saw that at once. This unfortunate individual was small and thin, like a piece of twisted wire. Unfortunately, Marie had forgotten to mention that he had been stabbed. For a moment, at the sight of all that surplus blood out of so small a body, I leaned against the door feeling thoroughly sick. Then I walked ceremoniously round him until I could see his face.

My heart cringing and thumping, I drew back. The man's lips were twisted away from his teeth into a grim sort of smile, and his sightless, wide-open eyes stared straight at me. I had never seen a dead man before, and the shadow from the pale trunk of a plane tree fell across one of his out flung arms. It was like a crucifix pointing the way to our front door. I felt shock and apprehension welling up in me . . . I heard Aunt Sophie toddling up.

"What are you doing here, Loreley?" she asked sternly, looking as if she expected to find the blood-stained knife overlapping one of the pockets of my dressing-gown.

It saved the outbreak, but I felt about six years old.

"I—I heard Marie scream—!" I mumbled, trying to edge past. The sooner this situation was left in my aunt's capable hands, the better. Besides, I felt sick.

Aunt Sophie, however, seemed to think that it was sufficiently unpleasant to draw a moral from it.

"Whatever Marie does or does not do," she decided, "is no excuse for a young English girl to go out into a French front-garden clad only in her nightdress and a dressing-gown. Go back to your room at once, Loreley!"

I might have replied with reason that I had not been, and had no intention of going, into a front garden of any nationality but the effort did not seem worth while.

"Yes, darling," I said instead—and hurried thankfully to the bathroom.

There is nothing more humiliating than being sick—unless it is being sick in public. It does seem so beastly futile not to be able to control one's own tummy. Besides, there was a splash of blood on my nightgown, and I had to wash it off. From the end of the passage, I heard Aunt Sophie, on the 'phone, her voice a little quivery now, rousing the local doctor and telling him to be sure and bring the local police force with him.

Marie, her face hot and shiny, hurried past me again as I opened the door.

"Breakfast will be ready in two minutes, *Mademoiselle,*" she gasped.

I had prepared myself for much—but not for breakfast.

"I have," I shouted back, "just been sick . . ."

Marie swung herself round and stared at me.

"Ah—*oui!*" she said at last; "I'll tell *Madame.*"

"I shall not," I continued with a careful assumption of dignity, "be wanting any breakfast to-day, thank you, Marie."

There was a quiet, detached look about the sunshine outside. I went out by the back door.

~ ~ ~ ~ ~

To a certain extent, Dr. Lemoine softened my next shock. I met him roughly an hour later, bouncing from the newly cleaned portico.

Somehow, this little Frenchman, who had already lived through two wars in his country and seemed to be quietly enjoying his third, was so comfortable a part of my everyday life, so comfortably round and bald, that I greeted him like a long-lost uncle.

"I have had the great misfortune to be laid up for eight days," he made proud answer to my query as to his obvious well-being.

"Oh!" I said.

"The neuritis," he said profoundly. We stood and stared at each other.

"Oh, I am sorry!" I said a little breathlessly; and, of course, I was. But in M'sieur Lemoine's face are two dark, twinkling eyes, and over those, debonair round pince-nez. The droop went out of me suddenly.

"What have they done with—with the body?" I whispered confidentially.

He quivered, and gave the ends of his waistcoat an important downward tug.

"The ambulance will be calling for it shortly, *Mademoiselle.*" He took off his pince-nez and polished them carefully. "In the meantime, *M'sieur* from the *Sûreté* is interrogating Marie."

It may have been the way he said it, but the *Sûreté* is France's Scotland Yard . . . *"M'sieur* from the *Sûreté?*" I repeated.

He swelled visibly, his eyes snapping.

"M'sieur Labourd, that one of the reputation of the highest, is undertaking the investigation, I understand," he explained. *"Mademoiselle!"* he struck an attitude, "I have the opinion that there is more in this regrettable affair than leaps to the eye."

"Why?" I asked very clearly.

He looked as if he were tingling all over.

"That one," he further explained, "he expects another murder here! *Mais, oui,* what do you think of that?"

I failed completely to see why I should simulate any enthusiasm. Then, seeing him breathing softly and with obvious respect over my head, I turned.

"That one" who was expecting another murder here seemed quite pleased to see us. M. Lemoine introduced me as if it were an honour. *M'sieur* from the *Sûreté,* that one with the reputation and apparently the expectation of the highest, managed to look faintly apologetic, and, before I had quite understood what was happening, had shooed M. Lemoine off the premises and me into the breakfast room.

"You remember me, *Mademoiselle, n'est-ce pas?* I had the pleasure of seeing you at M'sieur Treslin's party last night." Conversationally bubbling, he pulled one of Aunt Sophie's easy chairs forward for me.

I stood very still. My knees were so pulpy I could with dignity do nothing else. I remembered him all right. By night *M'sieur* from the *Sûreté* with the reputation of the highest was the mysterious stranger at Bobby's Château. By day he had come, like a big black crow, full of expectation, from our porch. Meeting fully his keen, interrogative eyes, I felt fear mounting in me, mounting until the dark eyes seemed to be glaring into my very brain. With a shiver, I remembered too my previous conviction that there was no love lost between him and Bobby.

"Please sit down," he invited. His voice had a slight, patronisingly Parisian accent.

I sat. Apparently he was anxious to know if I had seen any strangers in Vieux Bonnat within the last day or two. I kept strictly to the truth, because he said "in Vieux Bonnat," and Vieux Bonnat is a good half-mile down the road.

Even after half-an-hour's conversation, I was unable to help him in any other way whatever.

~ ~ ~ ~ ~

I tried to hide the burglar's mackintosh in Jules Sautier's onion field. It was a mistake.

I had found nothing very startling in the pockets. There were only a couple of white handkerchiefs—at least, both had been born white, but one appeared to have grown old, wiping away incriminating finger-prints. As neatly as possible, I did up the ensemble in a piece of brown paper from Aunt Sophie's waste-paper basket. I dared not ask for any from the kitchen. Aunt Sophie has, and has inculcated in Tante Theresa, such a strict moral sense. Black is black, and white is white. And I had a sneaking feeling that I was mingling with a particularly virulent shade of purple.

M. Labourd, that one from the *Sûreté* with the reputation so high, popped up from the other side as I was getting over the gate of the onion field. My guilty secret slid out from under my arm, and burst exactly at his feet. That I didn't run for my fife was due not so much to presence of mind as shccr panic.

There was a thin-lipped, man-of-the-world smile on his face as he apologised for startling me. I wasn't sure if I liked him any the better for it. Had he been sleuthing me, or was this third materialisation his Parisian luck? Quite apart from these possibilities, he was so sleekly self-reliant and sure of himself that my provincial spine felt like soap that has been left in the bath too long. To add to my confusion, I desired desperately to make a good impression on him. One had, I told myself, to use some social sense even with a super-policeman. It seemed easier with a super-burglar.

"Fancy," I said, gathering dignity in a sort of bunch, "seeing you again so soon, M'sieur Labourd!" Heavens, should I have called him "Inspecteur," or some such hard-won title?

He looked up for a second from his reassembly of my parcel. Suppressing a natural idiotic grin, I watched him. With all his superiority, I knew my package would beat him. He seemed surprised when the brown paper wouldn't meet.

"*Mais, oui,* I must confess I hardly expected to meet a companion so charming on my lonely walk," he said with Gallic politeness. And then, with a little hunch of the shoulders: "Are you going far, Mademoiselle Vance, so that I can carry this—er—thing for you?"

I couldn't decide whether this was official arrest, *la politesse,* or just impatience with the brown paper, but I thanked him and told him I could manage. He bowed again, and I gathered the naked incriminating mackintosh to me and departed. I could feel the dark eyes narrowing as he watched me out of sight. I think—I am not sure—he still followed me.

Wanted by the Police . . . Defiantly I hung the burglar's mackintosh on the hall stand.

Cook and Marie were happily distrait in the kitchen. Marie was of the opinion that the dead man in the portico had seduced another man's wife, and the other man had taken legitimate revenge. Tante Theresa thought it was a dirty Fifth Columnist who had suffered in the course of business. Both agreed that had he been a gentleman, he would not have made a mess of *Madame's* portico, and then Tante Theresa saw me and sniffed, and the subject was left in abeyance.

"Have you still the sickness, *Mademoiselle?*" they asked at once, in accents of grudging admiration. I judged that neither had, so far, achieved that delicate interior adjustment. With a hollow groan, I left them still wondering.

~ ~ ~ ~ ~

In peace-time, Vieux Bonnat would have been in the News. We automatically shifted the feeling of importance to ourselves, and even to such events as a visit to the dentist at Clermont Ferrand. Marie, Tante Theresa's niece, did much promenading in the village, negligently clasping my new hat in her hand. Had she not found the corpse in the blood-stained portico? Aunt Sophie, with a possible regard for complementary colouring, dressed herself in a much-disliked blue suit. M. le Cure, with the same earnestness with which he sipped his refreshment, deplored the modern lack of self-control, and was even more disgusted than Aunt Sophie that loose-minded poltroons, who should have been fighting for God and Liberty, were allowed to foist their crimes upon the innocent local areas. He failed to make clear, however, whether the ecclesiastical bias went to the Don Juan presented by Marie, or her Tante Theresa's Fifth Columnist.

"I've known some people have their gums terribly lacerated when they have a wisdom tooth out," mused Aunt Sophie, when we were changing buses for the dentist's. Needless to say, it was my tooth that was coming out. Aunt Sophie was still ruffled from a false alarm of enemy parachutists. She had been in the village at the time, and had been excitedly informed that a flock of them were hanging from her pea-sticks. The roads, we found, were packed, but so far Clermont Ferrand presented a creditably normal appearance.

"You're quite sure you won't have gas?" persisted my aunt. "I don't like these injections. Charles Yolette's wife was ill for days after one."

"I'll risk it," I quivered, trying to look unimpressed. My aunt slackened her stride and looked at me intently. It was the look they might have given Mary Queen of Scots. My head rose right royally to meet it. Surely murder itself couldn't be much worse than this?

"Oh, well," she sighed, "so long as he doesn't break it in and have to jab about for it afterwards, I expect you'll be all right."

It was not until the dentist and I were sitting side by side waiting for the immediate scene of operations to freeze, that I clutched again at my courage.

"Keep the mouth open, *s'il vous plait,*" said the dentist. I knew he was somehow linking the defeat of the Belgian Army with the fall of Narvik, but my mind wasn't on such wide ramifications.

At last he got up and prodded.

"Is it that it still hurts?"

I proudly admitted that it still hurt. We resumed our respective meditations. I learnt during this session that he had a weak heart, and was therefore incapable of fighting for *la*

France, a wife and four beautiful children, the youngest of whom had just had measles. All this information achieved, mark you, with my mouth agape and one cheek steadily icing. By the time he started on the tooth, I felt he was quite an old friend.

Scrunch, scrunch, went the tooth under the forceps. Had it broken off? Was he going to leave bits in to jab out afterwards?

He squared his shoulders like a true Frenchman.

Was I, English to the backbone, going to be a coward? Not I! . . . He got a grip well up in the gum . . . When I opened my eyes, there was the tooth, perched nakedly on the end of his forceps.

"She still looks a bit shaky," said my aunt critically, as I tottered back to the waiting-room. "Hold your handkerchief up, dear. This wind is chilly—and you might get an abscess in it."

Obediently holding my handkerchief up, but urged by some ill-chosen sense of humour, I so convincingly saw a pink elephant and a spotted monkey that we went home by taxi instead of bus.

My feeble flicker of humour fizzled out when I saw what was waiting for us in the porch. It was a sporting gesture which, in any other circumstances, I might have appreciated. The burglar was paying an afternoon call.

"Miss Vance is ill, I think," I heard him observe, as I peered at him.

"Yes, she's just had a wisdom tooth out," said my aunt. It was a full day, but one which I was afterwards to consider quite calm.

The burglar very kindly carried me indoors.

CHAPTER V

ART versus MORALS

ON SUNDAY, the burglar took us to the St. Jean Musée and Gaieties des Beaux-Arts. The better the day the better the deed, apparently.

Aunt Sophie, who greeted him like a long-lost son, was now an almost girlish example in brown marocain with white spots. He had an open car, at which her eyes lit up still further. I only hoped it was not stolen. The fact that it had military markings on it might in France at that time have meant anything or nothing. It was too late now—even presupposing an eleventh-hour burst of courage on my part—to tell her that our escort was a self-confessed burglar. I just hoped for the best, and expected the worst.

To my surprise, the burglar himself seemed primarily concerned with getting us out of the country. The last boat for England would leave any hour now. Even the English Consulates were closing down. On the roads north, panic-rotted civilians were strangling everything. Soon, the terror would reach here. *We just had to go.* That was what the burglar thought and, with calm determination, almost started picking up our neatly stacked suitcases.

My aunt poured him out an English cup of tea.

"In my opinion," she said, as if she were discussing the weather and not a move on which our lives might depend, "the Consulates were never very much good anyway. And if you think the fact that there are already several million people traipsing the roads is any inducement for me to join them, you are very much mistaken. I suppose all the *préfets* are leading the rot instead of dealing with it. They will rue it when the Retreat is stopped!"

"D'you know Auxerre at all well?" asked the burglar, politely smiling his thanks for the tea.

My aunt stirred her own tea vigorously.

"Yes, I know Auxerre is in flames," she said quite calmly. "If you expect me to gasp in horrified surprise, you're too late by about four hours. In any case, I have definitely ceased to be surprised at anything that happens in this war."

"And Touchy?" persisted the burglar, with a little frown.

"And Touchy," corroborated my aunt, unmoved. "There is also the small matter of some paratroops in my back garden." Not lightly would Aunt Sophie forgive those non-existent paratroops! "Now, you listen to me. I am not going to contract your blessed measles of panic, whatever you or Bobby Treslin or the radio say. Is that clear?"

"Almost dazzlingly so," said the burglar thoughtfully. I was rather surprised to find that he knew when he was beaten. My aunt settled herself snugly behind her teapot again.

A large removal van was driving away from the St. Jean Musée as we arrived there. We should most certainly have hoarded the burglar's petrol, but my aunt seemed to view its use for a non-panicky purpose as a personal challenge. She pursed her lips in mingled gratification and disapproval as we read the notice that this was the last day the Musée and Galeries des Beaux-Arts would be open to the public.

Inside we found the exhibits that remained neatly packed against the walls; to the few windows men were fixing black-out equipment. The authorities, however, still proudly showed a collection of stuffed fish. The premier sail-fish looked out at me from his glass case with dull, patient eyes. It was like this *he* had been hooked.

With a calm, proprietary glow, the burglar ushered us into the gallery of pictures. There were blank spaces on the walls.

"A subtle alternation of horizontal colour tones, allied to excellent unity of composition," hissed a skinny man of letters immediately in front of us. He had made his choice of a portrait of a woman in scarlet and gold doing her hair. My head craned upward with the rest.

"Striking chiaroscuro," ventured a secondary visitor, in uniform.

It didn't sound too respectable to me, but the burglar whispered that it meant light and shade. My aunt led us, and a couple of English Red Cross nurses, away. We learnt that the building was being taken over as a military hospital.

"Now this," decided my aunt triumphantly of her choice, "is a direct challenge to the distortion-non-representationist school!"

Where on earth had she found that phrase? I glanced doubtfully at the burglar, who was studying a nude. My aunt's choice was a gigantic *oeuvre* depicting *The Last Supper.* A stout-bosomed woman of the stern, northern type arrived simultaneously. Unlike me, however, she was seeking artistic enlightenment while there was yet time, and was further under the delusion that I was qualified to give it.

"Pardon the liberty, *Mademoiselle,*" she begged, "but are all these paintings, so *grand,* so *magnifique,* done by the hand or by the machinery?"

I dealt with this, and then, glancing round, I had my first shock of the day. Aunt Sophie was disappearing, under tow of an old but purposeful tug of an attendant, into the lecture room for a lecture in English on Pre-Historic Flints.

The burglar and I paced demurely to the same doorway. Here, not exactly to my surprise, he halted. I did likewise. The lecturer—a bald-headed, unobtrusive little fellow—had just stepped up for approval. The audience, quite half a roomful, made a sporadic attempt at applause. Aunt Sophie was being settled ceremoniously in a front seat beside a large gentleman in clerical grey.

I tried to catch the burglar's eye and failed. A lecture for the English on Pre-Historic Flints when, with the focal point not a hundred miles away, the world was locked in a struggle of modern giants! When emergency travel facilities had been in full swing getting the English away from France as fast as they could since early May! Irony? Or a pathetic last-minute parade of Allied unity?

"Ladies and gentlemen!" Obviously the lecturer had excellent command of the supreme language they had come to hear. "As will be clear to you, paleoliths presuppose the phylogenetic progress of the human genus—"

Aunt Sophie began to examine a nobbly piece of flint. A *Comédie Française* wink passed between the burglar and the attendant as the latter came back. The burglar took my arm, and five minutes later we were in his car on our way out of the town. In the distance, the mountains began to jag into the blue sky. Well, well . . .!

He did not drive at the speed I had expected; indeed, our pace was practically bed-ridden. To-day, so spoke every vital line in him, he was prepared to jettison the breakneck thrills of his profession and dawdle in the sunshine. I began to feel faintly superior.

"Do you work on your own, or are you part of a gang?" I queried prosaically.

He did not answer at once. Then—

"I must have notice of that question," he laughed.

"Does that mean you want it in writing?" I snapped.

"God forbid!" He turned dancing brown eyes on me. "I thought you were a pal!"

I grabbed at my cue and what I hoped was an attitude of blasé sophistication,

"Oh, I shan't give you away," I said. As I had already found, I could not, without incriminating myself. "It's up to you to take a holiday from 'business' while you're in this neighbourhood."

"It's a bargain," he said, holding out his hand.

I hurriedly shook it so that he could replace it on the wheel. What kind of life was it this clear-eyed young man of obvious good breeding had adopted for himself? That there was tragedy here was clear; and yet tragedy was the last thing one would have associated with him at the moment.

"Of course we do our grind as much as anybody, you know," he said, putting quite a wrong interpretation on my silence. Laziness was the last thing of which I would have accused him. "If you're not prepared to put in a definite number of hours, well, you just remain a semi-skilled burglar all your life; and I should say that is almost as monotonous as being a plumber."

"I suppose you're lording it on the top rung of the professional ladder by now?" For the life of me I could not keep the snap out of my voice. Apparently every time we opened our mouths we started scrapping about something. "It seems a pity you can't get medals or anything for it."

He raised both his slim, skilful hands from the wheel of the car, and lit another cigarette.

"Oh, I don't know," he said. "Our thrill comes when we're up against all the smug codes of law and order—and beat them!" He turned sharply to me. "Shocked?"

To my disgust, I coloured to the roots of my hair, and then, I think, to the brain itself.

"No, just interested," I said, my chin in the air.

He gave a suspicion of a chuckle.

"Don't you ever think of honesty? Of the value of other people's possessions?" I asked, with earnest gravity.

"Frequently," he said.

"I mean," I felt myself colouring again, "the *sanctity* of other people's possessions."

"Did Drake or Raleigh?" he questioned. There was that.

"Of course, I can see," I went on, stung by the look in his eye, "that there must be some sort of exhilaration—"

He threw back his head with a guffaw of unconquerable enjoyment.

I gave it up. So far as I knew, he had no connection with local crime. He was probably "resting" here from something far bigger. But it was no use moralising at him. His lack of social morals seemed more contagious than my promulgation of them. Minding her cow by the side of the tree-lined road, a dear old peasant woman, in bunchy skirt and rusty sunbonnet, smiled at us. I sat back more comfortably in the burglar's not too comfortable car . . . and almost began to see him as he apparently saw himself: a champion of a lost age of freedom; a standard-bearer against laziness and smugness and uneven distribution. We had to back into a field as a long military convoy bumped past us. They faced the right direction—towards the Marne—but why on earth were such urgent reinforcements on a secondary road like this?

There was a sudden stamping in the undergrowth, and a great Alsatian glided out to have a look at us.

The burglar snapped his fingers at the animal. In a couple of bounds, the dog's great front paws were on the burglar's shoulders, his red tongue panting puppy-like friendliness. The burglar, as he obligingly pummelled and tickled, laughed into my still somewhat scared face. The dog was pushing him towards me: I could feel the breath of both man and dog . . .

I glanced at the man's firm brown wrists as once more he set the car in motion. He would not let me down. There was a vitally reassuring quality about him that made me positive about that. I had a ragged feeling, however, that he was watching me out of the corner of his eye with alert interest. If he were looking for a lady assistant . . .? Possibly, opportunities for big-scale robbery were increasing . . .

Well, time enough then to make my position daylight clear. In the meantime, it was decidedly thrilling . . .

A long black car was creeping up behind. An arm in dark blue signalled in turn to someone in his rear . . . and we leapt out of our canter into something just over a mile a minute. "Is it—are they—after us?" I breathed. He nodded and pressed the accelerator. The evenly-spaced trees, the fields behind, became a leaping pattern, with one tiny thread of road between. He drove much as I had expected him to do. My heart bobbed up and down like one of those ridiculous rubber bath toys. Drake and Raleigh completely lost their charm. To die in a motor accident in the middle of a war sounded tamer than it felt. That I should be salvaged in little pieces seemed inevitable.

His hands slim and taut on the bucking wheel, there was a little frown of annoyance on the burglar's face, as if he had not expected official interference that day. "Are they up on us yet?"

Someone cried a triumphant negative. I recognised my own voice. A swerve that sent me clutching wits and windscreen, and we were off the road I had been so laboriously tracing. From the blue ahead, woodland shadows enclosed us like an envelope.

"Afraid we shall have to run for it," said the burglar, with a disarming grin.

I nodded in agreement and with the shock of finding myself still alive. In spite of my desire not to hinder him, I slipped twice in the soft pine-needles. But for these two unexpected checks, he ran in and out of the trees, head up, with the easy rhythm that comes of steady, secret training. Apparently it did not occur to either of us that he could leave me behind, and, willy-nilly, I kept up too.

Our flight was halted by the bank of a river, but I was too far gone to realise its potentialities. I stood panting at it, aware of a savage excitement.

I looked towards him mutely. I had absolute confidence in him.

He shook his head.

"Stay here," he whispered. I saw the flash of his coat, and then I was alone. I crept to a tree trunk and sat on it. Beyond the river there were more shadows, more trees. I told myself that there was nothing—absolutely nothing—to be afraid of. Yet, as the silence coiled itself about me, I held my breath, listening . . .

Suppose they caught the burglar and took him away? Suppose they came back for me? Suppose they didn't? Where was I exactly? Had I made a mistake about the burglar? Little shivers of fear were darting up and down my spine. There had been something odd about this sunlit drive of ours.

I leapt blindly to my feet. And then, somehow, I stumbled back. I had been told to wait, and wait I must.

He came back as silently as he went. His glance made me feel thoroughly ashamed. It was a straight glance, with the happy, challenging sparkle which spoke of the good companion. He took me by the hand, and we pressed still deeper into the wood. But now I didn't mind the shadows; they had lost their gangly menace; the silence was a friendly, picnic silence. I was a comrade, helping him in a situation of danger.

With eerie suddenness, the silence broke. It had split into a shuffling movement, first from the left, and then, as though on a prearranged signal, repeated immediately behind us. The burglar's arm reached out and drew me further into the shadows. I felt his breath coming quickly but noiselessly between his teeth; and yet, suddenly, as we stood close together, it seemed to me that *I* was the fugitive . . . He smiled down at me.

"A bird, perhaps." His lips formed the words almost soundlessly. I gave his arm a little squeeze. I didn't think it was a bird. Neither did he. Could it be that they had set the dog on him?

Footsore and triumphant, we finally crept back to our car. If a *gendarme* had interfered when we bounded out of the undergrowth like a couple of rabbits, I should have punched him on the nose.

~ ~ ~ ~ ~

I made him bring me straight on to Bobby's Château and go back for Aunt Sophie afterwards. Of course I ought to have guessed. He was not a burglar at all; but, according to him, on our first meeting I had "looked so expectant, it seemed a pity to disappoint" me. He had arrived later than was normal owing to the congestion on the roads; moreover, Aunt Sophie (who apparently knew his father very well) had not been expecting him until next month. But he was a respectable (?) representative of a Paris-London-New York art firm, and the reason Marie had been turning out the spare bedroom that morning.

Naturally, the long black car had had nothing to do with us this afternoon either. Although he had engineered this trip specially to explain matters and beg my pardon, he had not been able to resist such a heaven-sent opportunity of giving his joke a final full flavour.

I think he was genuinely surprised at my wrath. But surely I had reason! Thanks to him, from first to last, I had made a prize idiot of myself. My eyes pricked, even as I stamped my feet. It was all very well for him, with an unexpectedly shy smile, to admit that I had been "a real little brick." I felt like a house of them, all dropped.

I gave a vicious kick at a cushion, and sat myself down on Bobby's divan. Anyhow, for the first time that day, I had chosen my own parking place; perhaps I was learning from experience. Leaning back, I counted this and my one other consolation of the afternoon (as he had helped me over the fording place in the river, he had slipped back, zook, into it!) as a nun counts her beads. The water there had not been deep enough to be dangerous—merely undignified—and his seat had got exceedingly damp.

I stared round me. Bobby's old shooting jacket was thrown over the chair; a couple of filthy pipes awaited his return. The room, with its hangings of tapestry, had a sense of welcoming drowsy peace. I kicked my shoes from my aching feet and folded myself up amongst the cushions. Through the window, I watched the fastidious flutterings of a butterfly, and a couple of pigeons settled with a flourish on a lilac bush.

But once more my anger, which I had assumed buried under this cosy façade, flared up again. It seemed a pity to "disappoint" me, indeed! Did he think that living among the vineyards had left us dead from the neck upwards? We might be steeped in provençal respectability, but that was no reason to jolt us out of it as if we were some form of germs: little fat fellows, with goggly eyes and drooping whiskers.

The empty space where my wisdom tooth ought to have been gave a sudden jump, and a self-pitying tear which had threatened for a long time, trickled down my cheek. Let it trickle! There was nobody here to see it, and it felt sort of homely.

One trickled down the other cheek. With a gulp, I let myself go and buried my face in the cushions. I hated him! Hated his limitless art gallery immaculateness! Even though he was living in the same house, even if he got down on his bended knees, I would not speak to him again!

Feeling that, somehow, I had won after all, I raised my head. Something had disturbed me: a shuffling noise outside the door.

Feeling for my shoes, the tears still raining down my face, I saw the door open to admit a man. But I was no longer naïve and unprepared; I was ready for battle.

Three men.

The first was Bobby. A Bobby who was only just conscious. A Bobby with fresh blood streaming from his bandaged head.

I must have made some sort of noise. I saw Bobby's dull, horror-filled eyes, and then a hand closed over my mouth.

It was a man's hand, soft and repulsive, as was the whole body of the man who pressed himself against me. Without conscious thought, I bit down on the hand and used fists, feet and elbows on the body. The unseen owner gave little grunts of pain, I could taste his blood salt on my lips. The two men were dragging Bobby across the room.

Suddenly I heard Bobby give a sort of gasp, and I saw him and his captors disappear through a gap in the panelling round the fireplace. One of the men looked back at me. He could not have shaved for at least two days; his hair hung lank over a yellow stub of a cigarette behind his left ear; although quite young, there was a suspicion of unhealthy grossness about his body.

The panel closed. My arms were trussed behind my back and, for the first time in my life, I felt a gun in my ribs. I also saw the face of my captor. It was like a suet pudding, with grey, cruel eyes.

"Uh-oo!" I bleated, and gave no further trouble as he dragged me with him behind the tapestry curtain. In the deep window embrasure, with its unnatural darkness, he loomed monstrous above me. I could see him . . . feel the flesh of his body. It was flesh that rippled where it pressed; horribly live flesh.

It was an added horror that he seemed satisfied with me, as if I were behaving better than he had expected. The thought infuriated me. I opened my mouth to launch a good scream. Silently and effectively, he choked it off. Pressed close against him, I could smell, horribly, the perfume he had on his person. It was like crushed violets . . .

With an hysterical effort, I steadied myself. Of course, all this was really due to my hated, bogus burglar—

Suet Pudding stiffened. There had come the merest suggestion of footsteps steadily approaching along the cloistered path outside. Someone else was walking into this trap. I leaned confidentially across the horrible body, hoping to relieve the pressure of his hand on my mouth so that I could give eleventh-hour warning. It was like being matey with a large piece of india-rubber: a piece of india-rubber with deep-set, unwinking eyes glued to a gap in the tapestry curtain.

The window creaked.

My burglar came in looking mildly apologetic.

CHAPTER VI

AGAINST THE LAW

THE BURGLAR WAS SAYING SOMETHING about my *feet.* With a gasp of horror, I remembered two cruel grey eyes and a mountain of flesh frighteningly unlike the burglar's slim, muscled body. Rigid with anticipation, I stared around. The devil-man was gone. I looked at the burglar enquiringly.

"They were sticking out," he said, with an owlish profundity.

I nodded.

"You—you are all right, aren't you?" he persevered. Cautiously, I felt my ribs where the gun had pressed into them.

"Why, yes, of course!" I agreed, rather absent-mindedly.

"Your feet," said the burglar; "they were sticking out."

Sticking out? Oh, under the curtain, I supposed. I gave myself a little shake. Even if they were, there was no reason to harp on it. I fixed him with a stern eye. For the first time since I had known him, he seemed impressed by it. Ranging further, I saw that I was in the little toilet-room off the great hall, and that he had liberally sprinkled me with water. I gripped the edge of the basin to steady myself.

"Where is Suet Pudding?" I demanded.

"You mean the walking mountain who pushed you into my arms and bolted?" he asked still mildly.

"Of course!"

He nodded.

"It was only because I saw your feet under the curtain."

Oh, damn my feet! One would have thought they had hobnail boots on! Slowly, my grip on current events was strengthening. Suet Pudding had gone—apparently the burglar was not the man he wanted. I was in the toilet room with the burglar. Bobby—what about Bobby? Yes, Bobby had been dragged through a secret panel by another unprepossessing individual. The existence of a secret panel did not in itself alarm me. It was a habit these old Châteaux had. But if Bobby was unaware of it—as I knew he was—how had these horrible strangers found it out? I pushed the burglar out of the way with nerve-taut hands.

The *salon* was as I remembered it, with the panel still closed. No one would. believe that, not many minutes ago, men had passed through it. I swung back to the burglar, who had followed close on my heels.

"This is true, isn't it?" I panted accusingly. "It's not another of your idiotic jokes?" But all the while, I knew that this was not a joke. Bobby would not have taken part in a joke like this.

"I gave up pretending when I gave up being a burglar," said the man by my side quietly. There was a notc I had not heard before in his voice. Now it was he who pushed me out of the way.

I wanted to send for the rural *gendarmerie,* but he pointed out just how rural it was, and also the amount of time we should lose in getting it. All the while, his fingers searched deftly up and down, up and down, the intricate old carving of the panel. With sudden comfort, I realised that although he was not a burglar, he meant business all the same. *He* was not going to let Bobby perish in some mysterious dark hole behind this secret opening. The smoke-blackened woodwork seemed to smirk back at us. For all we knew every minute might count. The old clock in the far corner beat time to my thought. Might count, might count, might count, might count. Its smug yellow face had watched this frantic scene being enacted many, many times. It had a century of history to choose from. What did it care if we died of heart failure on the spot? What did it care that Bobby might be lying back there, dead or dying? He's dead! he's dead! smote the clock complacently.

"Our forebears knew how to hide themselves when the income tax man called. I'll give them that much," drawled the burglar.

"Yes, yes!" I said. He could give them anything for all I cared, if only he could get that panel open. It only he could break the spell of horrific expectation that was on me.

"Got it!" he yelped in tones of surprise almost equal to my own. The moving panel made hardly any sound, and a black gulf yawned at our feet. I folded my arms to stop them trembling.

"You stay here," snapped the burglar.

"I'm coming too!" I chattered.

His eyes searched my face with an odd look of resignation. "I'll go first then," he said, in that iron-studded, accommodating way of his, as he fixed the panel open to his satisfaction. I had no objection to that.

"Now! And for the love of Mike, hold on to me! We don't want to get separated!" I agreed with him.

There followed no sound but our questing footsteps on a rough stone floor, which all the time sloped downwards. The darkness closed in on us.

"See if you can touch the roof."

I reached up a cautious two inches at a time. There was nothing.

The air was cold and still; our whispers had a sort of stale urgency. Then the silence into which we were moving deeper and deeper smirked over us again, prodding ghostly fingers in our ribs . . . The figure in front of me became suddenly rigid.

I gave an hysterical tug on the tail of his coat. Had something . . . had somebody . . .?

"Sh-sh! The tunnel has narrowed, and I'm stuck!" hissed the burglar. "A clear case where mind is definitely subservient to matter."

The dark silence again . . .

"Shall I heave the matter backwards or forwards?" I whispered at last.

"I don't know. It has rather occurred to me that something pulverising might still be in working order here. Probably by exerting the natural pressure that you seem to desire, a row of mediaeval iron spikes dash out and into one's tummy."

Was he *trying* to scare me?

"Well, it's your tummy," I meditated. "Aren't you going on?"

He could not back out after that, however much he might doubt his ability as a spike-dodger. Besides, at the back of my mind, I wasn't sure I had forgiven him yet. The last thing I really remembered was swearing never to speak to him again.

He wriggled in response to my unequivocal prod. Iron spikes were probably a little above the ordinary accepted risks of his late profession.

"Don't scream!" he whispered; "I'm going to risk a torch."

I vacillated between anger and terror. And, with a zip, anger won. As if I should scream!

"It would be easy enough if you were a real burglar," I hissed like a serpent in his ear.

He switched off the torch, and my Dutch courage went with it.

"Must be some sort of leverage or balance here which swings this stone out as a barrier to check pursuit." His voice was without perceptible emotion. "Stay where you are for a minute—I may be coming back with some velocity."

I stood with my hands pressed against my sides, my eyes straining forward into the darkness. This exploration would have been fun if only I could have got Bobby's white, blood-stained face out of my mind. I tried to persuade myself it *was* fun.

"It's all right. I have once more achieved the impossible," came the whisper ahead. "I think you'll manage it all right."

To check pursuit. . . The words danced and danced in my brain.

I managed it all right. We were standing in a room or cave, and at the far end Bobby was lying on a piece of sacking.

"Stick 'em up there! And look slippy about it!" said a voice in soft, deliberate accents. In a sudden stab of light I saw the burglar's face. It was dead calm, but for little sparks playing like lightning about his eyes. There was a gun a couple of inches from his stomach. Obediently his hands went up. Mine were already there.

~ ~ ~ ~ ~

From the shadows behind the unshaven brute with the lank hair and leering face, two other figures moved menacingly towards us! The burglar was roughly but expertly searched for a non-existent weapon.

My breath so tight in my throat that for the moment it squeezed personal terror out of me, I saw Bobby lying there, his eyes closed, his body sprawled and still, like one already dead. It was more than I could bear. I must *know!* Guns or no guns, I skeltered across, and, throwing myself beside him, took his poor head tenderly in my lap.

"Oo-ow-w-w!" yelped Bobby.

"D'you mind if I put my hands down too?" came the burglar's voice across the intervening space. "I'm getting cramp or somethin', and in a few minutes I shan't be responsible for my actions either."

"Keep 'em up!" growled the other.

"Thank you," came the burglar's voice again, but I saw that he had lowered his arms. "And now that I am more comfortable myself, I should be interested to hear why my friend has blood all over his noble countenance, and what you thugs are going to do about it?"

They didn't seem to grasp the connection.

From an open gap in the rocky wall behind him, a new voice answered:

"Knock the fool on the head, and think it out afterwards!"

The burglar swung round.

"But that's against the Law!" he reproved.

I screamed a warning as the blow fell. The burglar went down like a sturdy sapling under the axe.

I fainted when they came across and kicked Bobby away from me.

CHAPTER VII

THE TRIUMPH OF PRE HISTORIC MAN

BY THE TIME I CAME TO, we had all been tied hand and foot. Bobby, by my side, his fair hair streaked with gore, his mouth indrawn with pain, was still unconscious. Across the cave, the hobbled burglar was eyeing me with a Pelmanic look. Yes, I remembered him too. As far as possible, I turned my back on him. I was glad, of course, that they had not killed him; at the same time, but for his finesse in playing the silly goat, we should neither of us have been here now. Maybe we were helping Bobby by giving him a bit of company, but I did not see that we were any other use. I wriggled and tugged at the rope round my wrists, ragged until I was dizzy with the pain and the mortification of it. The rope did not give a fraction,

As I involuntarily looked across at him again, the burglar gave a funny little grim chuckle.

"I ducked," he said, "and went down screaming!" And then, very gently: "Loreley, have they tied you up very lightly?"

I was touched by his concern—and the use of my Christian name.

"Not—not very!" I said, gritting my teeth.

"Good! Could you possibly roll towards me? It was painful, but I did it. I landed against him with a bump.

It was definitely more friendly, but, so far, it was I who seemed to have gained the bruises. Then I saw that the poor mutt was fastened to an iron staple in the floor, and my heart went down with the flood. We should never get free and be able to pull our weight against Suet Pudding and his gang of crooks! We were helpless until they chose to come for us! To shoot us! To kick us! Whichever best suited their humour or need . . .

My eyes, bulging with mingled terror and indignation, alighted on rough initials carved into the wall I had just left, the wall above Bobby's head. Close by was another iron staple, and clinging round it like a barnacle, a rusty iron chain. Rock-bound, chained, and perhaps starved to death! I took a determined hold on myself. That was one of the horrible things that made history so fascinating. . . . but it couldn't happen to Aunt Sophie's niece.

"Listen, Loreley," said the burglar above my head; "somehow you've got to get your hands into my pocket and take out a small stone wrapped in paper. I'll help you all I can. Ready?"

I twisted round and stared at him, speechless. To relieve him of the discomfort of a small stone in his pocket, I had thumped myself to pieces all over that awful floor . . .!

He grinned down at me, his eyes dancing and determined.

"I will do nothing of the sort!" I stated with equal determination.

"Pre-historic flint implements, my child; remember?" He smiled. "Inadvertently pinched by your own Aunt Sophie. It's a purely academic question, of course, and a bit of a bore for you, but if we can only get it out of my pocket, we'll soon see whether pre-historic man was right or not."

My head began to swim feebly.

"You mean—?"

He nodded. In this respect, luck was incredibly if only temporarily on our side. Could we take our due advantage of it? Suet Pudding and his crooks had searched him for a gun or knife, but they had overlooked A PIECE OF FLINT SHARPENED BY HUMAN HANDS MANY CENTURIES BEFORE THE HISTORY BOOKS.

Somehow, I got my hand into his pocket. Across him, doggedly, I rolled and squirmed. In spite of generous effort he could give me little help.

"It's useless!" I almost sobbed at last. "I can't get a hold of the darn' thing!" Nor, with all my struggles, had the rope round my wrists given at all. Rather, it seemed to me to have tightened and be biting back savagely into my flesh. In truth I was making an inglorious mess of things.

"Just one more go!" urged the burglar quietly.

I bit my lip until it felt numb under my teeth. For the first time this normally self-sufficient young man was really dependent on me. I must not let him down, and myself too!

My nails scratched at the flint . . . shifted it! It moved deeper and deeper into his pocket. Despairingly, without hope, my fingers prodded after it. Then, just as my arm and shoulder muscles reached the limit of their endurance, I had it!

My handling of that implement was even more elementary than primitive man intended. My hands being tied behind my back, I could not see what I was doing with it.

"May I remind you," said the burglar at last, breaking the sweating silence with preternatural solemnity, "that you are not preparing a meat stew? You may have misunderstood me, but my suggestion was that you got my hands free, not hacked them off."

My hysterical giggles did nothing to improve my aim.

But finally the rope at which I was aiming began to give . . .

"You two having an all-in wrestling match, or something?" came Bobby's voice, weak and drawling, from his corner.

Hooray! Bobby had now regained consciousness! It seemed a good omen. Soon we should know what this was all about! Not yet, of course, because Bobby would be too weak to talk much. But soon the burglar would be free . . .

He was. Pre-historic man had won—with the aid, undoubtedly, of me and Aunt Sophie. But our combination had certainly made a mess of the burglar's wrists. I watched him stagger to his feet, pick up the blood-stained flint, and start on me.

"Are you really all right?" I asked idiotically.

"Sweetheart," he frowned, "thirty seconds ago, I was a very sick man, and then a lovely lady stooped and put her soft touch on my fevered brow—and lo, I became healed!"

"Rather a solemn thought," grunted Bobby from his corner. "Now that you're free, too, Lorrie, what about coming over here and cleaning up my face a bit?"

We reeled across to him.

"Yes, it's certainly woman's work," decided the burglar. "My contribution will be a clean handkerchief, and you can be the purveyor of your own lick."

"There's a puddle of reasonably clean water on that ledge," suggested Bobby, pointing feebly.

"Now, Loreley," said the burglar, again busy with his flint, "put a jerk into it, there's a good girl. The gentleman's waiting!"

Through the blood, there was a martyr's smile on Bobby's face . . . .

"Oo-ouch!" he yelped a few seconds later, under our joint ministrations, "gently, you two! I'm still a sick man, you know!"

But he had asked for it, and we got him free and reasonably clean before we all staggered to the tunnel. Then—

THE STONE WHICH WAS ACROSS THE OPENING WAS IMMOVABLE!

"It doesn't appear to be quite so easy after all," said the burglar very quietly.

Bobby swayed and caught blindly at the rock to steady himself. A new sound beat upon my consciousness, a sound of water. Three paces from where we now stood, the floor sloped—gently at first, then with a great leaping stride. We all understood our geographical position at the same instant, I think. The cave mouth was in the rocky, unscaleable side of the gorge upon which the Château was built. Our cave was a natural prison, with that sagging, gaping mouth leading straight into the jaws of death below.

Inside the cave, the daylight was fading fast. Across the opening, a shadow flickered and was gone.

The burglar!

Without conscious thought, I made after him, out towards the smooth, sagging mouth of the cave prison. Instinctively, I took short, cautious steps. I was exploring as other prisoners must have done: hopefully, fearfully. . . . Enemies of the House of Treslin. Men who were now dead. I trembled to a standstill. I could have sworn that ghostly fingers had touched my face; that there had been the pressure of ghostly hands at my back, hands that remembered and wanted to share their own agony! The surging, tumultuous rhythm of the river below, now so persistent in my ears, bewildered me. It blanketed the sound of my footsteps. I slipped, could not stop myself! I was hurtling right out of the cave to my death! I shut my eyes, screamed, and the burglar was waiting for me.

"No way out for us here," he said.

The great hungry lip, the boulder against which he braced himself, held us. I fought my terror to a standstill, fought it until it seemed part of the matted growth on the opposite side of the gorge, part of the darkening sky we could just see above the gorge run, part of the tier after tier of straight, unshadowed pines that rose into that sky. And below, the waiting rocks with sharp peaks like little mountains . . . I was rigid with terror, yet I felt my body shivering. Whichever way I turned, there was a sense of unflinching, uncaring power. And no escape.

The burglar gave me one look, and then picked me up bodily in his arms and carried me back to Bobby.

"Oh, but I can manage," I tried to assure him, but my teeth chattered.

He made no answer.

"You poor kid!" he exploded so suddenly that I nearly shot from him, "it was a damn' shame to drag you into this! Somebody's going to get shot for it, I promise you!"

There was something in his voice that shocked me into silence. My head was practically touching his chin. A sense of extraordinary content began to creep over me. I hadn't felt quite like this since the week I had asserted myself with Aunt

Sophie over the rice pudding and got it transmuted into treacle tart.

I stole a look at the burglar's face. He was picking his way across the surface of the cave. Apparently sensing my interest, he became pontifically absorbed in the puddle of water from which I had washed Bobby's face. I think he was endeavouring to convey a tinge of reproach—and then, suddenly, we both laughed. It was stupid. I certainly wasn't sure what I was laughing at.

As I was laid gently beside him, Bobby opened one eye. "Hullo! Been for a stroll?"

"Yes; we've been admiring the crepuscular effect radiating its pleasing spell on the cretaceous striations immediately below us," said the burglar.

Bobby yawned.

"Yes, it's getting damn' dark this end, too," he confirmed.

CHAPTER VIII

SUET PUDDING

WE SAT CLOSE TOGETHER on a slab of rock.

"Sorry to drag you into this mess again, Pugg, old chap," grunted Bobby hoarsely.

The burglar's brooding face snapped into an alertness that had a comfortable undertone of sympathy.

"Oh, don't worry about me; I'm getting my two bobs' worth of entertainment value."

"Pugg," said Bobby, turning ponderously to me, "was in this on the night of the party. He forestalled an attempt on my safe, and probably saved my life. Remember?"

I remembered. So that was what had happened. It seemed poetic justice that my self-styled burglar had, even at that early stage, had to turn detective. But it all seemed a long time ago. And I was still in this cave. This was the important fact.

The burglar—I was still thinking of him as such—proudly massaged ear and tie. Bobby was gazing at him almost affectionately.

"And this," I enquired, surprised at the casualness of my voice, "is Pugg?"

"Eh? Oh, yes, good old Pugg! One of the best!" introduced Bobby, a little absent-mindedly. "Used to be at King's College together."

Ignoring the cave, I was suddenly infuriated with the way everybody except me knew this Pugg-man and without hesitation vouched for him. Perhaps I should feel better if I made brazenly public—at least to Bobby—my own naïve idiocy of the past few days.

The recitation of my woes appeared just the tonic Bobby needed. He looked as if I had presented him with a mug of English beer.

"Just like the good old days!" he chortled. "One day Pugg will bluff St. Peter himself into letting him through! The old war-horse hasn't changed a bit!"

I appeared to be getting the worst of the publicity again. I found I was clenching my hands. There was something else, too; something which was beginning to obsess me. It was like being shut in a clothes-closet, with unseen garments pressing and clinging round you.

"Bobby," I said deliberately, "did you see the man who keeps knocking you on the head?"

He rose to the bait.

"Damn it all, Brown Eyes, he's only had a couple of goes when I wasn't looking!"

"Was he like a mountain of blubber, with a grey, suct-pudding face and eyes like a man-eating fish?" I persisted. This was important! I knew it was important!

The burglar made a curious sound of appreciation.

"Anything else outstanding?"

This, somehow, was what I had been trying to keep to myself.

"He smelt," I whispered.

"Huh?"

"Scent," I said.

"Huh?" The monosyllable was again level, but I sensed a difference, a taut note, behind it. Both men were pressing towards me, their faces expectant, intent. And suddenly, all I wanted was to throw my arms round Bobby's neck and cry my eyes out. I felt as if I were betraying somebody. Which was ridiculous.

"Steady, Loreley," came the voice of the burglar. "You don't mind my calling you Loreley, do you?"

"I—er—no," I gulped. Bobby pondered on me. Then: "This scent, Brown Eyes—?"

Once more, the suffocating feeling of having burnt my boats . . . I flung up my head—

"Crushed violets," I made answer; and felt a fool immediately.

And, although it sounded ridiculous, foully ridiculous, Bobby let out his breath like a steam engine.

"Pal of yours?" enquired the burglar of him in mild surprise.

For the first time Bobby looked really alarmed.

"Good God, no! But Lorrie, good girl, has given me the clue I wanted. The gentleman on the job is Carl Vipoering!" He stared hard at our unresponsive faces and nodded, his breath whistling portentously through his teeth. "The most dangerous and unscrupulous S.S. agent at present in Europe," he elaborated. "With the best markets for blood and hate in the palm of his hand—so! Where he goes, expert in human suffering that he is, the Nazi 'tourists' soon gather, snapping and snarling."

I stared at him in blank astonishment. It was not Bobby's way to over-estimate, or under-estimate, either himself or other people. Such rhetorical description of his opponent was in itself something of a minor earthquake.

"And that's the lad who's after us?" asked Pugg.

A gentle, almost satisfied smile crossed Bobby's honest, stubborn-jawed face.

"It is."

"But *why?*" I squeaked, struggling with reawakened curiosity and sheer physical dread of Suet Pudding.

"Well," Bobby gave a self-conscious wriggle, "I happen to do a bit of work for the British Secret Service. But primarily he wants Leopold Rosbad of Troubania."

Glancing up at him, I saw that his mouth had become a firm, strong line. I looked hard. I had known, of course, that Bobby was a big, personable young man who liked the world and was generally liked by it, but the mantle of the Secret Service was almost too much for me.

"According to German sources, Leopold Rosbad's brain is going," he went on in reply to our unenlightened stare. "That, of course, is not necessarily correct. What is gospel truth is that, though at present swallowed up by the Axis,

Troubania is of great potential importance to the United Nations. Incidentally, Rosbad isn't a bad sort of guy—a bit dictatorial in his methods, but he suits Troubania very well. And, what's more, he's got almost a hundred per cent. backing of the Troubanian people behind him. The merest schoolboy therefore can see that in the scheme of things to come, Rosbad is a very useful card to hold . . ."

The burglar was sitting very still, staring with what was almost an air of challenge at the gloom, the gloom that was almost like a physical thing creeping towards us.

"According to present arrangements," resumed Secret-Service-Man Bobby, "Rosbad, who has already escaped from two German prison camps, arrives *here* in roughly an hour's time."

"Name of all the *chiens!*" Pugg's challenge swung to Bobby. "You mean—?"

"Yes, I have been honoured as his personal keeper, and probably his cicerone to England."

Still dumb with astonishment, we stared at him, his strained, bloodshot eyes, the tired pucker across his forehead . . .

"Damn it all!" he remonstrated under our inspection, "I'm not a new zoological specimen!"

I saw Pugg spare me a quick glance.

"Quite," he drawled. "Incidentally, I know we are only sitting close together on this slab for comfort and to keep our courage up, but I should just like to voice my displeasure that the portion of slab allotted to me is making slow, but irreparable indentations in my—"

"Tut, tut!" smiled Bobby, taking his cue. Their sudden change of front, I knew, had been for my sake, in case I had hysterics.

Dear old Bobby! If anything . . . serious . . . had happened to him, forty million Suet Pudding Carl What's-His-Names wouldn't have held me down! No, I felt like an emotional volcano, but they need not be afraid that I was going to have hysterics.

I set my chin grimly in the air. There was an agony of chill in the cave now that the sun had set; a faint, unclean smell . . .

"Mind if I smoke?" asked the burglar quietly.

Something had got into his lighter. Bobby tossed him a packet of matches. In the flickering triangle of yellow light, I saw Bobby's face against the initials tooled into the prison wall—and all the fears and terrors which I had been challenging snapped down on me.

I threw myself on Bobby and clung convulsively.

"What is it? A mouse, or a spider?" he enquired.

"Oh, Bobby," I sobbed, "I *am* frightened—and there's no getting away from it!"

Very gently, he ran his fingers through my hair.

"I know you are, my dear. That's why—" His pause convinced me that there was more reason to be frightened now than before.

"Y'know," I heard his continued murmur as he slipped an arm firmly round me, "somebody's been leadin' me up the garden path. I always understood that the female of the species was more deadly than the male . . . Don't shake so, you great cry-baby," he broke off; "you're more like a jelly than a genuine 100 per cent. accomplice."

I stole a watery glance at the burglar. He was puffing away at his cigarette, his eyes once more on the gloom by the lip of the cave. I straightened my spine resolutely. Even if I suffered from inhibitions ever afterwards, I wouldn't give him the opportunity of saying I had been a coward. Not that he would actually say it, of course.

There came a sound from behind the boulder. Still sitting stiffly upright, I found myself, not between two men, but ALONE ON THE SLAB.

Then I saw that Pugg was standing a little in front of me, to the left, with Bobby against the wall immediately to my right. Two virile, very tense shadows in the darkness.

The next few minutes I shall never forget. Neither of the two men made a sound. Their very silence added to the nightmare quality of the pause. The sound of the river gurgled in our ears with a suggestion of eerie, hungry life. We waited. At any moment, the boulder which kept us prisoners would roll back. We should be picked out by light . . . menacing . . . blinding . . . like red-hot pokers prodding at us.

Desperately, I clenched my hands. This was the moment we had been waiting for. Something wet and creepy ran over my wrist—and the nearest manly bosom again got me in a heap. It grunted but accepted me without question. It belonged, I found, to Bobby.

The boulder rasped.

The beam of a torch fastened unerringly on us. Almost as in my imagination, we were shackled in a pen of light. Bobby put me gently from him.

I reminded myself proudly that, thanks to me, we were not bound and helpless. The leading man spoke. To my horror, I recognised his voice. Suet Pudding Carl Vipoering, expert in blood and terror, had come in person.

"Mein Gott, a team of escapologists, I see! That is splendid!" he approved.

The burglar swung away from me.

"Stand still, you bastard!" came a second voice from the shadows; "move another inch, and I'll plug you!" Bobby took a pace forward.

"That is admirable," Suet Pudding again approved. "It is you, Herr English Spy, that I want! Your stupid companions," with a nod in the direction of the burglar and myself, "can wait."

Bobby, his eyes narrowed against that damnable light, again moved forward. Swaying as he walked, he came abreast of the burglar. Then things happened.

The burglar made a lunge forward.

A shot.

A terrific thud.

The enemy torch spun in the air. To my everlasting pride, I caught it, and held it steadily down to the scene of action. It was the least I could do. The burglar, apparently, unscratched, was standing on Suet Pudding. Bobby had the second man by the throat and was banging his head on the stones. The latter's colleagues mistakenly thought it was time to intervene. The burglar flung them, one after the other, over his shoulder, where they lay beautifully still. I gave Bobby most of the light, because I felt he needed it. Finally, his patient also seemed to lose heart. He was a raw-boned, nasty-looking customer, with a beard that must have given Bobby a lot of trouble

"And now, what?" asked the burglar, glancing at Bobby for further instructions. Panting, I slipped off our slab of rock on which I had been standing out of the way. This was more like the Adventure I recognised. My heart sang as I danced round from one fallen foe to the other. Yes, there was Suet Pudding Carl Vipoering, with a trickle of blood down his chin. It seemed odd that I had been so dominantly afraid of him.

"Oh, there you are, Loreley!" said the burglar pleasantly. "May I congratulate you on the fielding of the torch? It was nothing short of brilliant. You are, if I may say so, one of those rare women who combine a striking personal beauty with a fairly robust intelligence. For just one second, you allowed me to see the face of my current assailant clearly, and the sight inflamed my soul to unprecedented deeds of valour."

I bowed my head humbly on his chest.

"My hero!" I worshipped. But I think he understood. He brushed a speck of the cave off my shoulder. Bobby made unintelligible noises in his throat.

"Well," I fumed, for some wild reason defending the burglar, "if Mr.—" (dash it all, I still didn't know the man's proper name!), "if Mr. Who-is-it hadn't done his ju-jitsu stuff, or whatever it was, we should have looked pretty silly."

"Call him *Pugg,"* said Bobby, with what practically amounted to brotherly love. "Do we leave 'em here, d'you think?"

"Just as you like," said Pugg obligingly. "How much time have we?"

Bobby flicked back his cuff.

"Not more than half an hour now."

"Then we leave 'em."

For the moment, I had forgotten about Leopold Rosbad, his charge from Troubania. My, this was lovely! Spies in the cellars—for this could almost be called a cellar—Fleeing Dictators on top . . .

"Come on, Bobby!" I cried, "let's fix the boulder so that Suet Pudding can't get out!"

Hurry, ingenuity and brawn co-ordinated. I, who knew nothing of the mysteries of counterpoising, kept out of the way as much as possible and held the torch ready to "douse" at an instant's warning.

The burglar stopped for a moment to raise a quizzical eyebrow at me, and all at once, the scene—the gaping throat of the cave; the smooth, evil lip down to the gorge; the snarling, unconscious figures of the enemy; the dark secret tunnel back into the Château—rocked before my imagination and left it icy cold. Bobby, too, had stopped work, and was breathing tensely down my neck.

"What is it, Lorrie?" he whispered at last.

I realised that I had unconsciously "doused" the torch, and they were waiting for me. I gulped and switched it on again. The boulder rasped forward, quivering like a man disturbed from sleep, and then, with scarcely a sound, sealed the secret cave behind us.

"Yes, I see the idea. A very fine piece of work on the part of my ancestors," said Bobby ungrudgingly.

I had to drag both of them away from it. Admiration could be overdone. To me, this ingenious stone was like a nightmare hand, clutching down upon us; a hand like Suet Pudding's—that specialist in blood and terror.

It was the burglar who placed me in the middle of our small procession back through the secret tunnel, and Bobby who almost irretrievably stuck in the "bottleneck" a few yards further on. My spirits rose as we went. We were leaving Carl Vipoering and that dark cave with its clutching boulder hand, behind us. In a few minutes, seconds perhaps, we should be safely in Bobby's familiar *salon.* I had stepped into the middle of a tremendous, pulsating Adventure which meant not merely my life and death, but the lives and deaths of thousands. All I needed was a banner, and a flag to stick on the top of the Château.

Here, almost exactly where I had expected it, was the secret panel which led back into safety.

The panel was shut. Something in the opening mechanism had been put out of action. Brittle with terror, a terror that was like the smell of dried blood, I realised that we were trapped in the secret tunnel.

CHAPTER IX

THE UNSEEN NOOSE

"HOW LONG NOW?" jerked the burglar. Apparently their thoughts were not for themselves but Leopold Rosbad, but they had spoken in a staccato circle of whispers of which I was, mercifully, a part. Outside, somebody must be waiting, listening for every move.

The torch was hot and clammy as Bobby handed it back to me. I saw temper rising in his face, and when big, easy-going Bobby gets into a temper, things happen. They were going to break down the panel by sheer force.

"Directly the panel gives, Lorrie," he said, with faint, unconscious arrogance, "blind them with the light directly into their eyes. Eyes, remember! We haven't time to go back for your Suet Pudding, or we'd extract him and use him as a battering-ram."

The hair rose all down the back of my neck, There was something about the very mention of scent-drenched Carl Vipoering that sucked up my courage like a sponge. My fingers trembling on the switch, I flashed the torch back along the tunnel, almost surprised not to find the jelloid Nazi figure swaggering up on our heels.

"One . . . two . . . *three!*" said Bobby . . .

But the panel did not give. It had been built to withstand even 20th century manhandling. But Bobby would not have it so. He was berserker with effort. Blood and perspiration dripped from him as he and Pugg hurled themselves on it again. I stood on tiptoe, tensely hugging the torch, my heart nearly bouncing out of my chest.

With uncanny certainty, I knew that they would not smash down that door. We were trapped like rats in a sewer. What was happening behind and before us? Outside the arc of our own activity, I had a horrible awareness of life and movement.

"Take it easy for a minute, old chap!" said the burglar. There was an odd, startled note in his voice.

Desperately, I flashed the torch. *Eyes!* That was my job!

Something was touching his head. A smooth leather noose, a hangman's halter!

Without hesitation, the burglar put his hand on the evil thing.

"Oh, be careful!" I moaned. The echo of something dead and horrible seemed again to vibrate about us.

I felt my nails biting into the palms of my hands. Their ferocious onslaught must have jerked the thing loose from some unseen hold. An unseen noose, an unseen hold, more insidious croakings of things unseen!

The burglar's strong, lean fingers were round it, jerking it sharply towards him. For a second, nothing happened. Nothing but a fury of expectation. Then the panel slid slowly open.

The main opening mechanism might have been put out of action, but the craft of many centuries ago had prepared for just such a contingency. That the auxiliary mechanism had been brought to our notice surely proved that Lady Luck was still sitting on our shoulders! In accordance with instructions, although my hand trembled, my torch shone out bravely.

Another hand, warm and steady, gripped mine and deflected it lower. Of course, what a fool I was! One did not look for a clever enemy on the ordinary eye level, but lower, lower, crouching down, almost on hands and knees, creeping nearer and nearer . . .

Bobby went first, gun in hand. Then the burglar. Then a hand closed over mine, drew me out, and pressed me back against the wall of the room. This, I thought, was Bobby.

Someone switched on the electric light.

This was the burglar.

Bobby was still beside me, even his hair looking actively belligerent. The burglar remained by the door, his tie a little skewed, but otherwise still looking uncrushable.

I heard Bobby deflate his chest.

"Dash it all," I burst out as I caught his eye on me, "how could I focus eyes that weren't there?"

Barring ourselves, the room was empty of friend and foe alike.

"No eyes," agreed the burglar sympathetically from across the room.

Was it possible that we had the entire gang bottled up below? I stared round the room. One thing was obvious. They had made a pretty thorough search for something here. Indeed, it almost appeared that, before finding the panel, they had looked for a trap door in the floor.

"*Nom d'un chien* of all the *chiens!*" yelped Bobby, "he'll be here in a quarter of an hour! You, Pugg, keep watch on the gallery and stairs, while I toothcomb the rooms for any loiterers—ground floor first. Loreley can have this," tossing a spare gun out of his pocket, "and stand guard here."

I handled the gun reverently. I was getting all the handy oddments one way and another.

Bobby closed the secret panel that had seemed so immovable only a few minutes before. I stared at it. My chief feeling now was bewilderment. What I had expected I hardly knew. It wasn't this.

"Looks to me," said the burglar, "like the first stages of a Grade A spring-clean. What's your opinion, Loreley?"

Once again the man voiced so exactly what had been in my mind that I could only nod helplessly.

"Don't you worry about that yet," ordered Bobby. "If anything moves behind the panel, fire at once! Stand over here," pulling me across; "you can also keep an eye on the door and the window."

For a novice, I appeared scheduled for a full time.

"Do I fire at *anybody* that comes?" I asked brightly.

Bobby rubbed his chin.

"Well, you might leave us out," suggested the burglar. "All friends, as they approach, will whistle *Rule, Britannia!*"

"Fire into the air, Loreley," said Bobby gently. "We'll do the rest."

"That's right," confirmed the burglar. "Your only object is to make a noise. As a matter of fact, standing there with that gun, you present a picture calculated to strike fear into the stoutest heart; and a girlish scream would really do more damage than the gun!"

Bobby took him away before I wreaked girlish vengeance on him. Nearly ten minutes later, I realised that my rage was running the exact course he had mapped out for it. If an unregistered head had popped in anywhere, I could have gone for it with a mallet let alone a gun. Some day, this Pugg-man and I were going to have a real stand-up fight.

There came now occasional, stealthy movements overhead, but otherwise the old Château was furtive with silence. I perspired with responsibility and memory of Pugg.

But my ears were strained to attention, and I heard a footstep in the cloister-like sixteenth century arches outside the window. I would, I decided, both fire *and* scream at sight. If that didn't give the burglar a jar, nothing would. I licked my dry lips, but the sound outside was not repeated. I hardly knew whether I was glad or sorry.

I stole a glance at my watch. They had been gone now for exactly ten minutes. The chaste stone staircase seemed to lead to a mountain of emptiness . . . When the burglar came back, whistling *Rule, Britannia!* it was all I could do not to throw my arms round his neck.

"Well, that's all right then," said Bobby's voice from immediately behind him. "We've got three minutes now to stage the reception. Lorrie, you can take the soft furnishings."

The burglar took the gun from my hand and laid it on the great beam across the fireplace; then rushed to Bobby's assistance in time to avert tragedy among the decanters, as Bobby made his first onslaught on the old Italian cabinet which now edged the other furniture in the centre of the room. Slowly, but appearing to me in the guise of a miracle, the room began to take on its normal, gracious appearance. I felt flurried with satisfaction. "Two minutes!" said the burglar.

I prodded under a chair and triumphantly excavated the last cushion.

"Time!" said the burglar.

We all stood to attention, breathing heavily.

"The clock's stopped!" panted Bobby accusingly.

The burglar got there first. After all, we could not let Allied hospitality down like this.

"What now? Just wait humbly until the procession turns up?"

Bobby nodded, his eyes still roving anxiously. I could sympathise with his obvious state of mind.

"Didn't we ought to meet the Great Man, or anything?" asked the burglar, also giving the matter profound thought.

"Eh? Oh, no! That's all arranged at the other end, thank God!"

The interval passed slowly. I could not but admire the whole-hearted manner in which the burglar had thrown himself into his friend's political cauldron. I watched him as he crossed to the window to let in a little fresh air. But for Bobby and the Secret Service he would, I decided magnanimously, have been wasted in Vieux Bonnat, even for a fortnight.

"Well, Loreley might as well sit down, anyway," he said.

Bobby hesitated, then nodded. I sat on the extreme edge of the divan, ready to fly off it the instant the great bell rang. Reaction had once more set in. I felt very small and insignificant, and kept my nose strenuously powdered.

How did one greet a Dictator? Give an unsmiling, dignified bow to indicate one appreciated the gravity of the situation? Smile and say "How d'you do?" as to an ordinary mortal? Or just stand to attention with downcast lids waiting for the Great One to speak first? I mentally practised standing to attention.

Suddenly, I remembered to report the footstep I had heard outside. Stiff with uncertainty, I watched the burglar throw open the window and disappear. He returned with a quizzical shake of the head which once more roused all my worst passions, and, pocketing his gun, came and sat down on the other end of the divan. From then on, he didn't look at me. Just pulled up the knees of his trousers and relaxed comfortably among the cushions. I continued to sit bolt upright some two feet away.

I kept a surreptitious eye on the clock. Aunt Sophie must be furious, but whatever the hour, I was determined to wait for the Dictator's arrival, the grand culmination of our night's adventure. Besides, I should have the burglar as escort. Our spare room would be swept and garnished for him by now.

I was galvanised by an entirely new line of thought. Although he had arrived a little prematurely, my aunt had been altogether too secretive about this young man's visit. Was she going all matrimonial on me? Was it of guile aforethought that I had gained the impression we were having something definitely antediluvian? Or hadn't I been listening properly? Yet my aunt had always complacently assumed that some day I should marry Bobby—or so I thought. Neither Bobby nor I had put forward any real complaints. I shot a wary glance at what had arrived.

"Pugg"—what was his proper name? It was ridiculous, but I still didn't know, and I was dashed if I were going to ask him! "Please, kind sir, can I know your name?" What had Aunt Sophie called him this afternoon? I tried racking my brains, but all that emerged with any clarity was a vision of her sitting with determined concentration over a flint implement that "Pugg" had since presented to me as a memento for my grandchildren.

"Stick 'em up, there!" The sharp command came from the door. "I've got you all covered!"

CHAPTER X

LOST AND FOUND

AFTER ONE PARALYSED SECOND, my hands shot up as to the manner born. The burglar lifted his gently. Bobby went limp over his tobacco jar, then straightened slowly like a fish coming back to water. He turned, his hands starting the fashionable upward journey. Then suddenly, they stopped.

"Oh Christ!" said a voice from the doorway, "you needn't bother! It seems I'm too late!"

"Procrastination," said the burglar graciously, laying his hands with great circumspection on his knees, "is ever the bane of the human race. It demolishes empires, and it lands men like you and me in the Divorce Courts. What can we do for you, laddie?"

"A brandy and soda, if you don't mind," said the newcomer hoarsely.

It was then that I recognised him. Slipping off the divan, I poured the poor man's drink.

"Here you are, Mr. Tampler!" I called cheerily.

Up to this glad moment, he had obviously only seen me as a misty, sexless blob. He was mud and blood-stained, and could hardly stand.

"Why, Miss Vance!" There was a flattering mingling of joy and apology in his voice. I remembered the last time I had seen Dickie Tampler: dazzling in white flannels at one of the village fetes, handing me a strawberry ice. My world was widening rapidly. Apparently he, too, was in what I was already calling the "Service."

"Yes," broke in Bobby callously; "but what the devil are you doing here? I thought you were at Bouillaise."

"I was—God help me! If either of you want a one-eyed hole for a honeymoon, Bouillaise will do as much good in a fortnight as any other place I know." The slow, good-natured smile that was Dickie Tampler's chief asset stirred beneath the mud and blood, and his tired blue eyes radiated gratitude. "Thank you, Miss Vance. That just about saved my life! As you may have noticed."

"I take it," pursued Bobby relentlessly, "that you didn't get into your present reprehensible state at Bouillaise?"

"No, damn it! In your beastly Château! Bouillaise was only a damp squib." He staggered across the room and threw his gun on the table.

"Is that a spare portion of the re-armament programme I see on the mantel-shelf, old man? This blasted one's jammed."

I stared, helpless between admiration and a sense of having been shamefully fooled once more. We had been held up by a jammed gun! There really WAS something in this bluffing business . . .

I found that Bobby was speaking again.

"And so you traced Carl the Abominable here. He was then—?"

"So far as I was allowed to see, supervising some form of earthworks with the furniture in this room. Unfortunately, also watching the fun was one Herwigler, Carl's chief lieutenant, and I simply got scooped up on a plate."

The disgust in his voice made me squirm uncomfortably.

"Incidentally," he went on, his voice clouding, "you'd better take it easy while you can, seeing that they've lost your bloke from Troubania."

Bobby shot up.

"Lost him! They can't!"

Dickie Tampler's head slumped down on his chest.

"Sorry, but they have. 'S Bible truth." Suddenly, he raised his head, a fierce alertness back into his tired eyes. "Didn't Cyclops tell you?"

"Cyclops is out," said Bobby. His succinctness seemed fiercely aimed to penetrate Dickie's tiredness. "They got him on the road. He was found on this young lady's doorstep. It's the first house before you come to Vieux Bonnat."

For a second, Dickie's eyes remained unblinking.

"Poor devil!" And then, again, he stretched himself.

I stared from one to the other, my heart shivering within me. Once more, the fun was gone from our Adventure. Even more horrible in remembrance than it had been at the time, I saw those evenly spaced blood-marks, a man's life-blood, that had led from our front door out to the road. My mind fashioned the necessary material to fill the gaps that remained in the story. The man who had died in our portico was Cyclops and Cyclops was also in the "Service." Sheer instinct, and traditional determination to get his message through to his colleague at the Château, had brought him, slithering inch by inch, to within reach of help . . . and then, as his hand stretched out under the shadow of the plane tree, the unrung bell had been answered not by dark, alert-eyed Marie, or my impeccable aunt, or myself, but by the greatest leveller of all . . . Death.

Now, in a country already divided more against itself than the enemy, they had lost Leopold Rosbad, the man who mattered more than death.

Bobby's eyes were snapping in a haggard face as he flung himself heavily into a chair.

"It can't be!" he gritted; "and it's me the lousy skunks will stand up against a wall for it!"

"Incidentally," drawled Dickie Tampler, scratching his head vigorously, "the Government's not settling too well at Bordeaux. One or two little birds have whispered something about nesting in your part of the country. Vichy was mentioned as a hot favourite."

"*What?*" Once more, Bobby hurled himself to his feet. A conspiratorial look of understanding passed between the two men.

"Yep. Turning their faces away from the Empire and back to the enemy," drawled Dickie Tampler.

"Capitulation?" Bobby almost whispered the word.

"Maybe. *Sauve qui peut.* It's a great life while it lasts."

"Do I understand that we've lost the war?" came Pugg's enquiry. In its broad, clean-cut audacity, it was typical of the man.

"God knows," sighed Bobby. "Somebody appears to have thrown a whacking great spanner into France's military machine, and everybody in France, from the Premier downwards, is on the conveyor belt of that machine. Still, I may be wrong. Maybe it just means that they're making a strong stand." He turned to me almost savagely. "Your confounded aunt ought to be chloroformed into making a bolt for it!"

What did he expect *me* to do? Under Bobby's continued glare, I turned helplessly to the burglar.

"If you intend to try it, you're a better man than I am," declared that individual.

I turned back to Bobby with a sigh of relief.

Bobby's hand and eyebrows went up simultaneously in that one French gesture which the centuries had left him, and then, typically and unconsciously British, he dug his hands deep into his trouser pockets and stood legs astride.

"My old governess stayed too, in a peaceful little sun-drenched place leading down to the river. So did roughly four thousand other women and children and old men. Three days ago, the Nazi dive-bombers came. When they left, three thousand seven hundred and seventy-three of those women and children were dead." He had made his point without raising his voice, without shifting his bulldog position.

And for the second time, I saw Pugg shaken out of his imperturbability. There was a blazing spark of sheer fury in his eyes and in his cheeks. But he, too, spoke quietly, even more quietly than usual. And his words had a force that was grey and firm and somehow like the thrashing line of a row of battleships.

"It's time," he said, "that somebody put a stop to this devil's work. It's gone on too long."

"Agreed. And we shall, old man." Bobby, too, was very quiet. It was like a dedication between them. "In the meantime . . ." He audibly gritted his teeth. "God!" he burst out, "what a mess we're in! It's like being shut up in a mad-house!"

"Goo-goo!" said Dickie Tampler, and slumped helplessly back among the cushions.

Slowly, I went upstairs to get the handkerchief that I had left there on the night of the dance. I was tired and dispirited. There was nothing but bad news whichever way we turned. They had even lost a human landmark like a Dictator. How could we expect to win a war? The sooner I was tucked up in bed the better.

Yet, contrariwise, the more I realised the necessity for haste, the slower became my progress. The great carved and painted beams interlaced above my head. I knew the Château so well, yet until these last few days, I realised that I had never really looked at it before. Its beauty, its dignity, in some way almost frightened me. It seemed already alien and strange.

My handkerchief was lying in front of the cherub-fringed mirror. I added another layer of powder to my nose without noticeably improving it. Gosh, I was tired! Yet, still with that odd sense of bravado, I would not hurry. It was far better to be hung for a sheep than a lamb. Stifling a yawn, I looked with a trace of longing at the big Empire bed. It was, I knew, as comfortable as it looked.

I choked off a scream of horror.

Underneath the bed, facing me, his chin unshaven, his mouth rigid in a snarl of hate, lay a man.

That he was dead I had no doubt until, with a movement like a tiger pouncing on its young, he leapt up, put a hand over my mouth, and dragged me back with him under the bed.

With the bed covering down, we were shut off from the room outside. I could hear his throaty breathing beside me—that was all. I tore at the hand over my mouth until it almost stifled me.

When he started to chuckle over me, I went completely limp.

"Much better, little one," he approved, releasing me. "No one is going to hurt you. I," his access of dignity crashed his head on the mattress above, "am Leopold Rosbad, of Troubania!"

CHAPTER XI

SNAKES AND LADDERS

"I KNOW," I GULPED MISERABLY. From the first, I had no doubt as to WHO it was I had found. I was chiefly concerned about getting help. I could see him faintly now, a mass of controlled, powerful insanity immediately above me. His face was a grey blur, with unshaven jowls vaguely darker than the rest. They moved, apparently moistening dry lips. His grasp on me tightened, and my wits seemed to desert me utterly.

I had found the man they were scouring the country for, but what on earth did I DO?

Chuckling, he pulled me across to the far corner of the bed. He pressed something into my hand. It was a dice box.

He lifted the corner of the bed-clothes. Something spread in front of me had a strange but familiar pattern. It was a snakes-and-ladders board. Was I going mad, too?

"Game for the English. You play first, little one!" He pressed a counter into my hand. His touch was hot and clammy.

I played first. Sometimes it was his clammy, bony hands that moved my pink counter; sometimes my own trembling ones. It might be a game for the English; it was an un-English way of playing it. I expected assault and battery at any moment. I finished the first game in safety. He won. We finished the second game. He won. The third spun itself out in, on his part, unbearable excitement. Finally he won.

Unlucky at dice, lucky in love. The maddeningly silly tag kept repeating itself in my head. Yet my wits were slowly tottering back again. Surely Bobby and Pugg must have missed me by now? But perhaps they would assume I had gone home? I had to contact them, and quickly. But HOW? I was even more a prisoner here than we had been inside the tunnel. If I made a move to get out, this maniac would strangle me. I had no doubt of that. Yet there must be some way . . .

Leopold Rosbad's excitement was now increasing unpleasantly. I was within three spaces of winning game No. 4. His staring eyes on me, he threw the dice . . . and sent my counter down the back of the largest and blackest snake on the board.

"*Rule, Britannia! Britannia rules the waves!*" I piped, suddenly and stridently. After all, in a moment I might be dead.

"*Britons never, never, never shall be slaves!*

Leopold Rosbad was looking at me curiously.

"*La—di, da-d*a*—!*" Like so?"

"Like so!" I laughed crazily. Merciful heaven, even if I retained my life, in a few minutes I should be as mad as he! "*La—di, da-da—!*"

This was unexpected success. Our combined effort under the bed became deafening. We thumped on the floor for greater effect. We rolled, we bellowed. Surely Bobby and Pugg would hear?

It was because I was listening for it that I heard the door open.

"*La—di, da-da—!*" bellowed the madman.

He did not notice my silence.

Suddenly, he heard the footsteps in the room. I felt the tensening of his body, of his grim, bony hands . . .

I dared not make a sound, but the footsteps were inexorably coming towards us. In another instant, I should see Bobby's blessed face peering in at me. Or perhaps it would be Pugg—the 'burglar.' I prayed for Bobby. Desperately, I prayed for Bobby. I didn't feel equal to meeting Pugg's comments just then.

"I know you're there," said a voice. "Come right out if you don't mind." It was a soft, cultured voice, with an evil, clinging purr behind it. It was the voice of Suet Pudding.

The madman beside me also recognised it. Beads of sweat stood out on his forehead. Then he gave a short, mirthless laugh. It was ghastly. Clinging to the bedclothes as though they were a solid protection, I heard Suet Pudding Carl Vipoering move closer. The stench of violets seemed poised over us.

I braced myself . . . and then, with one of his swift, powerful twists, the man beside me leapt out into the room. Suet Pudding had a gun in his hand, but he took no notice of it. Straight he went for Suet Pudding's white, suety throat, and his bony fingers closed round it. Nothing human, I thought, could have stood up to that mad onslaught, but I saw then a brute endurance such as I hope never to see again. There was muscle behind Carl Vipoering's dough-like exterior. Muscle and—dragged out against my will, I had to give the man his credit—a cool, quick-working brain. His right arm was twisted behind him. The hands were around his throat. His gun thudded to the floor. His left arm worked like a piston. He dragged the madman with him, and his right knee stabbed into his enemy's stomach. I saw his face. It was a curious grey-white, and his eyes were bulging . . .

Feeling sick, I crept out and grabbed the gun. Without conscious thought, I knew what I had to do. My hands were steady. I was going to fire, and if I killed that gross monstrosity . . .

Only I must not hit Leopold Rosbad . . .!

My finger pressed the trigger. The gun smoking and smelling in my hand, I knew I had fired at the ceiling. The report was deafening. The two men had ceased fighting. I fired again, my finger coiled desperately on the trigger. I could see nothing, hear nothing. Smoke and noise were about me like a cloak of invisibility.

Then Bobby and the burglar crashed into the room, and I saw that Suet Pudding had gone, and Leopold Rosbad was lying in a huddled heap on the carpet.

There was a strange look on Bobby's face as he rose from the prostrate figure.

"Good dog, Loreley," he said quietly; "where did you find him?"

I gulped air back into my lungs.

"Then—then—I h-haven't k-killed him?"

"So far as I know, your conscience is innocent of the death of even a mouse. He's just knocked out—that's all."

I regret that I burst into a torrent of tears. The maniac from Troubania had been enough. Bobby might have made sure that Suet Pudding was not loose on the premises. A distorted vision of Suet Pudding rose like a grey balloon in front of my eyes. Balloon-fashion, he seemed to stir the atmosphere around me—sluggishly, like a pond in which mud is busy settling.

Bobby, reviving and valeting the guest I had found for him, waved aside my disapproval. It had been best to let Suet Pudding go, but they had been keeping a watchful eye on him.

I murmured "Oh yeah?" as darkly as I could, but Bobby met my watery eyes with such candour that my amateur criticism died. My mouth was dry and my throat ached. With a fatuous sense of shock, I found that Pugg was presenting me with a cup of tea.

Leopold Rosbad sat up and drank whisky. Then I found that we were all on our feet, and Bobby was formally introducing me to him. Good heavens, did one bow now, or just look honoured?

"Enchanté, Mademoiselle," he said, holding out his hand. Except that he held mine a little longer than was strictly necessary, he now seemed as sane as anyone present. Those bony hands were, I saw now, finely shaped. He carried his head well on a sturdy figure; his eyes were grey and quite steady . . . That knock on the head had certainly improved him.

I began to understand a little why Carl Vipoering wanted this ex-President of Troubania so badly. And the idea suddenly filled me with dumb, personal fury. After all, I had found him—and scared off Suet Pudding . . .

Why had Bobby released that hated Nazi master-spy from the cave? Why not keep him and slowly starve him to death? It would do him all the good in the world. Never had I so hated and feared anyone as I did him. The sheer neck of the man, sneaking back into the Château, and nearly sneaking out again with our trump card before we knew we had it! It sounded disloyal to Bobby, but his next visit might be more successful.

Moreover, in itself, custody of Leopold Rosbad gave a feeling of living on the top of a time bomb. Excitement leapt up at me. Within the walls of the Château, which had witnessed the conquests and failures of many a *grande intrigante,* of wits and fools of four centuries, lay a modern jigsaw which must be very much to its taste. To my excitement-biased eyes, the sword scabbards interlaced under the delicate flower fresco seemed to vibrate with hope and fear, and a curious exultation.

"Well, a bath and a shave is the first thing, I suppose," said Bobby. His matter-of-fact air of possession was suddenly very reassuring.

"And then—?" I breathed, pulling him back by the sleeve as he was following his charge out.

He scratched his ear.

"Well—er—then I'm afraid we just wait."

"*WAIT?*"

"You heard. Priority instructions just come through. If I don't want to be hung, drawn and quartered, I remain seated on my little behind, with or without the Dictator, until young Dickie Tampler romps back with another set of Great Thoughts from the Great Ones."

"But—but Bobby—that's almost suicide!"

"I know. But England expects, etc." Suddenly he turned to face me, his tanned, clear-eyed face unexpectedly grim.

"Listen, old girl; that wait may not be so long as it sounds. May be only a matter of a few hours."

"But why wait at all?"

"Search me! Perhaps there's another of 'em to pick up somewhere."

Even at this stage, it struck me that one was quite, if not more than enough.

"Whatever happens," continued Bobby steadily, "I've given Dickie Tampler his marching orders to see that you and Aunt Sophie are all right."

I rubbed my hand up and down his coat sleeve. There was a great lump in my throat. I swallowed hard.

"O.K., Chief," I gulped.

He swung me into the air as if I were a little girl, and kissed me.

"*Au 'voir,* Brown Eyes. God bless."

"God bless, Bobby," I gulped back. "Just in case we don't see you to-morrow."

Aunt Sophie was waiting for us at the gate, with panic wrapped round her like an apron. She had had three lamb chops cooking since seven o'clock. Under direst pledge of secrecy, directly the burglar and I were inside, we whispered about Bobby, and the Secret Service, and the Dictator of Troubania. But she was not greatly impressed. I must admit that the chops were a trifle over-cooked.

For the first tune I noticed that I had torn my frock in my under-the-bed struggles with the Dictator. To deflect Aunt Sophie's attention from it, I moaned about a tiny jagged end of my tooth which had escaped the dentist.

Aunt Sophie decided that with the first available transport to-morrow we would hie us back to the dentist in case I got cancer of the tongue.

She called the burglar "Mr. Walnutt."

CHAPTER XII

AUNT SOPHIE TURNS SLEUTH

IF ONLY WE HAD BEEN ABLE to borrow the burglar's car, much mental and physical wear and tear would have been spared us. But on sighting the house on the return journey yesterday, the burglar's big end had gone.

Curiously enough, also, Aunt Sophie's forebodings seem quarantined to the trivialities of life, such as walking on wet grass, or getting to bed, or a meal a quarter-of-an-hour late. So far as can be seen, they never function when everybody else's hair is standing on end.

The dentist had just bowed us out when it happened. Straight in front of us, we saw Aunt Sophie's double walking out with the lank-haired man who had kicked Bobby in the cave! I wanted to shout FIRE! and MURDER! and several other snappy comments, but, without an instant's hesitation, Aunt Sophie decreed that we quietly follow as fast as our legs would carry us.

"But—but—Aunt Sophie!" I demurred weakly, "what can we do about it anyway? You can't start a minor war just because somebody looks like you!"

"I'm curious," said my aunt, tucking her little double-chin in militantly. "And when I'm curious, I'm curious."

I made one more attempt.

"But the man she's with is one of Suet Pudding's gang! You can't tackle the whole gang single-handed!"

Even as I said it, I had a ghastly suspicion that she could—and would.

"I never saw such a girl for making arguments. There's a police force in this town, I suppose."

Yes, but not in the part to which we seemed to be heading. I shrugged my shoulders. It was Aunt Sophie now who had the bit between her teeth. And that was that. Opposition would only make her more determined. Besides, with one half of my mind, I was worried sick about Bobby. Papa Jean, the milkman, reported that there had been no sign of life at the Château that morning. Which might mean anything—or nothing. Aunt Sophie had not allowed me time to go and see for myself.

I became aware that we had travelled farther than I realised. We were now in a part of the town completely unknown to me. A little dazed, I looked deliberately and in vain for a landmark I knew, and surreptitiously pinched myself to make sure I was awake, and not dreaming it all. This was the same Adventure, but with an important difference. We had no masculine support. Had Aunt Sophie and I sufficient courage and ability to face the fireworks on our own?

The street was old and narrow, with tumbledown façades, and a vaguely unsanitary odour. Pale-faced *ouvriers* seemed to walk along it for perhaps a couple of hundred yards, and then disappear again in one of the tiny alley-ways. I became more and more saddled with imagination. We had found the ideal setting for a double murder. I pictured myself being dragged into one of those alleys . . .

We turned into another street, a street where there was not even an *ouvrier,* but an almost equal preponderance of alley-ways in which they could be swallowed up.

A man came sneaking out of one of them with a basket of fish. I shall remember the smell of that fish to my dying day. My aunt, having eyes only for her double, cannoned straight into it. We, the man, and the fish, became unsalubriously intermixed for several minutes. Our quarry was still striding along ahead of us.

"Have you seen a big, fat man, with a dough-like face, about here lately?" I asked the man, on a sudden inspiration.

The man spat reflectively into his fish basket. He had a dark, straggly circle of beard round his face, and his eyes were shifty. He was fingering the good French francs which

Aunt Sophie had dispensed for his fish. With a communal sigh, I opened my bag and, in turn, fingered a note.

"*Mais, oui,* now, of course, it returns to me!" he said eagerly. "A man *trop, trap gros!* To me, it occurred that he might be a *salle Boche!*"

"Yes, yes," I said; "go on." I had to reinforce his memory with another note.

"It is strange, *Mademoiselle,* but even these past days have I seen him down this very street. *Mais, oui,* this street, and no other. Never does he go further than this street, *Mademoiselle.*"

"You're sure it's the same man?" asked my aunt suspiciously.

The fish-man bent towards me. I hastily retreated a pace.

"*Mademoiselle,* he not only looks. He smells." He winked. "Like the flowers that my little bitch of a niece—*votre pardon, Madame*—sells in the Place de la Cathedrale."

My aunt reluctantly but hurriedly paid over another note. Her double and the escort with the lank hair had almost reached the corner. And at that moment, without a backward look, they disappeared into one of the tall, deserted-looking buildings.

Naturally, we followed until we were level with it. On the wall of its accompanying alley-way, a weather-beaten notice board promised "*A la Riviére.*"

"Do you want to see the river?" asked my aunt in a sepulchral whisper.

I shrugged, excitement clouding my common-sense. Having come so far . . .

Our backs as stiff as soldiers on parade, we proceeded down the alley-way. Half-way down was a roughly boarded-up window of the building into which our quarry had disappeared. Aunt Sophie gave me a curious look, and then stood on tiptoe to peer between the gaps.

She saw what I saw.

Aunt Sophie No. 2 was a man.

"Come along, my child," said Aunt Sophie. "This is no place for us."

"Let's run for it!" I whispered . . .

We were too late. Between us and the street a door was opening.

"Then the boss comes here as usual at fifteen hours today? We are to leave everything ready for him." The voice was immediately behind the door. If it was Lank Hair speaking—and I felt it was—he would recognise me at once, of course. Yet there was nowhere we could hide. Unless . . . unless we could get into the building on the other side of the alley!

"He arrives alone, *bien entendu.* The others will arrive at 15.30." The voice was even more distinct, almost as if he were peering round the door. In another second, he would be out in the alley-way. I wasted no further time. The door handle into the other building gave to my hand. I did not stop to reason why it should do so. At the exact instant that Aunt Sophie and I stepped inside, I heard the opposite door bang, heard footsteps mounting towards us! I fancied they stopped for a moment outside our new refuge. Then they passed on.

I allowed my constricted lungs to breathe again, and looked round to see where we were.

It was a bare, dusty room, evidently part of a warehouse of some nature. For the first time in her life—so far as I knew—my aunt looked definitely scared. The footsteps started to come back down the alley-way outside. There was obviously no way out for us there.

After some minutes we plucked up sufficient courage to cross the room to the other door. We looked out on to a long straight passage, with doors from which savage heads might pop out on either side. But we were in luck. At the far end was the front door.

Aunt Sophie kicked over a bucket.

"*Qu'est-ce que vous étes? Qui est là?*" The irate voice came from the hidden rear of the building.

Quite frankly, we ran for it. If there were any heads, now was the time for them to start popping. The very air, so still and heavy that we could almost taste it, made me feel captive.

Footsteps again were hurrying after us. Each door as we came to it was mute and loaded with destiny. And, horror on horror, despite our speed, the footsteps behind were gaining on us as if they belonged to a leaping beast.

It was not until my trembling fingers had shot the heavy bolt of the front door and I saw the sunshine white and hot on the opposite pavement, that I began to feel faintly human again. I caught my aunt's arm, and regulated her pace a little. We were not only human: we were ladies. Ladies did not burst out of dilapidated warehouses like rabbits.

To my relief, the building next door now showed no sign of life. No sound came from the alley-way which we had to pass.

Sweating at every pore, we passed it. There was a feeling of movement from it, which was probably our imagination. The sentinel, if there was one, remained silent and unseen.

Past the place where we had collided with the fish-man. Back, back, nobly resisting the temptation to cast furtive glances over our shoulders; back to the normality of the Place de la Cathedrale; the familiar striped awnings of the cafes.

Aunt Sophie did not complain even when we had to wait half-an-hour for our bus in an almost tropic sun. Our faces were bourgeoise with sweat and our hands still clammy. I gave her arm in mine a good squeeze. I was dying to explain to her our FULL importance, namely, that we had made a discovery which, if Suet Pudding knew of it, would not leave our lives worth an instant's purchase. But anybody—even that fat little woman in front of us—might be one of Suet Pudding's Fifth Columnists. There was a girl selling roses not far away. I wondered if she were the relative of the fish-man. Red Cross vans seemed to be everywhere. There were a few troops . . .

If only Bobby had not already gone! If only my information had not come too late! Almost dancing with impatience, I repeated to myself for the umpteenth time Bobby's undertoned remark to the Dictator, a remark I had not been intended to hear . . .

"If only—if *only*—I could find the secret G.H.Q. from which that rat of a Nazi is operating round here . . ."

Aunt Sophie and I had found it for him. Without their manly escort, we hadn't done so badly. No, sir!

~ ~ ~ ~ ~

Bobby was not gone. After his first paralysis, he took me again and again through all the details of our afternoon.

"It's great!" he admitted magnanimously at last. He enfolded me in his arms and waltzed me around the room. With even greater clarity, I visualised him, and the reinforcements he would probably be able to gather, smashing open one of those dirty doors on a startled, unprepared Suet Pudding. And although the ultimate credit would be Bobby's, I should have been a sort of *deus ex machina.* Laughing, breathless, we practically telescoped Pugg as he was making his usual impeccable entry into the room.

"Children! Children!" he remonstrated, manfully trying to massage all the injured portions of his anatomy at once. With a horrible grin fixed on me, he hobbled forward.

"May I have the next dance?" he gritted.

Then he had to be told what all the fresh excitement was about. At the expression of awed surprise on his face, I felt a sense of exhilaration which might have been the envy of any peacock. Bobby ordered Pierre, his handy man, to have his rattle-trap of a car ready at fourteen hours without fail. Pugg pressed chocolates on me. Where or how he had got them I did not enquire. Then Bobby took me out into the garden to look at his roses.

"Isn't this a lovely bloom?" he asked, bending over and sniffing at a scentless Daily Mail rose. I smiled at him encouragingly. After all, he was going out on dangerous work. Men did not confide in women in these circumstances. "Now, listen, my child," he went on, "and try to look as if you were enjoying the beauties of nature that I am providing for you."

I sniffed at his rose. It was as I thought. Not my favourite at all. I prefer a rose that does its own advertising.

Bobby snapped it off, presented it to me with a flourish, and sucked his finger.

"Do you think we could get Leopold Rosbad into a barrel?" he asked softly.

In sudden, cold, sheep-faced astonishment, I stared at him. He motioned my eyes back to the rose.

"Have you gone mad, too?" I piped, when I found my voice.

He bent over a second rose.

"Not so loud!" he whispered. "I have a feeling that these old castle walls of mine have grown ears. And I'm becoming suspicious of shadows. You see, when I go out this afternoon, I want Leopold Rosbad with me."

"Why?" It was the best I could do for a few seconds. "Isn't that asking for trouble?" I went on doggedly.

"I don't think so," smiled Bobby. "Perhaps I ought to add that one of the people to whom I am not paying a visit is your dear old Carl. And please," as I opened my mouth again, "not so loud this time, if you don't mind."

"Cold feet?" I cooed.

It was hitting beneath the belt, and I knew it, but I didn't care. He broke off another rose for me with loving care. This time it was I who sucked a finger.

"Yes," he said meekly. "Cold feet of as pretty a trap as I ever wish to see. Come on, step out of it, Angel-face! Unknown, unseen ears around us told Suet Pudding of your visit to the dentist. That is the part that worries me: the ears seem to be incredibly efficient. However, in arranging his play, Carl the Abominable paid you a graceful compliment. Even after a session at the dentist's, he knew you would still be interested in a couple of suspicious characters."

Of course, it was Aunt Sophie who deserved this herbaceous bouquet. I had just followed Aunt Sophie. I felt myself trembling like a weeping willow.

"You mean—you m-mean it was arranged that we should follow them right down to that b-beastly riverside place, and—and overhear w-what we did?" I stammered.

Bobby nodded with a sympathy for which I could have killed him. It was a sympathy somewhat akin to that with which an hour or so ago I had regarded Aunt Sophie.

"Exactly. Incidentally, do please be more graceful with those roses. Remember that where there are ears, there are often eyes as well." He patted me tenderly on the shoulder, his eyes suddenly dancing. "Don't worry, Brown Eyes! It is giving me the greatest pleasure to reflect that a gang of toughs are going to waste a beautiful afternoon garnishing all the darkest and most uncomfortable spots of an empty warehouse."

Waiting for Bobby to walk into MY trap . . .

Yes, I saw the whole beastly scheme now! I shuddered. Once Bobby was in their hands, there were ways and means of making him talk!

"But you ordered the car!" I gasped.

"I did. And in good time, too, as you may have spotted. My pet hide-out may be a trifle primitive, but little Leopold will have to put up with that." Bobby's clear eyes and stubborn chin smiled down at me. "Official stink, or no official stink, it's my job to see that Suet Pudding and his mob don't get at him—and I'm going to do it!"

"Hear, hear!" I cried, waving the two roses. Bobby folded his arms like a mighty Trojan. With yet another shock, I realised in a heap what a bad enemy this old pal of mine would make.

"But how do we get the Dictator into a barrel?" I asked doubtfully.

Bobby screwed up his eyes against the sun. His arms were still picturesquely folded.

"Oh, there are ways. Strictly speaking, it is not a barrel, but a rather novel form of air-raid shelter which, as I shall broadcast to all and sundry, I am taking to a friend in the vulnerable town of Clermont Ferrand. That should satisfactorily account for my early start."

"Yes, but—"

Bobby dug his hands into his trousers pockets, and shuffled his feet.

"Well, in analysis, the actual barrel is a series of rubber tyres, braced together and reinforced to resist almost unlimited pressure. It is on the market the other side of the Channel and, to a certain extent, over here. Technically, you just crawl into it and let the house fall down round you. When the dust settles, you crawl out again as safe as the lady who has been sawn in two. Ingenious, isn't it?"

"Very," I agreed.

CHAPTER XIII

THE DICTATOR RIDES IN A BARREL

THE DICTATOR REFUSED to be put in a barrel of any sort. He had taken a fancy to the Château. He did not want to leave the Château.

From the expression on Bobby's face I saw with horror that he would be leaving the Château right on the scheduled minute—which was less than a quarter-of-an-hour ahead—probably under the influence of a sock on the jaw. I trembled with foreboding. The effect on a Secret Service Man's career of a sock on the jaw of the Dictator of Troubania, I did not know—but I thought I could guess. There must be some other way! I glanced desperately at my watch.

"So you refuse to go for your own safety, for the future safety of your country?" demanded Bobby.

Leopold Rosbad looked at him and then suddenly looked at me.

"I will go," he said handsomely, "if the little English girl goes too."

"Oh, but I can't!" I gasped, going completely haywire. "Aunt Sophie is waiting for me!"

Bobby looked at me. "You must," he decreed.

We fitted Leopold Rosbad into his barrel. He wriggled out again, said it smelt, but made no other complaint.

"You don't want me to go into another barrel, do you?" I smiled, secretly aghast at the thought as it passed my lips.

He looked at me and bowed charmingly.

"I do not think that will be necessary, my dear young lady."

"I do," said Bobby.

It was when, I judged, we were on the Clermont Ferrand road, that I heard a faint bass proceeding from my fellow barrel.

"*Rule, Britannia! Britannia rules the waves . . .*" I piped in unison.

It was our theme song.

Suddenly, I felt Bobby accelerate madly, felt the tension in his hands shivering through the aged but willing car.

"Quiet the happy chansons, you two!" he shouted back. "We're being followed. I only hope to God we're on time!"

Whether the barrel accentuated the feeling of speed, or whether Bobby's car was making a supreme effort, I never knew, but the application of our brakes, even though it followed a sharp, official order to halt, brought a faint measure of relief. Now, if I still wanted to, I could be sick in comparative comfort. My oral senses were, I found, especially alert. I heard the rattle of bicycles, and the chatter of voices about me. I judged we must have arrived in town. I heard men piling out of the car which had presumably overtaken us. Then their heavy official tread . . . crunch, crunch, crunch . . .

I held my stomach tightly with both hands and decided that, after all, this was not the time or the place to be sick comfortably. Bobby was angrily demanding what the hades they thought they were doing?

They wasted neither his time nor their own. With flagrant determination, they wanted to see what was inside his two barrels.

To my horror, I found that Bobby was accepting defeat. I myself had not considered seriously before the possibility of defeat. *Mon Dieu!* in the middle of a country which bulged with friend and foe alike, what was the penalty for Dictator-smuggling? Should we be shot at dawn, or just shot? I felt more sick than ever. If Suet Pudding had his way, he would want something sure and sharp.

Yet what else could Bobby do? With a crock of a car that could not be relied on to out-distance anything more than a pony-cart, he was caught in the act. He could, perhaps, attempt a personal escape, leaving us in the barrels, but I did not think that would appeal to him anyway.

"In the name of the Law, remove those barrels from your automobile, and open them up!"

"Perhaps you will be kind enough to assist me, *M'sieur?"* said Bobby, with grand irony. I heard a smothered but appreciative titter from somewhere, and judged that now we must be collecting a crowd.

We and the barrels were lifted out and thrown heavily on the ground by the side of the car. The crowd, I reflected bitterly, was going to get its full money's worth in a few minutes. There was a packing of rags at both ends of the barrel. After the rags would come us.

I felt my barrel roll a little, felt one end of it touching the mudguard of Bobby's car. With my heart in my mouth, I waited Bobby's signal.

Bobby had roused himself to fresh wrath.

"Though why the hell I should play kids' games with a covey of plug-uglies already lousy with the money of the *salle Boche,* I can't think." He tapped, two quick raps, on the side of the barrel.

"Hold your tongue, *M'sieur.* We carry out instructions."

"That I don't dispute. I only wondered whose instructions."

"That you will find out in due course, *M'sieur.*"

"That again I don't doubt. You seem to be an unusually truthful set of ruffians."

With trembling, haste-ridden hands, I was pulling out the rags nearest to the car. Bobby had assured me that there would be sufficient space underneath his rattle-trap to crawl out and hide. Only too glad I had not the bulk of the Dictator to manipulate, I hoped he was right.

My head was already out, my shoulder following, when some instinct caused me to scuttle back. The next second, my world heaved round and round. Something had happened to my barrel. Either by accident or design, it had been rolled away from the car, and out into the middle of the road!

"For your own good, *M'sieur,* I advise you to be more careful in your language to the police of this country. This is not England."

"My God, what a mine of information you are! As a matter of fact, you're from Alsace, is it not?"

"What if I am?"

"Pure biological deduction, *mon cher.* The German blood in you stinks *aux ciels,* that's all. Your father, I take it?"

The murmur of the crowd was much nearer to me now, an ominous undercurrent of whispers and shuffling feet.

"Unfortunately, *M'sieur,* you cannot answer to me at the moment for these insults. Doubtless that situation will be remedied soon. Leave that barrel alone for a moment, and open this one."

Me? Or the Dictator?

"Okay," said Bobby.

Someone heaved at my barrel. I gave myself up for lost. Then I found I was rolling not to, but *away* from, my captors. Aided, no doubt, by the camber of the road, I was rolling, rolling, right into the feet of the crowd.

In a flash, I saw my opportunity. The barrel was fortunately commodious enough for me to reverse myself. I again snatched aside the rags. Yes, I had bumped right on to the pavement. There was a pair of honest peasant clogs immediately in front of me. Some voluminous peasant skirts. Then some wrinkled trousers . . . Feeling like a worm which might be sectioned at any moment, I crawled out among them. To my unutterable relief, they closed like a solid phalanx behind me. A motherly woman stooped and crooned over me, lifting me to my feet. In my relief, I almost sobbed my heart out on her ample chest.

"Pack the rags back in the barrel end, you great fool!" I heard the tense whisper go out before me. Brokenly, I tried to thank them.

The man in front of me spat on the very small area of pavement allotted to him. "*Salle Boche!*"

I forced myself to peer between their shoulders on to the drama in the road. Bobby had won their sympathy to good purpose. Had the Dictator managed to crawl out also? Vying with each other in their excitement, our would-be captors were peering inside his barrel.

"Y'know, all this interest in my air-raid shelters is very flattering, but what the blazes did you expect to find in them? A covey of turkeys?" I saw Bobby take a casual look inside. "As you see, no turkeys."

"It is not turkeys for which we search, *M'sieur.*"

I felt the motherly arm around my waist tighten.

I quite agreed with her. I was not a turkey. But at that moment, I could have gaggled and cackled with the best of them. For obviously the Dictator had also quitted his barrel.

I crawled back into mine when they had inspected it. After all, however friendly the inhabitants, I did not want to be left stranded, literally without a sou, in a strange town. Bobby rolled me back to the car. I braced myself for the upward heave. Soon, thank God, we should be out of this mess.

"I am still not satisfied, *M'sieur,*" said our chief captor. "I must request that you accompany me to the *Bureau.*"

At first, I mistook the two raps above my head for the first claps of the end of the world. Then I realised that I had to crawl out again and join the Dictator who was presumably still under the car. Though what use it would be to us when the car moved off, to be left lying in full view in the middle of the road, I could not think.

Still, orders were orders. I joined the Dictator under the car. He was lying tense and flat. All we needed was his snakes-and-ladders board.

I nearly let out a piercing yell as I found the ground give beneath me. A man-hole or something was opening!

CHAPTER XIV

UNDERGROUND

"NOT A WORD, BUT HURRY, SIR!" came a *basso-profondo* whisper from the depths. Hands simultaneously grasped my dangling legs, and the whisper, equally *profondo* but decidedly less *basso,* said: "Oh, my God!"

In a business-like manner, the hands (whether of friend or foe I could not be expected to tell) pulled me lower into the blackness below. My feet suddenly found for themselves an iron ladder. At the same instant, a pinpoint of light struck on my face.

The unidentifiable man beside me sighed.

"He's still up there!" I whispered. And ten feet up it must have been by now.

"I see. Another couple of rungs, and you'll be on terra firma. Wait there."

The terra firma was wet and sticky, and smelt. With darkness swelling about me, I watched the light above become smudged out. My escort had reached the top again. I cursed myself for not sending the Dictator down to safety first—if this was safety. But underneath that car, there had not been room for full-scale manoeuvres.

The Dictator, breathing heavily, was coming down the ladder. Above him, the man was sealing up the manhole. We had exchanged our barrels for a sewer. Pray heaven we were not caught like rats in it!

Flashing a high-powered torch, the man came down the ladder with the speed and abandon of a monkey. For the first time I saw that the sewer had a sort of branch line to the left.

Afraid we'll have to wait a second or so here, sir," said the man with a look of bored respect at the Dictator.

The Dictator bowed.

"*Dickie Tampler!*" I yelled.

"In person," replied that young man. He cast a still respectful but sidelong glance at the Dictator, who was not paying the slightest attention now to either of us, and then drew me a few paces down the branch line.

"But what the hell in harness," and underneath his cool, drawling voice I sensed that he was genuinely annoyed that I had been foisted on him, "do you think you are doing here, Mademoiselle Vance?"

"Being pushed and pulled from one foul spot to another, it seems to me." I, too, affected a boredom I did not feel.

"Yes, but do you realise that, having been told to assist very reverently a middle-aged gentleman, I nearly passed right out when I got a grip of what was coming down to me?"

"I didn't notice it," I said severely. After all, though I could sympathise with him, it was a bit humiliating to feel I was so *de trop*—especially when I was there by special request of the great Dictator himself!

"Hark to the lady! She didn't notice it, and only a miracle saved her from slipping through my nerveless fingers and smashing her brains out on the cold, cold floor below."

"I didn't know I kept my brains in my feet. You're thinking of the scorpion's sting or something, aren't you?"

"H'm, there seems to be a war on. Well, put your little trusting hand in mine and see what Father Christmas has in store for you now." The faint smile left his lips. The Dictator was still in absorbed contemplation of the drain pipe by which he had come down. "Ready, sir?"

"Pardon? Oh, yes, ready, certainly!"

For the first time I saw that a tiny light above our heads was glowing; I saw too that a door in the side of the sewer was slowly and silently opening. Dickie Tampler pushed me through first.

Air thick with wine and sweat struck me in the face so that I almost gasped. We were in a cave-like room occupied by a group of men who sat at a long trestle table. A pile of francs tottered or sprawled beside each man's elbow. Every eye was intent on the hand of the thrower of the dice. It was a long, thin hand, almost like the claw of a skeleton. The hand performed its final gyration, and, with an air, threw the dice.

The dice rattled on the bare table, stopped.

Someone spat noisily on it. A little man with a straggly beard and a bright red necktie leapt to his feet and harangued it blasphemously for a full five minutes. Then he kicked his chair and sat down again. He and the other players resumed the game. Except one. The thrower of the dice.

"In case you're interested, he didn't repeat himself once," mouthed Dickie Tampler down at me. "Excuse me a minute, I must pay my respects to *Le Bébé.*"

I was hardly surprised to find that these were couched in an argot completely unintelligible to me, but of which Dickie Tampler seemed to have his usual bored control. My attention was held by the face of *Le Bébé.* Over the high, skeleton frame of his cheek bones, the flesh was pink and absolutely unlined. Round his face and bare skull was a fringe of soft, baby hair. Not once did he look at us, yet I had a feeling that every detail of our appearance had been noted on his memory.

His companions continued their dicing. A player at the far end burst into a violent fit of coughing. Someone pushed a gourd-shaped bottle across to him. He drank noisily and fell silent, eyes avidly following the dice again.

"Who *is* your pal?" I asked Dickie, as we left through another doorway.

"Le Bébé? Oh, he doesn't really belong hereabouts. He comes from Paris—the second-best forger in Europe."

"And the others?"

"Bit of a mixed bag, I admit. One or two Communists, one or two burglars, a newspaper-hound who followed the scent too far, a couple of murderers, and so on."

"You—you're pulling my leg!" I gasped.

He turned a completely humourless face to me.

"Good Lord, no! Why should I?"

Still dazed, I passed through two more doorways, then without structural warning, the tunnel opened out into a large cellar.

"The refugee section. Jews," obliged Dickie Tampler.

The cellar was packed to overflowing. From each huddled heap dark eyes peered at us. There were men and women, but the eyes seemed sexless. Only a question remained, and even that question was becoming dulled by time. A tall, strong-faced woman rose from the side of a rough, low bed.

"It is useless, *M'sieur.* He does not know anyone any more. It will not be long now."

Dickie Tampler nodded gently. The features of the man on the bed had once been fine and strong. Now, something—something horrible had happened to them. Dickie Tampler, as he pulled me away, whispered that he had been a justly celebrated surgeon.

A group of children were playing tig-tag round our feet. Except for one little girl with long, dark plaits. She was standing against the doorway, rubbing one black-stockinged leg against the other, her dark eyes wide and piteous on the man on the bed.

The man of healing was dying painfully.

Dickie Tampler threw a handful of small coins to the surrounding children. They scrambled for them, yelling lustily. Only the little girl still stood aloof. Gravely, almost reproachfully, she turned her eyes on us. Dickie Tampler's lean, severe-looking face broke into that nice slow smile of his, as he held up an apple. Her face suddenly alight, she danced across, and made a little curtsey as she took it.

I found another door close to my elbow. Next we were in a dank stone passage. At the end of this were steps up, with a rusty iron handrail at the side.

"Careful! For God's sake, don't slip!" said Dickie, a steadying hand on each of us.

Neither of us misbehaved in any way. We passed through another door at the top and into another passage-way.

So silently that I heard nothing, a man sidled up to us. One dark, ferrety eye was closed and reddened with a sty.

"*C'est vrai,*" he whispered, and just as suddenly departed again.

I felt my eyes growing bulbous and shiny with excitement.

"*Nous allons,*" drawled Dickie Tampler down at us. He just looked bored to the limit.

I caught another glimpse of the man with the sty. He was sliding open a great door. Nor did any sound come from the door. There was just a strip of daylight growing steadily wider and wider.

Presumably he shut it after us. I heard nothing, but when I looked round it was shut tight as the grave.

Around the corner of a dirty, overhung street, a car was waiting for us. We piled into it. Dickie Tampler drove in silence, and, as the streets became more crowded, with more caution than was usual.

In spirit, I scorched ahead. Dickie Tampler could only be our emergency escort. At the very first opportunity, he would park us back with Bobby—if Bobby was, mercifully, still a free man.

"Good heavens, Dickie," I suddenly yelled, "weren't you supposed to be getting some further instructions for Bobby?"

"I was. In fact, I'm on my way."

I nodded profoundly. And then—

I sat there suddenly frozen. For Dickie Tampler had accelerated, and, in my growing experience, acceleration meant the discovery of fresh danger.

"Oh Christ, the hunt's up!" corroborated Dickie.

We missed six cars by a hair's-breadth, and a donkey by a couple of inches. Then—

"Keep your head down and yell as hard as you can!"

I didn't stop to reason it out. I just yelled. It was quite easy, for Dickie Tampler had swung the wheel round and was crashing at full speed into an ornate-looking restaurant.

By the mercy of God, the loudness of Dickie's claxon, and my yelling, people sprang away from our path in time to avoid the carnage that for one palsied second seemed inevitable. There were screams, and probably some cuts, because glass was flying. We finished up inside the private office. With a whine like a fallen angel, our two front tyres deflated at the same instant. Bricks from the opening we had made in the wall were still falling as the Dictator and I were dragged out. There was even worse pandemonium now, outside.

"Quick, *Messieurs, Mademoiselle!*" adjured a new and breathless voice beside me. "They are almost here!"

I saw a little man with the correct beard, the correct dark striped trousers, everything correct except the snap in his eyes and the way he bundled the three of us inside a smelly cupboard.

"Mother of God! is there likely to be much more of this, M'sieur Tampler?" asked the Dictator.

"I hope not, sir." To my surprise, I heard Dickie Tampler chuckle. "Er—that is, I hope not, sir. This is where I leave you anyway."

"Not—not in this closet?" I gasped.

CHAPTER XV

BABES IN ARMS

BEFORE DICKIE TAMPLER COULD ANSWER, the pandemonium outside had become a hullabaloo inside. Quite a lot of people seemed annoyed that we had quitted the wrecked car. Rising crescendo above them all, the little man with the correct beard—presumably the manager of the place—was calling richly on his own vocabulary to describe the damage done to his so beautiful building.

I heard a sound as if he were being taken by the scruff of his immaculate neck.

"Never mind your pigsty of a building. I demand of you where are the villains? *Vitament,* their descriptions, *s'il vous plait!*"

M'sieur the Proprietor's memory of us was a trifle odd. It seemed that we were two girls, and that we had run off screaming down the passage and out through the service entrance which was immediately opposite.

"Did no one stop them, *imbécile?*"

"It was not my affair, *M'sieur.* I regret the passage was at the time empty." M'sieur the Proprietor's voice still carried well. "I am a hotel proprietor, *M'sieur,* not a collector of doubtful women."

Suddenly, everybody seemed to be issuing instructions at once. I gathered that Jules and Jean were to search this, Fluchard and Sebastian to search that. The rest was lost in an urgent scurry of heavy boots. To add to the confusion, another part of the wall came down.

I felt myself counting the seconds. Surely the obvious place to search was a closed cupboard?

I clutched the Dictator hard. He stood stiffly to attention. It helped neither of us when the door of our cupboard slowly began to open.

"Quickly, *M'sieurs, Mademoiselle!*" came the whisper from M'sieur the Proprietor; "you have, I should estimate, ten and a half minutes. You know the way."

In a room on the top floor they proposed to put the Dictator into a voluminous black alpaca skirt. He gave it all one look—the skirt, the jacket that was to go with it, the rusty sun-bonnet—and flapped his hands energetically to heaven. Doubtless, he conceded, everybody was acting for the best, but he had been born a man, and he intended to stay a man. From which arrogant attitude nothing would shift him. In despair, they sent for Dickie Tampler, who, in the excitement, had disappeared.

"There's a cordon round the building. Every exit's watched," he announced calmly, as he strolled back. "We've got about five minutes now before they get sufficient reinforcements to raid the place." To the Dictator, who was standing glowering into space: "Do please hurry up, sir!"

"I am ready," scowled the Dictator.

"You are not," said Dickie bluntly. "For God's sake, get into that skirt! You can keep your trousers on underneath, if you roll them up to the knees."

With hunched shoulders, the Dictator drove his hands into his trouser pockets.

"No Troubanian of my sex has ever donned women's clothing."

The two Frenchmen hovering round us nearly swooned on each other. Dickie Tampler remained unruffled.

"I would not suggest, sir, that no Troubanian has ever before been chased over Europe. That would be an insult to your countrymen. But no Troubanian of your *importance* has been in that position before."

The Dictator smote his forehead, paced like a caged lion up and down the small room.

"Four minutes," said Dickie Tampler.

"But my honour, sir!" It sounded a clarion call deep-throated and menacing. "My honour!"

"If all goes well, who will know?"

"And if all fails?" It was a wail from the lost regions.

"Who will care?"

The veins in the Dictator's neck were swelling. Good heavens, if he went mad again now, we were hoisted with our own petard! I sweated without reserve. My fellow-countryman ought to be warned!

"You have a daring tongue, *M'sieur l'Anglais!*"

"And I hope, sir, a clear head. Nevertheless, the choice—the terrible choice—is yours, and yours alone. Your honour! Or the honour of Troubania! And may I dare to remind you again, sir, that time presses?"

The Dictator made quite a passable woman.

"Can you handle a baby, sir?" enquired Dickie. "I mean, you know which of the ends to hold?"

"*Mon Dieu!*" whispered the Dictator, his hands, well hidden in rusty black alpaca sleeves, dropping helplessly at his sides.

"Wait a second. I'll get you one to practise with!" There seemed nowhere to run to, so we waited. In an incredibly short space of time for the production of a baby, Dickie placed a lusty infant in the Dictator's arms.

"It is for Troubania!" he whispered sympathetically.

The Dictator's arms in their alpaca jacket flexed manfully about the infant.

"For Troubania!" he cried, raising it aloft like a banner.

One of the Frenchmen surreptitiously wiped his eye.

"For Troubania!" we all chorused, making for the door.

"Could you—could you possibly look a bit more *maternal,* sir?" piped Dickie Tampler after us. "Miss Vance, how the hell do women hold babies? It's not like that, I know."

Unfortunately, I was very much in the amateur class, but one glance at the Dictator, and I agreed. The Dictator's elbows were sticking out like girders for the Forth Bridge, while the poor little mite's feet dangled.

"More like a sheaf of lilies," I suggested. "By the way, what is it—a boy or a girl? Didn't we ought to know?"

For the first time, Dickie looked a little distracted.

"It's got a label on it somewhere."

Throughout the proceedings, the baby regarded us with big, solemn blue eyes. It was a girl, of the name of Marie Agathe Chavannes, and was ominously marked No. 13. It was, it appeared, one of a bunch that we were taking to safety, the expedition being vaguely connected with the American Red Cross. We joined the rest of the bunch in a private room on the ground floor.

To my biased eyes, mothers and infants seemed to sprawl all over it; nevertheless, we were packed expeditiously and safely into the bus with the rest. Two policemen scrutinised our little mob, but their eyes were bored. They were doubtless sick to death of the sight of such parties.

Truth to tell, I hardly recognised myself. They had strained my hair back under a pink cotton handkerchief, and scrubbed my face clean of whatever powder and lipstick persisted in adhering to it. I had been re-christened Elise Bordelais, and draped for travelling in a long dust-coat. The Dictator was my Aunt Thérèse. I must say I looked the part.

As the bus moved off, there came a terrific banging at the front of the restaurant. The police had arrived!

~ ~ ~ ~ ~

We were almost in the middle of the bus. All the windows were shut. In fact, I do not think the makers intended them to open. To the right of us, feminine tongues chattered. Before us, feminine tongues chattered. Behind us, feminine tongues chattered. With the addition of the yells and gurgles of the children, it was rather like being shut in a monkey house. The Dictator wisely closed his eyes and pretended to be asleep.

Little Marie Agathe's blue eyes also closed, one chubby fist tightly clutching the alpaca. But before long she must have had a nightmare. Her yells pierced the ear-drums. They ran the gamut of infantile terror, of soul-destroying agony, and utter boredom. Even in that bus, they rose supreme, defiant and attention-compelling. All other vocal effort stopped with a jerk.

The Dictator made gallant crooning noises, rocked it, chucked it under the chin, twisted its little soft tuft of fair hair. All these operations I watched breathlessly, but they were of no avail. Marie Agathe just got her second wind, while the Dictator lay back exhausted.

One of the women obliged with her own infant's bottle.

The Dictator, roused to life again, took it with an immensity of earnest felicities and thanks, and then sat looking at it blankly.

I assisted him to place the right end to the baby's mouth. Marie Agathe did the rest.

Five minutes later, she also did the inevitable in the Dictator's lap.

I shall never forget the look of pained disgust on his face.

Fortunately, my infant was some three years older, and a model of good behaviour. He was also, I found, Marie Agathe's brother. He made only one *gaffe.* That was when he clawed out a hand to the Dictator's knee and lisped penetratingly:

"Nasty man! Don't like nasty man!"

The journey seemed to go on and on. There was to be a 10-minute halt—so we had been told—at Château Dominique. At Château Dominique, Bobby would be waiting for us.

At last we stopped. No one got out except one woman.

"Is this Château Dominique?" I enquired anxiously. There was no sign of Bobby, no sign of anything except a wine-shop and a few tumbledown cottages. It was dismal, and somehow forbidding. French peasants seem to accept a squalor that no English family, however rural, would tolerate for one second. I felt a curious, unexplained relief when I found it was not Château Dominique.

The woman who had got out came hurrying back. She had news to impart—news of importance!—so much was evident. We all looked up expectantly.

"*Quel horreur!*" she gasped. She was a big, heavy-breasted, heavy-stomached woman, and she completely filled the bus door-way. "The police, they are searching for a criminal the most dangerous, a criminal, *mon Dieu!* who has basely disguised himself as a woman! It is said that he comes this way, *le canaille!*" Her seat was just behind us. She started to sway down the bus. "Let me get these hands on *le cochon!* I'll teach him, *n'est-ce pas,"* she dug the Dictator in the ribs, *"Madame?"*

Once more all eyes were on us. The Dictator did the best thing possible in the circumstances. Mutely, he raised a clenched fist. We all raised clenched fists. The bus sped on its way. The digger-of-ribs subsided in an ungainly heap.

"Next stop, Château Dominique," sang out the driver half-an-hour later.

With my heart working double overtime, I saw Bobby's familiar car. Apparently it had broken down again. As we passed, he cheerfully waved a spanner at us. We all waved back. We stopped only just round the corner.

Three minutes later, we had parked Marie Agathe and her brother. The brother was inclined to be peeved about it, but Marie Agathe was the most placid infant I ever hope to see.

CHAPTER XVI

PUGG PROPOSES MARRIAGE

OUR NIRVANA—the haven for which we had been making in such a shuttlecock service—was a wooden hut in the mountains. At first sight of it, my state of beatitude proved more difficult to analyse than I had expected.

"It's a bit primitive . . ." Bobby had said.

I had not, of course, expected the Ritz, and "primitive" described it fairly. It matched our pre-historic flint implement. Pugg was there, too, and he made himself equally at home with it. Truly he must be heaven's own gift to a hard-pressed Secret Service man.

Not that I was not glad to see him! He had a kettle boiling on a brazier, a spread of cracked white crockery, and a perfect galaxy of bedding and bedclothes, all unblushingly out in the strong, bracing wind. After our high-pressure progress through cellars and sewers and brick walls, the healthy Boy Scout atmosphere was a little sudden, but gradually I found my heart opening to it like a noble flower repatriated to the ducal flowerpot.

Bobby left us, with the assurance that no one would find us here in a thousand years. With relief, I recollected my scrawled note to Aunt Sophie (which she must have received by now) explaining, as far as I could, my absence.

The tree-limned scenery was magnificent. So, I believed, was that surrounding the original Sleeping Beauty.

The Dictator's first action was to throw off his dishonouring alpaca. As he unfurled the legs of his trousers, he almost purred.

Pugg combined look-out duties with general exercise. The Dictator, after one stern glance at the interior of the hut, set about mat-making with some form of mountain rush. I naturally became maid-of-all-work between them.

I was tired, perhaps, but very exultant. This, after all, was Life. Life a trifle in the raw, but throbbing with the species of rich red blood we had never known about in Vieux Bonnat. There was another point I was not so sure of. The more I looked at the Dictator, the more disappointed I became in him. He was too human. Moreover, discounting his lapse at the beginning of our acquaintance, he appeared as sane as ourselves. Perhaps I had expected too much. After all, a Dictator must start human, however he finished. I almost dropped one of Pugg's precious cups in sudden fright. Surely there was no real mistake? Surely the British Government were not taking all this trouble on purely humanitarian grounds?

His hands, as I had already noticed in the bus, were calloused with recent manual work. One Dictator had apparently been in enforced co-operation with his more successful brother. What a mess it all was! No wonder the poor man had broken down! This time, I nearly dropped the teapot. Suppose his madness was not genuine, but part of a brilliant, pre-arranged Plan? Even with the toe of excitement pushing me on, I could not get very far with this, however.

My thoughts became sleepier as I turned them to Bobby. Suddenly conscience-stricken, I remembered the distorted smile on his fair, tanned face as he had given Pierre his final orders to close and bar all the shutters of the Château; of Pierre's sad-eyed obedience. Pierre, who was only a *cocher* and general handyman, had understood the bitterness of that departure, while I had been too preoccupied with my own mounting troubles. Le Comte Robert de Treslin, hereditary heir to the Château des Roches, had to flee like a criminal from it. Poor Bobby! He was, I knew, just a little bit vain of that Château. It pleased him to think that he was as good as, if not better than, his true-French ancestors. How this furtive leave-taking must have stung him! With very real if belated sympathy, I made up my mind to be extra nice to him when he came back.

My thoughts roamed off again. Count Robert! It sounded like a nickname for a London policeman. And, in a way, although I was still staggering a little under the weight of the discovery, Bobby was a policeman. Not the same kind as M'sieur Labourd, that one with the reputation so high from the *Sûreté,* of course. Our adventures of this afternoon would have been very different if he had been. With eyes suddenly alert, I found myself studying the landscape to make certain that no further excitements had broken out on it.

I cannot say that I was consciously worried. I was just geared to tension. Surprisingly enough, up here the war seemed nearer to me *personally* than it had been in Vieux Bonnat, or even in Clermont Ferrand, or Château Dominique. It was as if a hand had snatched us out, first from peace, then from great danger, for a particular purpose. From this eagle's eyrie, France was spread before me. *La Belle France.* France, over whose cherished soil, rumbling nearer and nearer to us, and to England, the Nazi tanks and guns were already pouring a hell of fire and death and a stinking dishonour.

I did not hear Pugg approach, but I knew he was standing beside me even before he placed his warm hand over mine.

"I suppose," he said, quite diffidently, "you wouldn't care to marry me when this is all over?"

"M-marry you?" I repeated, *à la* the village idiot.

His eyes rested on me, gravely, steadily. I saw the sensitive lines of his mouth relax into a faint smile.

"Yes, believe it or not, people do marry sometimes, y'know. In fact, taking it by and large, it's fairly popular."

Yes, I knew that, but somehow I had fallen into the assumption that it was Bobby I was going to make happy. Pugg was a new candidate.

"Do you know," I said severely, "I don't even know your name yet, Mr. Burglar Pugg Walnutt?" He smiled.

"You won't like it when you do."

"No?"

"Well," he gently massaged one ear, "it's—Jonathan."

Jonathan . . . But I did like it. it suited him. Jonathan Walnutt. It was polished, satisfying, and somehow distinctive.

"And that," he grinned, "is how I came to be known as Pugg."

Jonathan—Jonathan Walnutt. Yes, I liked it. But I was unaware that I was rehearsing it aloud until he gave a wild whoop.

"Say it again!" he commanded. "There is a certain cadence in your voice that is most becoming to it. After all these years, my mother's choice is suddenly becoming understandable to me!"

"Something to do with the altitude, perhaps?" I mocked. Again his dark eyes were fixed on mine. They danced in his finely etched face with the reflected mountain sunlight, but somehow they were as inscrutable as Destiny itself. And we were destined for something. Of that I was becoming more and more sure.

"The gods have been even kinder to me than I knew," he said gravely. Almost roughly, he pushed me back to the hut. "Run along and get some supper ready, my dear. Bobby will be back soon."

And I went. With yet another problem hammering at my brain. He had been fooling, trying to cheer me up, perhaps. I suppose I had looked like the figure of doom contemplating the graveyard of France. I found myself chuckling, and quickly gagged myself. Why did I always want to chuckle at the wrong moments? Pugg—I meant Jonathan—had been fooling, of course; he hadn't even waited for my answer. He had, indeed, sent me in like a good girl with a new toy. I began to resent that a trifle. Yet he had undoubtedly been under the spur of some unusual emotion. What it was I did not feel qualified to say; but it was obviously not uncomplimentary to myself.

And suppose he had not been fooling? Was it disloyal to Bobby to consider it? No girl married to Pugg would have a dull time, anyway.

I became aware of movement, violent movement, in the hut to which I had obediently hurried. Leopold Rosbad had discarded mat-making. His calloused hands clenched and shook in front of him. His sturdy body writhing like a spring, his breath whistling sharply past his outflung tongue, he hurled himself straight at me.

His outspread fingers grabbed at my shoulder like a crane. Second by second, I expected them to creep up, to stretch round my defenceless neck. About his madness I could have no complaint now. We were back at the snakes-and-ladders stage.

To my dazed, uncomprehending relief, he released me and hurdled round the hut again. His face now was grey. Grey eyes. Grey hair. Grey, too, I realised, his coat. He was a wispy horror of grey.

I was too paralysed to move. I just stood there, screaming at the top of my voice for Pugg.

Pugg's feet sounded outside, like easy-going pistons.

Leopold Rosbad heard them, too, and his face worked in demoniac rage. I heard Pugg coming, knew he was there, but still I could not stop myself screaming.

"Here, I say, this won't do!" said Pugg mildly, from the doorway. Feeling suddenly foolish, I stopped yelling.

Surprised either at the silence, or by the arrival of an exceedingly self-possessed young man, the Dictator stood stock-still, staring, staring, at the intruder, drops of saliva dribbling from his chin on to his stocky chest.

Then I saw his muscles ripple, and my tongue cleaved to the roof of my mouth. Was it possible that Pugg didn't realise the danger, the mania-charged strength of this man? I tried to choke out a warning to him, but the only sound I made was a frightened hiccup.

With incredible speed for his bulk, the madman sprang. The hut seemed to shake as to the tread of a wild beast.

"I'll kill you!" he screamed. "Kill you, KILL . . . KILL!"

Pugg side-stepped, and the whirling fists rammed into the jamb of the door. His face puckered like a child's, the madman stopped and inspected his damaged knuckles.

With a leisurely air, Pugg picked up a pillow, stuffed it into a sack, and tied it tightly into a sort of neck about a quarter of the way down. The way he held it, it was ridiculously life-like. I giggled. They were all mad . . .

The sound swung the Dictator round to face us again.

Pugg held the effigy at arm's-length and took a violent punch at it.

"Come on, let's finish him off!" His enthusiastic yell made me jump like a performing flea. "The devil's weakening now! Look, my friend!"

Leopold Rosbad gave a tiny guttural grunt. Concentrated in his eyes was a blaze of cunning hate. I watched his clenched fists, his crooked, punch-drunk arms . . . Pugg placed the sack between them.

The Dictator became very quiet. One hand crept up slowly to the neck of the sack. I watched him, breathless, fascinated with horror. His clutching hand tightened! Now it was *squeezing!* And out of his own mouth choking breath gurgled and panted . . .

Pugg laid his hand gently on my shoulder. The saneness of that touch steadied me in time.

Squeezing . . . squeezing . . . I saw the whiteness of the knuckles round the neck of the sack . . . Then, deliberately, as a terrier shakes a rat, the Dictator shook it, and then, slowly, allowed it to slip through his hands.

Pugg quietly stepped forward. My heart somersaulted with apprehension.

"That's fine, sir! You've killed him this time all right. See!" With one, well-aimed kick, he shot the sack out through the doorway and on to the path beyond. "Look!" he repeated back at the Dictator, "he's lying quite still—quite dead now."

The Dictator's breath was heavy.

"Yes," he said, a little uncertainly. "Quite dead now."

Slowly, like an old man, he stumbled to a seat. His head drooped on to his arms, and I was sure I heard a thick, guttural sob. The utter misery in it went to my heart like a knife. And my swamping tide of terror incontinently left me. I felt oddly mature, and very sure of myself. One bony, despairing hand was outflung on the rough table. I laid mine over it. For a long time neither of us moved. When at last he raised his head, his eyes were gentle and sane again—as I had known they would be.

"My little sister was very much like you," he said. "The only human being I had to love!"

"Where is she now?" I breathed.

"They kicked her to death," he said simply. "She had brown eyes too—until the red blood closed over them."

I don't think I shall ever forget my rush of pity.

"And you never married?" I said, after a pause.

"Married?" He seemed genuinely surprised. "Marriage is not for such as I. If you ever have a son, pray to your God that he be ordinary, commonplace, stupid even, but not sensitive, or brilliant, or outstanding in any way above his fellows." His voice dropped. "Then he may find—happiness."

Pugg went out on his everlasting guard-duty.

Leopold Rosbad watched his retreating back, his eyes puckered into a quiet little smile.

"Our young friend will catch something sooner or later," he mused, "even if it is only a big fish . . ."

CHAPTER XVII

I AM CREDITED WITH TOO MUCH INNOCENCE

I SHALL NEVER FORGET the look on Bobby's face when he brought back the news. The Dictator was gently completing his fourth mat; with Pugg's help, I was opening the second tin of soup. The tin-opener fell from his hand like a thunderbolt. We hardly noticed it. The silence of the mountains closed about us, as it had closed about the heart of France.

Reynaud had resigned, and Marshal Pétain had applied to Hitler for the conditions for a cessation of hostilities.

"You were right," said Pugg at last, in a curious voice.

"Yep."

"But—but it's *madness!*" The shocked horror with which Pugg voiced the all too-familiar state brought my face into an instinctive half-grin before I could stop it. Surely WE were not in a position to throw stones at any form of insanity?

"Yep." Bobby, too, seemed blissfully unconscious of the domestic parallel.

"But will the French people take it?" Pugg was unusually vehement. Even his nerves, it seemed, were rattled now.

"Probably." Bobby had—thank goodness!—not said "Yep" for the third time. His hands and eyebrows went up simultaneously in that one French gesture of his. "Doubtless there will be a flood of tears and histrionics, but, with the best will in the world, the alternative of becoming a temporary German as opposed to a dead Frenchman may have quite a mass appeal. And I can't say I blame them. Wait till the poor devils get fed up, that's all. That'll be our day!"

"Then you don't think the panic has spread across the Channel?"

Bobby laughed shortly.

"We don't get even honourable mention in the News Bulletins, so there'll still be hope." My dazed mind swung back like the pendulum of a clock to the personal. Bobby looked so tired and worried . . .

"The devil of it is that the only order I can get through from the powers-that-be is an even more emphatic instruction to *stay put.* What do they think I am? A blasted monument around which the Storm Troopers and the Gauleiters will do the goose-step?"

"An inspiring thought," sympathised Pugg.

"Of course, I know that Dickie Tampler will juice things up all he knows, and Dickie's a good lad at the high-pressure stuff—none better. But damn it all, he's only human. And, blast their whiskers, I want to get moving! France isn't becoming too healthy."

"Any idea what you're waiting for?"

"Not an earthly. Maybe for the pearly gates to open, or just for a new moon. The whiskered brigade like to go all mysterious on us sometimes, you know. Keeps up their self-respect."

"Hmm. I think—that is, if Jerry permits—I'll stick to Art rather than Intelligence. Despite the post-impressionism, the cubism, the surrealism, the naïvism, the fauvism, and all the other isms, that started with Cezanne, there is, after all, a certain sense of continuity in Art. A Breath of the Eternal, as some of the critics like to call it. Has Paris been taken yet?"

"About a dozen times, if report is anything to go by. But the muddle-headed nitwits haven't the guts to say 'Yes' or 'No' to it. The rot in this country has indisputably started at the top—and God, what an excellent job they've made of it! I tell you, it just about breaks my heart—" He broke off suddenly. "Winston knew his basket of fish: 'We fight on—if necessary ALONE' . . . I wonder what they made of that over there?"

"Probably turned it into a victory march. NOW we know where we stand—and God help everybody!" I began to realise why Jonathan Walnutt had been re-christened *Pugg.*

Standing there, puffing strenuously at his cigarette, he had a marked and, in the circumstances, comforting resemblance to a statue to Graceful Pugnacity. "How long are you thinking of waiting for your boiled shirts in Whitehall to do their stuff?"

"God knows! That's just the point: I'm not thinking! I'll see that Lorrie and her aunt and you get safely aboard something, and, if things look too bad, I'll push the Dictator off on to somebody, but in these days I simply dare not quit myself until I know what it's all about. By the way, how are you off for ready cash?"

Pugg pulled out his wallet and both men peered intently into it.

"Put it back," said Bobby resignedly. "Fortunately, I didn't intend you to go first-class."

It was then that I found both men were listening, every nerve in them strained to attention. I could hear nothing. I became more scared of that NOTHING than anything that had gone before.

Bobby saw my white face and indulged in a hearty laugh.

"Well, anyway," he grinned, "we're all right for the time being. No one can find us here."

"You're sure?" I began to feel more brave already.

"Sure as eggs," he replied cheerfully.

But his eggs must have been addled, or something.

There was somebody watching us through powerful glasses about two miles down the mountain track. I bit my lips to keep my mouth steady. Even here, Suet Pudding had tracked us down. Was there nowhere we could lay our heads in safety?

But danger was the right medicine for Bobby. His tired, worried face became set into lines of quiet efficiency. His blue eyes seemed to take in at a glance every object in our immediate terrain, including Pugg and myself, and classify them in order of importance. We, like the rest of France, might be on the conveyor belt of the military machine . . . but we were obviously going to fight—if only as a British example.

I saw that Pugg had slipped away from us. What, for mercy's sake, was the plan of campaign? The night had a thousand eyes, and we but two each. Nearer and nearer, borne on the wings of danger, every evil, growing shadow cowering round him in craven allegiance, Suet Pudding and his attendant jackals were striding up the mountain toward us. He was the Nazi lord of the shadows, and the things of the shadows. He was almost the lord of France.

"Everything is all right, yes, no?" asked a voice behind us.

But it was only Leopold Rosbad, our charge, sniffing the evening air.

"Everything is not all right," snapped Bobby; but swiftly recovered his temper. "You will greatly assist me, sir, by keeping to the hut and in no circumstances leaving it until I say so."

The Dictator raised his hat and turned obligingly on his heel, possibly to start another mat. He obviously thought he had stumbled out on another situation *à deux.* I had never felt less romantic in my life, but Bobby gave a fairly satisfied grin. It was not a point that he would miss.

"That will be your job when things break," he said unromantically, jerking his head backwards to the hut; "guarding the door."

"With what?" I asked, trying to sound equally matter-of-fact.

He had, however, prepared for that with a carefully whittled piece of wood which, handled even by me, would have split open a man's skull. Standing there in the fading mountain light, I began to feel club-conscious, as though the veneer of civilised centuries was slipping away . . .

Bobby again appeared satisfied.

"That's the spirit, my wench!" he said cheerfully.

We became aware of a faint, stealthy scrambling up the path by which Pugg had disappeared. *This was the decisive moment.* Bobby and I flattened ourselves against the wall of the hut. Every nerve in me was alert with warning, but I was too excited now to be really nervous, too thrilled for real apprehension. The shuffling grew nearer, and suddenly—

"*Hist!*" said a voice.

Pugg's voice.

Bobby did not move.

I saw Pugg. He had in tow another figure. A short, squat figure with a curious-shaped head, and a curious method of walking. I saw that Pugg was dragging him.

Still Bobby did not move.

"Raiders past!" came Pugg's voice again; "I've got the only bird there was."

"Good!" said Bobby quite casually, and we went out to inspect our prize.

Mon Dieu! Surely I recognised those boots, that long camel-hair coat? In my new excitement, I am afraid I got horribly in their way, but they good-naturedly treated this as a prerogative of my sex. I did not dare yet to open my mouth.

That peculiarly shaped head was, I now saw, caused by the fact that, right down to the middle, the prisoner was enveloped in Pugg's ubiquitous sack. The poor human inside it must be almost stifling. Marching like a Roman conqueror, Pugg dragged his prize inside the hut. Bobby followed grimly. I kept close behind him,

"Now," said Bobby, "we're going to learn a thing or two."

"Mother of God! what is it?" Leopold Rosbad had come from the inner part of the hut. He had obviously been disturbed in the act of combing his hair. Grey and wiry, it stood up straight round his lined face. His eyes, I saw, were sunken, with great dark pouches underneath them, but, to my inestimable relief, they were completely sane. He was peering at the sack with frank astonishment, but it appeared to evoke no unpleasant memories.

Pray heaven they got it off before . . . A hand loaded with ice seemed suddenly to have me in its clutch. Then—

I didn't know whether to laugh or cry.

Pugg had nipped off the sack.

And there, her best toque rammed down over her nose, her sleeves pulled up to her elbows, and her chin covered with dirt from the sack, *stood Aunt Sophie.*

I shall never forget Pugg's face, nor Bobby's silence, nor the Dictator's startled grunt.

My aunt found her voice.

"You f-fools!" she said. That was all. Two words. She was really magnificent. I rushed in and wiped the dirt off her poor old chin, and we all tried to help her to a seat. She flung us off with a gesture as statuesque as her dishevelment allowed. Aunt Sophie had found us out, and had taken our measure.

Never had I expected to see Pugg's aplomb so shattered. After one forlorn, irrevocable moment, he walked out backwards, and came panting back with a cracked cup of water, which he presented almost on his knees and with an expression of such dog-like entreaty in his eyes as should have melted any heart.

Not Aunt Sophie's.

"Brandy?" breathed poor Pugg, his chunky brown hair falling on to his forehead.

"No, thank you," said my aunt primly.

And then she relented a little, and—because, I suspected she badly needed it—accepted our help back to the chair. She sat and surveyed us sternly.

"I'm not even going to say I'm sorry," said Pugg, nervously getting out a cigarette and then, even more hurriedly, putting it away out of her sight. "Words aren't much use really, are they? But you do believe it was a horrible mistake, don't you?"

I think we all held our breath. Aunt Sophie's mouth twisted into a faint smile. It was only this morning that she had told me she had nearly married his father. Like father, like son?

"It was a horrible mistake all right," she said.

"I could wring my own neck," said Pugg and, to his credit, he looked as if he meant it.

The Dictator stumbled out to finish his toilet.

"I always said," he remarked gently, clapping Pugg on the shoulder as he passed, "that sooner or later *you* would catch something, my friend—even if it were only a big fish."

I think that jest was the beginning of my aunt's dislike of the poor man.

Bobby made sorrowful noises in the background. His intention was obviously of the best, but I must admit it lacked subtlety.

My aunt swung round on him.

"Bobby Treslin, I would never have believed it of you!" she said, and to my surprise, and Bobby's horror, there was a clear sob in her voice.

My head was whirling. What on earth had *Bobby* done to Aunt Sophie?

"There are some things which are below contempt," she pursued. "Mr. Walnutt's father was a great friend of mine. I should never have believed his son could sink so low, unless I had actually received proof in black and white. As for you, Bobby Treslin, I have treated you as my own son. I have placed no restrictions whatever on your seeing the girl. You, anyway, knew that she was a mere innocent child—"

I think Pugg and Bobby began to understand at the same instant, To my delight, Bobby crimsoned to the roots of his hair. Pugg rubbed his hand gently up and down the seat of his trousers, then he smoothed his hair back, and his eyes twinkled.

"But, Aunt Sophie—!" began Bobby.

"Don't Aunt Sophie me!" snapped my aunt.

"B-but, look here—" Bobby had been sorely tried that day. I saw an explosion was imminent, and interposed myself between the two warriors.

"I think there's been a mistake," I said sweetly. I faltered a little as I saw that Pugg's eyes were lowered and his fingers crossed so that he should not be blasted by too much local "innocence." Bobby was staring at me straightly, waiting for me to go on.

"I—I haven't been kidnapped!" I gasped. Dash it all! the dear old soul ought to have had more sense. She might believe it or not, but, dash it all! I was not so innocent as all that, and what she was hinting was sheer insult to two of the straightest, cleanest men I ever hope to meet.

"Didn't you read my note properly?" I demanded hotly.

She took out of her pocket a scrap of crumpled paper which I recognised.

" *'I am being taken somewhere, I don't know where, by Bobby and company,'* " she read austerely, and prepared for further battle.

I stared at her, stupefied. Had I actually worded my message as badly as that? It took us a quarter of an hour to undo the wrong I had done. By this time, I felt even more miserable than angry. Knowing Aunt Sophie, I ought to have been more careful, but I had been so obsessed with the idea of secrecy that my ordinary precautions had sideslipped completely. But then, the "Service" had recruited me with rather a jolt.

"I still think it unconventional and very undesirable," said Aunt Sophie thoughtfully at last, "but—well, I suppose we had better let bygones be bygones." Her eyes, I saw, were on her battered toque, and she determinedly sucked a scratch on her finger lest it turned septic with mountain dirt.

"You're trumps, Aunt Sophie!" said Pugg, and he meant it.

She was, too. Dragged up that mountain-side, half smothered, full of outraged guardianship and heaven knew what grade of foreboding, she had tracked us down where men trained to the task had failed. True, she had family knowledge of Bobby's hide-out . . . I put my arms round her and hugged her tight. We were all together again now, and things didn't seem nearly so bad. When luck favoured us, we could escape from this ravaged country in bulk, as it were.

She patted my hand soothingly, as if I were the one who needed comfort.

"You may smoke if you want to, Mr. Walnutt," she said graciously.

And suddenly, the smile on my face stiffened. The door had opened soundlessly. In the opening, gun in hand, stood the man I feared more than anything on earth: the Nazi Suet-Pudding spy, Carl Vipoering! And behind were the grim faces of his bodyguard.

CHAPTER XVIII

THE TERROR IN THE HUT

BOBBY LEAPT FORWARD like a paranoiac victim who, having made up his mind to suicide, miraculously sees his opportunity. But evidently Suet Pudding wanted him alive—if possible. One of the jackals used the butt tend of his gun. Bobby went down and out. Pugg surrendered more elegantly.

Aunt Sophie was honoured by the supervision of another jackal. She looked mildly surprised.

Carl Vipoering beamed his sunken-eyed, suet-pudding smile all round.

But without warning, almost without sound, Bobby reentered the fight. Twice I thought he was down for good, then he was wading in again, his fists ramming scientifically into every enemy he could still see. But the punishment he was taking was murder. Desperately I wrenched my eyes from his whirling fists and grim, blood-streaked face.

Through the mist, I found Pugg, his eyes shining like a schoolboy's, his feet literally pawing the ground in his excitement. Perhaps fortunately for him, one of the jackals had taken the precaution of tying his hands to the beam of the hut.

Aunt Sophie continued to sit on the seat we had, in calmer moments, provided for her. I crouched against the wall, the violence of the scene in front of me fascinating me against my will. Bobby was being battered and was battering the bodies of his enemies into gory pulp. Pugg was helpless. I alone was unwatched, unnoticed! I caught Pugg's eye, and nodded.

Somehow, I must get Leopold Rosbad away from this hut before anybody noticed me. How, or what I should do with him afterwards, I had not the faintest idea. *Now* was my testing time, and I was not going to funk.

Aunt Sophie's eyes widened as I sidled back into the inner part of the hut. For one ghastly second, I thought she was going to voice her instinctive disapproval. I put my hand frantically and mesmerically to my mouth and shook my head. She shivered from stem to stern and reluctantly withdrew her gaze from me and re-focused on the fight. Whether at that time Aunt Sophie did or did not understand the importance of the stake at issue, I was never able to fathom.

Now I was in the tiny rear portion of the hut. As silently as possible, my fingers trembling a little, I closed the creaking door. Leopold Rosbad was standing against the far wall, waiting . . . waiting for the jack-boot of Suet Pudding and his concentration camps to fasten on him again. Never had I seen on any face a more poignant, a more bitter acceptance of defeat—no, not even on the faces of homeless refugees. When he saw my comradely entry, he relaxed a trifle, his lips curved into a faint smile of welcome, but his waiting eyes went beyond me to the door for the next.

I stared round the tiny "room." The very air seemed poisoned with a mental tiredness it was impossible to fight. Once again walls seemed to be closing about me like a trap. But I knew now what I and the Dictator had to do. Bobby couldn't hold out much longer.

I set my chin stubbornly. It was my fault Suet Pudding was here. Aunt Sophie had followed me. Suet Pudding had followed Aunt Sophie. We had made it just as easy as that for him. And I was furious.

By this time, I had torn down the rusty wire netting that was over the one small window. The Dictator watched me idly. Perhaps he, not being imbued with the heroic violence of the scene I had just left, did not think much of our chances even if we got outside the hut.

But he came forward instinctively as he felt the clean, cool evening air blowing in on his face. I measured his bulk silently as he stood there, and decided that, with a little assistance, he would get through.

He did—though I think I badly bruised his august posterior in my excitement.

At that moment, the hut shook. Bobby had gone down for the last count. Desperation like a ravening wolf at my heels, I tore my frock from waist to hem as I scrambled out through the gaping window. As I heard the rent, my blood boiled even faster; and then, with an odd sense of its importance, I remembered wondering what sartorial damage the Dictator had suffered. He was waiting for me, and fortunately—because I was now a mass of barely-controlled panic—he took charge.

I heard Pugg's voice raised inside the hut. Raised intentionally I knew, so that I should hear it and be comforted, in that he temporarily was holding the fort.

This was again fortunate because we had to circumnavigate the rear of the hut to get to the part of the wood the Dictator had chosen as our refuge.

"Indignity of the spirit I can bear with a high, noble fortitude," said Pugg. "But indignity of body, no! As a very special favour, would you mind asking your good-looking henchman here to withdraw his ramrod from my ribs?"

Good old Pugg! Pugg, I knew, would give them something to think about. And every moment they were thinking, we could creep nearer and nearer to safety.

I heard some form of a blow, and it was the skin on the back of my head that did the creeping.

"Extraordinary," I heard Pugg's voice again. And there was not a tremor in it. "As Ariosto puts it: 'It came upon them like a blast from Astoipho's horn'! Or perhaps you do not remember 'Orlando Furioso'?"

And that, I knew instinctively, with a shiver of sheer horror, was the way he would walk to his death, his eyes laughing at it, gentle, polished raillery on his lips. I restrained a maddened impulse to rush back, to say that I was here, that poor Leopold Rosbad was here, that Suet Pudding must, on no account, touch either Pugg or Bobby again.

The Dictator, with abnormally quiet tread for one of his bulk, was moving with the steady momentum of a train. As I trotted after him, Aunt Sophie entered the verbal ring back inside the hut.

"I never mind being told if I am wrong," she said. "Please correct me if I am. But I believe I am right in assuming that you"—there was a typical Aunt Sophian pause—"gentlemen—are looking for one of the name of Leopold Rosbad?"

"We are, *Madame.*" We were still so near to the hut that I could hear every word distinctly, and I could picture Suet Pudding's cold, appraising eyes fixed now on Aunt Sophie, his gross body bending toward her with mock deference . . .

"Then you're a fool to come here," said my aunt sternly.

She had chosen a critical moment to be so revoltingly personal. Though, honestly speaking, the moment had been thrust upon her. I halted, holding my breath.

"Will you kindly explain?" Suet Pudding's voice was, to my astonishment, a little thoughtful.

"Certainly," said my aunt crisply. "You imagine—why God alone knows!—that Mr. Treslin and Mr. Walnutt have some association with this Leopold Rosbad, Dictator of Troubania."

"We know that to be the case."

"You do, do you?" The words came like icicles. My aunt, I knew, pursed her lips. "Then, my earlier remark is self-explanatory, I think."

Leopold Rosbad, his gait still steady, was disappearing into the shadows of the trees. I had to follow him! I could not be left here alone! I hurried along. My aunt's voice with its next incredible assertion came faintly after my flustered back.

"I think I can associate myself with Mr. Treslin and Mr. Walnutt in this. The gentleman who was our guest was no more a Dictator than I am. Good gracious, man! anybody could see that with half an eye!"

The Dictator smiled at me as I kept pace by his side, away from Aunt Sophie, and from all the friends I knew. A little waveringly I smiled back. Aunt Sophie was adding her full quota to Suet Pudding's discomfort, but she was also adding to mine. It was ridiculous to worry about it, of course, but she had voiced something which had been nagging at me for hours. And of course it was ridiculous! Bobby and the whole of the Secret Service were solid behind Leopold Rosbad. They could not be mistaken in him. The issue was far too important.

That he had, in addition to making mats, already explored his surrounding terrain, was evident. In the dimming light, he followed the mountain track unerringly. Fresh unease flickered into my mind. As darkness hovered and almost settled upon us, he led me off the path into the wildness of a stony outcrop that appeared untrodden by human foot since the beginning of time.

Moment after moment, we pressed on. My mind fastened on a new and exceedingly prosaic danger. One false step on that dark mountain-side could well mean a broken neck. As though to augment the warning I felt the Dictator's hand on my arm, firm, and intensely strong . . .

As my feet moved cautiously forward, darkness clamped down on me. I became conscious again of walls . . .

The Dictator had brought me to the mouth of a cave. Helpless to resist, I squirmed through the opening he indicated, and he followed hard at my heels.

There was a moment of utter silence, and then I heard and felt him breathing heavily over my shoulder. I was pushed forward . . .

There was a click, and a thin pencil of light travelled slowly round the cave. I turned sharply. To my surprise, the beam came from a torch in the Dictator's hand.

"Good!" he said at last, with a sigh of satisfaction.

And, on second thoughts, I had to agree with him. It was a commodious cave, dry, and, but for ourselves, unoccupied. The Dictator smiled down at me that quiet little smile I was beginning to know and trust. I smiled back. With those boulders behind us, shielding us, the darkness was now friendly and comforting. True, a thousand miles from Suet Pudding's pale, podgy hands would have lent it even more enchantment; but here was valuable, if only temporary, sanctuary from both him and the treacheries that surrounded us like a ring of wild animals.

And, with the dawn, who knew what might come? Unaccountably, I shivered.

Suet Pudding would spread his net wide with the ghoul-like expectation of finding our dead or exhausted bodies in some crevice or track miles away. It was Leopold Rosbad, the man by my side, he wanted, and Leopold Rosbad, the man by my side, he must have. Probably he would leave Pugg and Bobby and Aunt Sophie in the hut. We could slip back and cut our friends free, and then—

Why, what was I shivering about? It was wonderful! We should all be together again and be able to sneak out in Suet Pudding's own tracks to safety! With all his skill and his gross triumph, we had outwitted Suet Pudding Carl Vipoering. And for the second time! The blood rose hot in my cheeks in excitement. It was a little terrifying at times, the cave too was somewhat chilly; but it really was Adventure Supreme. The kind of thing that Aunt Sophie would never let happen to me again in her life-time. I had better make the most of it while it lasted. The Dictator—a man with more than a price on his head—and I had outwitted and outclassed the Nazi master-spy, Carl Vipoering!

Whew! It was lovely!

CHAPTER XIX

DEATH AROUND THE BRAZIER

SUET PUDDING CARL VIPOERING found us as dawn was breaking. Never in all my life shall I forget our stumbling return to the hut. Little wreaths of mist rose over and hid things that rustled in the undergrowth. My feet moved automatically. One of the jackals was leading the way with a pine torch. It was a nightmare walk in a nightmare light. The Dictator's face, which I had last seen reflecting my own now punctured triumph, was grey and almost inhuman in its bloodlessness. My hands, I saw dully, were purple with cold.

Inside the hut, a fire had been started in the brazier. By it sat my aunt, her feet attached to it by a rope, her eyes dark-ringed with fatigue and, I suspected, anxiety for me. She just nodded her head as I was prodded inside.

My eyes went beyond her. Had anything even more terrible happened in my absence? My horror-propelled hands flew to my throat. They felt like dabs of cold fish.

The only light in the hut was that from the brazier, a blood-red glow which hit my eyeballs like hot pincers. I stumbled forward. Two bound figures lay on the floor like sacks. The jackals smirked warningly over them, like viciously accentuated figures in a Goya painting.

One of the figures moved, and was kicked into immobility again. Was it Bobby or Pugg? Thank God, anyway, they weren't dead.

I shied like a horse as rope touched my own wrists. The snake-like encirclement of it filled me with a red frenzy of terror. And then they pulled it tight, tighter, until I nearly screamed.

"Steady, wench!" came Bobby's voice from one of the sack-like figures. There was a paternal, admonitory note in it as if I were letting the Secret Service down. I answered to it immediately and stopped kicking.

"A chair for the lady," came Suet Pudding's voice ironically behind me.

One of the jackals, still smirking, drew up an empty packing-case to the brazier. It was, I flattered myself, like a perfect lady that I walked across to it and sat on it.

The Dictator was standing just inside the prison door, staring, staring at me . . .

" *'There was a young lady from Bonnat—'* " chanted Sack-like Figure No. 2, thus enabling me to tag it definitely as Pugg.

A coal clattered off the brazier. For a second, I honestly thought my last hour had come. Suet Pudding laughed.

"Nerves, I fear," he chortled. "Most gratifying."

"It's a pleasure," I snapped, and he seemed quite surprised. On the whole, we must have been a fairly surprising gang. Not that he allowed surprise to interfere with his cursed efficiency. Pinpoint despair and triumph filled the hut. I was shivering in spite of the heat from the brazier. Without reason, I hated that smug little fiery furnace. It was the furnace of all our hopes, the end of Leopold Rosbad, of Bobby and Pugg, the end, perhaps, of something more important than any of us.

But Suet Pudding's fat, sunken-eyed egotism was not yet satisfied. If he had had a whip, I knew he would have cracked it. Instead he clicked his heels smartly to attention. And, for the first time that night, I smelt the stench of crushed violets.

The Dictator slightly shook his head. Since our capture he had not said a word. His eyes were tired and sunken back into his head. He met Suet Pudding's jeering salute without change of expression, without altering the position to which he had been pushed.

At last Suet Pudding smiled, a viperous smile. Rightly had he been named Vipoering! He was as slimy and treacherous as anything that crawled on its belly.

"Leopold Rosbad, Man of Iron, Provider of Medals!" he chortled. "*Gott ein Himmel!* Very soon you shall have a medal even on your chest. *Ya!*" with sudden ferocity, "on your back, too!"

I found that the Dictator was crossing the space that separated them.

My eyes ached with strain and smoke from the brazier. Both men, now standing heavily face to face, were of the same height. Both were sturdily built, with broad, sloping shoulders. Both their faces had that demoniac glare from the brazier on them.

"Listen, Carl Vipoering," said the Dictator.

Suet Pudding breathed heavily into his face.

The Dictator pursed his lips judicially.

"We met once before, Carl Vipoering, as I see you remember. I had the honour to show you to the door."

I could hardly breathe. Did that explain the obvious personal hatred between the two men? The air was full of it; it vibrated like a wire between the main protagonists and set the note for the more than normal malignancy of the jackals towards ourselves. I saw Bobby and Pugg raise their heads. I saw the jackals kick them and then themselves strain forward.

"In any fight for freedom, in any just and good cause such as I believe mine to be, there looms a frontier stronger than race or country," said the Dictator. "It is a dark river of something common to both man and animal. It is," from that touch of sombre rhetoric he snapped out the accusation with the harshness of breaking off a stick, "good, honest contempt."

Again, before Suet Pudding could speak, before the jackals could move, he went on:

"Just as, at this moment in secret places all over Europe, men and women are taking a new and bloody oath, just as they will one day wrench freedom from the Nazi gutters into which it has been kicked, so my life—waking, sleeping, dreaming—has been given to the service of my country. Mother of God! have I not been wounded often by the paucity of the work I have been able to do? Yet, at others, I have felt the consuming fire of achievement leaping up in me! *Grâce à Dieu,* it is not for me to judge the merit, or the demerit, of my efforts. Least of all for you."

"Very proper," said my aunt.

Trembling, I stared from one to the other. As we already knew, Carl Vipoering was a cultured beast. But Leopold Rosbad was beginning to show what had made him—and, providing his brain had not suffered irreparable damage, would make him again—a great Dictator. A Dictator who would—and I felt absurdly proud of my deduction—be loved by the people rather than the politicians. If, in his opinion, either needed discipline, with honest, Presbyterian ruthlessness they would have it . . . I had liked the man who was so important to Troubania before: he was our charge and our responsibility. Now, with a thrill that set me quivering from top to toe, I was proud of him. As I had found already, in that atmosphere of supercharged emotions, one did not dislike—one hated with the ferocity of an animal. Similarly, at that moment, had it been asked, I would without question have given my life for Leopold Rosbad.

My aunt would not have said "Very proper" to that. . . .

"And towards the end, I have even found friends," went on the tremorless voice. "Good friends, with young, happy blood in them." Above the dark pouches, his eyes smiled at us. "I would like to thank them from the bottom of my heart for all that they have done, and all that they have tried to do." We were all dumb. His glance travelled back, as though reluctantly, to Suet Pudding, and the face that had relaxed so naturally stiffened into those new grim lines.

"You, Carl Vipoering, have found enemies!" Of a sudden, he flung out his arms, and his voice blasted into the hut and out into a France that was rapidly becoming Germany. "Enemies, Carl Vipoering! Enemies all around you! Don't you ever wake in the night and feel the breath of the oppressed ruffling your hair? Don't you feel all over Europe the dedication of brave men and women to blast you and your kind from the earth? Don't you ever regret?"

He waved aside Suet Pudding's attempt to speak. I could see the great veins filling in Suet Pudding's forehead, his deep-set eyes sinking further and further back into a brain that was as evil and cunning as the devil's.

"But no, it is your shame and your doom that you never regret," said Leopold Rosbad. "You seek to apply the role of the serpent and the tiger to the ordinary business of buying bread. You worship power only for what it brings you. But you too will find that what it breeds is Courage and Hatred, and—much as you try to overlook the fact—many masters . . ."

His eyes ranged over his enemy with something of the other's own grim appraisal. He sighed, almost imperceptibly.

"That is all, Carl Vipoering. Now have your way. And, until the Army of the Oppressed marches, God save Troubania!"

It was then, for the first time during that terrible indictment, that I breathed again.

For a full twenty seconds, there was no movement in the hut, and, with a hot feeling of suffocation that was so unbearable that I nearly shrieked with it, I knew that I was seeing my last of a great man. Fool that I had been to doubt him! For the moment, he had put illness aside and stood out in royal purple, but it all linked with the skilful resource he had shown in taking me to the cave. Bobby, the Secret Service, had been right. Aunt Sophie, intentionally or otherwise, had been wrong.

"I am sorry," said my aunt, "but I still maintain that that man is no more a Dictator than I am."

"My dear good lady!" expostulated Suet Pudding, with creditable mildness.

My aunt positively glared at him.

"Are you, or are you not, telling me I am a liar?" she demanded.

"Say rather I think you are mistaken," almost purred Suet Pudding. And suddenly snapped: "And foolish, very foolish."

I turned beseechingly to Aunt Sophie. Heavens, the man was capable of anything! What had happened to all her usual forebodings?

My own jaw dropped, my eyes goggled, I stared dazedly. "Should I do this to a Dictator?" enquired my aunt. And her tongue shot out at my new hero.

I heard myself gasp with an indignation that demanded some sort of physical effort. I would have liked to have shaken her until her teeth rattled. Politics aside, here was I doing my hardest to behave like a lady, and Aunt Sophie was putting out her tongue!

Suet Pudding gave her a long stare, during which I cooled down a trifle.

"Feminine logic, Carl," laughed Pugg from the floor; "you can't beat it!"

To my surprise and horror, Suet Pudding turned to me.

"And does Miss Vance also subscribe to this—shall I say strange—belief?"

It seemed sacrilege to say I did. With the tired grey eyes of Leopold Rosbad smiling at me with the quiet, reserved little smile I had come to know so well, I felt like Peter denying his Lord. Yet, if we could sow some seeds of doubt in Suet Pudding's mind, it might achieve more than we knew. My aunt never did anything without good reason.

But I had hesitated too long.

"Thank you, Miss Vance," smirked Carl Vipoering. My aunt clucked.

"So you *are* calling me a liar?" she demanded. "In which case, I wash my hands of the whole lot of you. . . . What do we do now?"

Leopold Rosbad went mad.

CHAPTER XX

NOT ENOUGH DICTATORS . . .

THE SMIRKING FACE OF THE MAN who hated him was his target, and Suet Pudding, totally unprepared, went down before him as from a scythe. In that small hut, the pandemonium which followed came like the end of the world.

"Dear me!" said Aunt Sophie, and at last rose from her centre pew. If she had forgotten that she was attached to the brazier, she just dragged it with her when it was brought to her notice.

Leopold Rosbad took on all comers, his face so drained of normal expression that it looked like a grey mask. A grey mask gushing blood. Lacking Bobby's skill, he yet worked systematically and with a horrible enjoyment. After one or two preliminary tries, he threw Jackal Number One, easily but heavily, into a corner. Jackal Number Two started firing as if in a shooting gallery. His last bullet pinged on the wall beside my ear, then he was tossed to the side of his groaning companion.

Number Two didn't groan. His neck was broken.

I looked round feverishly to see if there were a safer spot for us non-combatants. Non-combatants because we were too tightly bound to be anything else. But we had all instinctively rolled or shuffled—whichever the method dictated by our bonds—to the farthest wall. Unfortunately, Suet Pudding was lying only a few yards away.

Perhaps it was the very look of Suet Pudding that scared me. Moreover, as I knew well, youth and training were on the side of the remaining jackals. Yes! our man was flagging already! A shiver ran up my spine as, spitting out a couple of teeth, he started to *sing.* It was a mournful, strongly-accented air in, I supposed, his native tongue. It was uncannily suggestive of death and desolation; of sightless eyes and sagging jaws; of mighty mountains closing icy fingers on their prey; of slowly congealing rivers of blood . . .

The jackals didn't like it a bit. It jarred them, sending red-hot and frightening barbs into something primitive in themselves. It was beyond their comprehension. Insensibly, their guard slackened.

Zog, zog! went the Dictator's choicely-aimed fist into one chin. I heard the jaw smash. So quickly that it was like a dream, only one man, spouting blood from eyes and mouth, faced him.

The rhythm of Leopold Rosbad's song changed to a sort of rumba. He snorted over him, he charged like a war-horse! Mad! Horribly, gloriously mad! I was yelling war-whoops at the top of my voice.

I saw Bobby tearing at his bonds until the sweat poured down his face.

"They'll tear us limb from limb for this!" prophesied my aunt steadfastly.

"Don't be silly!" I gasped. But, in some measure, I knew she was right. When the madness ebbed, as soon it must, Leopold Rosbad's superb strength would be gone. And Suet Pudding, struck not only in body but in his colossal vanity, would return to consciousness. With the whole force of that vanity, he would exact penalty.

Leopold Rosbad would pay first. We should follow as a sort of dessert. Sweet to the tooth if hard on the digestion.

The Dictator finished with his last man. His eyes were distended with blood-rage.

"What do you do with your pet when he gets like this?" It was Suet Pudding's voice, calm and slimy, and unwarrantably frightening, as usual. How long had he been conscious? Watching . . .! watching . . .!

Without warning, the Dictator leapt at his large, prone body, and started a slow, heavy-footed dance on it.

"Treslin!" Carl Vipoering shrieked the order with venom dropping from it. "Do something, you palsied, white-livered swine!" He was trying now—too late—to get to his feet.

"How can I, you fool?" snapped Bobby tersely.

Carl Vipoering screamed, but made no other reply. The Dictator stepped away from him, apparently satisfied.

"Quick!" came Bobby's urgent whisper.

All around the hut, except for Suet Pudding and his jackal with the broken neck, men were stirring to some degree of consciousness again. Moving like a great cat, his eyes blazing in the red light, the Dictator came straight for us. A trickle of blood slobbering down his chin, he straddled Bobby . . .

In his hands gleamed a knife . . .

Would he cut his throat? Somehow, horribly, I knew he would. Then, after Bobby, perhaps me! I stood there dazedly. I had gone through too much even to feel fear. I was numb.

Then, to my surprise, Bobby was free. The Dictator's knife had gashed not him but his bonds. I saw the agony that returning circulation caused.

"You'll feel this for days, Bobby," said my aunt.

Then, somehow, Pugg was free, too.

And maintenance repairs were being done with the rope to the stirring jackals.

I couldn't believe it. I must have fainted; this was not reality but a borderline vision.

Then the Dictator was breathing on me, heavily. The knife was still in his hand. I screamed at the top of my voice. I saw Bobby and Pugg and my aunt jerk round like marionettes on a string. The brazier toppled beside Aunt Sophie.

Pugg hurled himself on one of its hotter portions to steady it—and cursed fluently.

I drew my hands across my eyes. My hands! Yes, they were free! So gently, so carefully, the Dictator had cut them free.

I turned to thank him, but there was no one there. Then I saw him standing in the doorway, looking out into the quiet dawn. As I watched, as we all watched, his strong, sloping shoulders shook.

No one inside the hut said a word.

Suet Pudding had, Pugg thought, a few ribs broken, but he was not seriously hurt. We trussed him before he regained consciousness once more, and shut him in the dignity of the inside compartment of the hut. The jackals we spaced neatly about the main compartment. Their more than adequate arsenal we shared between us. Once more, I found myself holding a gun, of which I was secretly scared to death. Aunt Sophie voiced open disapproval of it.

"You'll shoot yourself in the back, or something!" she moaned.

"Well, she'll make a noise with it, anyway," said Bobby, somewhat ambiguously, I thought.

My aunt refused to be the possessor of anything more lethal than an iron poker. There was still the circle of the moon above us, a faint dawn light to encourage us, and a couple of pine flares to show us where to put our feet.

"Where are we going?" I ventured, when I could keep silent no longer.

"God knows!" said Bobby.

I could have cried.

"And what happens to the family party we've just left?" enquired my aunt.

"They'll be able to tackle their own difficulties in about half-an-hour," said Bobby shortly. "I've left them the brazier. Another few seconds, and I should have burnt myself loose on it. If they haven't the guts to try it, well, that's their misfortune. We ought to have liquidated them anyway. It's probably us or them, and it would have saved us a hell of a lot of trouble."

"Bobby, you foul-mouthed ghoul!" yelped my aunt. "And," she added, "I think it perfectly criminal of you to drag a young girl into your disgusting schemes."

Pugg had her by the arm and was leading her gallantly down the path.

"Loreley will be all right when the shock wears off," he said paternally. "After all, it was a case of the devil and the deep blue sea, y'know."

I studied that remark from several angles. Did he intend anything personal?

"Mr. Walnutt," I enquired at last, "I hope you aren't insinuating—"

"Hackles down, Brown Eyes," said Bobby.

And down they went. I was horribly tired.

We stumbled down that mountain-side for hours—or so it seemed—until we found the car which Bobby had hidden. We piled into it without a word. Bobby switched on the engine. After a couple of agonised whirrs, it started. Still nobody spoke. Our nerves were geared to movement. Movement only could satisfy us. Fast movement.

It was only when I saw Bobby pull up his coat collar that I realised that we were actually off. I turned round to inform Pugg. With a shock, I saw that his chinky hair was standing straight up with the force of the wind. Aunt Sophie's toque was battened down over her eyes. Bobby's car was giving of its best. We were indisputably moving.

Away from Suet Pudding. A few miles nearer to England! No one who has not been hunted in a foreign country can ever hope to understand how I groped even for the memory of a familiar London bus, a familiar smoky train fussing into Victoria. It all seemed so far away, almost as if it were in another world. Bobby had said that he would see that Aunt Sophie and I got safely away. . . . Good heavens! I felt my eyeballs freshly glazing. Aunt Sophie didn't know yet what was in store for her! Personally, I was too tired to fight, even if I was being shipped to China; but I didn't think Aunt Sophie would be. Aunt Sophie's active resistance loomed large and heavy before us.

Miserably, I anticipated more trouble. Miserably, very soon I got it.

"Now," grinned Bobby, with a casualness that was a trifle overdone, "for a nice deep, water-tight hole where we can decently inter ourselves—"

"I don't want a hole of any sort, size or description," said my aunt, pursing her lips disapprovingly. "Loreley and I are going home."

Bobby looked ingenuously horrified.

"And be arrested as undesirable aliens?"

"*What?*"

"Well, after to-night, they'll hunt you down with the zest of the devil—two devils, in fact!"

Involuntarily, I winced. Already I had been hunted quite enough. What I wanted was sympathy, not a couple of red-hot pokers.

"Well, you needn't be so ghoulish over it, my lad!" I said indignantly. "After all, you dragged us into this!"

He deliberately winked at me.

"Frankly, your arrests will be given priority . . . but I expect they've already started rounding up the English in any case."

My aunt stared at him incredulously.

"Rounding up the English! Bobby, you're mad!"

Bobby shook his head.

"Solemn oath!"

"Do you mean to tell me that France won't let us out of the country even if we *want* to go?"

"The last boat left yesterday," said Bobby dreamily. "We warned you, you know."

"Good gracious!" said my aunt. "But," settling her hat more firmly on her head, "I still think you're exaggerating."

I saw Bobby inaudibly pray for strength. My own eyes opened to further possibilities. He had, as we could witness, tried peaceful means. If these failed . . . if he could not get her conscious co-operation, he was now desperate enough to knock her on the head and shanghai her.

"*Once aboard the lugger, and the girl is mine*," whistled Pugg, with a damnable look of innocence on his face.

"See here," resumed Bobby, with saintly, unnatural patience, "we're going to get Leopold Rosbad and ourselves across to England, Home and Beauty even if we have to commit every crime in the book to do it, and," he paused portentously, "if you ask me, it'll be a nasty blow in the eye for Hitler when we do."

"Quite," said Pugg.

"H'm," said my aunt. To my relief, the idea of doing Hitler in the eye met with her approval.

"Now," resumed Bobby, "when Dickie Tampler brings back the official word GO, we ought to find things smooth out nicely. Maybe they'll send out a bit of the Fleet for us. How would you like to be piped aboard one of His Majesty's destroyers, Aunt Sophie? Or on to a nice, sleek-looking submarine?"

"By that time, probably I should be too seasick to worry whether I was being piped or not," said Aunt Sophie prosaically.

A bird started to sing on a nearby tree . . . or was it only in my heart? True, Aunt Sophie's resistance might become active again at any moment, but, to date, Bobby was winning! Perhaps his triumph made him a little light-headed.

"They'll probably give you hot rum toddy and make you thoroughly drunk, and stalwart arms will carry you off at journey's end."

"I have never been drunk in my life, young man, and I certainly do not intend to start with the Navy. In my opinion, it shows an unwarrantable lack of self-control."

"Oh, no! not the Navy!"

"As you know quite well, I was not referring to the Navy."

"Thank God for that! Then, I take it," reverting to pompous-eyed solemnity, "that your self-control is strong enough to leave everything to Uncle Bobby for a space?"

"How long?" queried Aunt Sophie bluntly.

"Must you be so explicit? Maybe hours, maybe days. You see, they may have to shift the Fleet from the Gulf Stream or somewhere."

"Yes," said Aunt Sophie in all seriousness. "Incidentally, your instructions will probably be waiting for you at the Château!"

"No," said Bobby so decidedly that even Aunt Sophie blinked. "They haven't arrived there yet."

"I see," said Aunt Sophie blankly, after a little pause. "As a Commanding Officer, you fulfill my worst expectations. What are we waiting here for?"

"Everything okay by you, Pugg?"

"Definitely," said Pugg.

There remained only Leopold Rosbad.

"Before we go any further," said Leopold Rosbad, "I think I ought to tell you something."

Rather belatedly, it occurred to me that the moment of crisis was only just looming on us.

"This lady," said our guest, indicating Aunt Sophie, "was quite right earlier this evening. I must congratulate her on an exceedingly shrewd knowledge of human nature . . . *I am not Leopold Rosbad of Troubania.*"

In the short but eloquent pause, Aunt Sophie smiled. The road started to heave up and down before me. This—this was all we needed to turn us into raving imbeciles!

"Really?" said Bobby with extravagant politeness. His fair head swayed towards me. He mouthed words at me, gangster-fashion.

"Can't afford to let him have another bad spell now. Better humour him, Brown Eyes!"

I nodded, opened my mouth brightly, then closed it again. So many things were becoming clearer, and so many fresh possibilities were dawning, that polite small-talk was impossible. From the back seat, grey eyes met ours, gentle but in some way as grim as steel. As though on a swivel, Bobby's wholesome face gaped backwards and forwards from me to him.

"I am not Leopold Rosbad, Dictator of Troubania," repeated our charge patiently.

Aunt Sophie beamed encouragingly at him. With a hollow groan, Bobby rocked backwards and forwards, his head clutched in his hands.

"God! I'm mad *now!* Call a vet, someone! Get the Army out! I shan't be responsible for my actions much longer!"

Nobody even looked at him. Our charge had the floor.

"I am Yusef Skuteszky, scientist, at your services, *Mesdames, Messieurs.* Unfortunately, I have no more idea where the great Leopold Rosbad is than you have. You understand, yes?"

"No," said Bobby flatly.

"One can hardly blame you. I must apologise."

"H'm," grunted Bobby.

"It appears," the lines on our ersatz Dictator's face deepened a trifle, "that my physical likeness to a great man was of more use to my country than all my years of scientific research. Under certain circumstances, they mistook me for him. Apparently, they have been satisfied. Who was I, Skuteszky, to complain?"

Drawing a deep breath, I thought of those tired, tortured eyes, those brutally callused hands, the hands of a scientist . . .

Bobby pinched my knee.

"You really are hearing what I'm hearing?" he demanded pathetically.

Aunt Sophie sniffed. It was the kind of sniff that said: I TOLD YOU SO, DEAR BOY! in Hindustani.

But I could sympathise with Bobby. This stab in the back, our latest discovery, was deadening. Moreover, there was the future to consider. His bosses in Whitehall had commissioned the Dictator of Troubania. A scientist substitute named Yusef What's-his-name would be no use to them.

I started violently. Nor was a scientist-substitute of such major importance to Suet Pudding! Did that apostle of savage intrigue know that we had only the Dictator's double? Was he perhaps using him as human bait?

Once more my brain refused to follow all the ramifications of the situation, and once more, I reverted to the personal. Bobby was the stool-pigeon to be shot at by all parties concerned, even though it was no fault of his. He had been told to receive a madman. He had received a madman. Now, cut off from official back-chat, surrounded with the 3 Ts of

Tanks, Treachery and Terror, our wits needed sharpening on a grindstone.

If we were caught, Bobby and Pugg would, with the usual preliminaries, be shot as spies. Possibly Aunt Sophie and myself, too. Strange . . . I had always thought the female of the species were long-legged creatures in black velvet, women with green or violet eyes, tempestuously breaking men's lives. Svelte houris that even Bobby would not dare to call "wench." But then he wouldn't want to marry them either . . . He let in the clutch with a jolt that shook my back teeth.

"Is there a corner in insanity in Troubania?" whispered Pugg.

Bobby shook his head.

"No, just priority," he replied bitterly.

CHAPTER XXI

THE MAN WITH THE DIMPLE

I FORCED MYSELF TO RELAX in my seat. We might have snaffled the wrong man, but we were getting away with him from Suet Pudding—that was the main thing.

At that instant, the tyre nearest to me burst.

"Hell!" said Bobby, glaring at my startled face.

Even less politely, the tyre nearest to Pugg burst.

Nobody said a word.

That our car did not overturn was due entirely to Bobby's skill; but our skid faced us back to Suet Pudding. Which, even regarded as an omen, was bad enough.

Had luck completely turned against us? Surely two punctures at once was a refinement of cruelty?

Pugg pronounced it sabotage.

"Of course," said Bobby. He had not even troubled to get onto "Nails, or slash?"

"The very devil of a slash." Pugg was leaning against the car, his hat pushed to the back of his head. His alert face was superficially unruffled, but he looked older.

Suet Pudding had backed himself both ways. We might conceivably escape his clutches at the hut, but we should not get very far. The man was a model of inhuman forethought.

"How many kilometres to the nearest pub or human habitation?" drawled Pugg.

"About fifteen," said Bobby, with grim promptness.

Fifteen kilometres! Nearly ten miles! And, assuming that Suet Pudding had not garnered us in, then what? I dared not ask if we had sufficient money to hire somebody else's car. My courage was too low. I could just hope—and I think I prayed.

We piled numbly out of the dusty, useless car. With the exception of Bobby, we stared at it with dull, hostile eyes. Bobby's face was whipped to a healthy glow. His eyes and lips were swollen, but somehow he looked alert and well-fed.

"You know, I felt quite proud riding in that thing to-day," said my aunt introspectively.

Bobby slipped out an arm and put it around her shoulders.

"Poor old lady!" he said gently.

It was some minutes before my aunt said "H'm!"

Between us, we coaxed the derelict into obscurity behind a low belt of trees. The exercise made me remember afresh how hungry I was. Hopefully, I searched the car's pockets on the off-chance of finding a stray piece of chocolate. There was nothing. Aunt Sophie took out her poker, and in blank silence we set off.

That the *bon Dieu* had never intended either my aunt or myself to hike to freedom became quickly evident. The stones bit through our thin shoes which, all too soon, began to feel over-full of feet. In contrast, my tummy grew emptier and emptier . . . I decided I would be the last to mention such a thing, but didn't Bobby and Pugg feel hungry, too? It was bitter irony to think that we had started out on this trip with a surfeit of rubber tyres. With the road waving up and down before me, I smelt again the odour of our "barrels." Not that tyres which had been intended for bombs would be of much use even on Bobby's car, of course . . .

"*Hist!*" said Pugg.

I swallowed a thin scream, and stared fiercely in the direction from which he appeared to scent fresh danger.

Away to our left was a grey wilderness of mountain scrub. In the middle of this was a light.

"What is it?" I breathed, my full-blooded imagination prompting ghostly visions of will-o'-the-wisps, and then transforming them into hordes of Germans looking for us with a light.

"Cottage window, I think," said Bobby, but he appeared undecided. "Probably some farm hand."

"Then he ought to be more careful with his black-out," said my aunt.

"Yes," agreed Bobby. "Yes." But I knew him well enough to sense the excitement in his voice . . . an excitement which communicated itself to every nerve and muscle in me.

"Bobby!" I shouted; "breakfast!"

"Yoicks! and tallyho! Maybe a horse and cart, too!" supplemented Pugg, hands dug deep in his pockets. "And," *sotto voce,* "maybe not."

Without much difficulty, we traced the light. It was not until we were practically on the threshold of that workman's cottage that I realised what they were afraid of. There was only one road down from the mountain. Had Suet Pudding planned for us to come here?

We stood without moving. The cottage was a dark shape ahead of us. Dark save for that one unwinking eye of light. And as we stood there, the light went out. To our right was another long low mass of dark sheds. From these came the sound of beasts stirring and rustling in their straw. To our noses came the accompanying smell.

"To be or not to be?" whispered Pugg.

"I don't like it," said Bobby. "But Aunt Sophie and Lorrie can't go on much further."

My aunt tapped on the door for them with her poker.

It opened almost at once.

The dawn light fell on a figure in a long, shapeless coat. The interior of the cottage was cavern-like behind him. The figure peered at us without speech.

I knew that under the shelter of their pockets, Bobby's and Pugg's hands were at the right end of their guns. I suddenly remembered that I had put mine in my hand-bag for safety!

It was while Pugg was apologising for our intrusion that I noticed that the light in the window was on again. Our car, I gathered, had broken down on the mountain, and we were cold and hungry. Quite accurate. And then, somehow, we were all inside the cottage.

The room into which we groped our way was small but comfortingly warm. An oil lamp hung from smoke-blackened rafters, and an iron kettle sang cheerily on the hob of a big open fireplace. On the substantial shelf above hung a row of gleaming saucepan lids. Nor was there anything incongruous in the heavy patchwork curtain that hung across one end of the room. It was blurred with the same use, the same age . . .

"The future, it is a puzzling thing, is it not?" said our host, smiling at us from the doorway. He spoke in cultured, Parisian French. "One never knows what it holds, yes?"

"One never knows what it holds, *no!*" said my aunt decisively.

We decided, heaven permitting, on bacon and eggs *à l'anglaise* for the first step.

The young man from town in the shapeless country coat seemed delighted to oblige us. He was very pale, I saw now; his fair skin had the drained pallor of one who has been ill a long time; but his blue eyes were roving and merry. Perhaps he was convalescing in the country. That would explain his presence here. He was obviously no farm hand. Nor did I now think this cottage was a trap of Suet Pudding's. In all probability he did not know of its existence. After all, the man was not omniscient.

"Probably glad to have someone to talk to," suggested my aunt, continuing my own line of thought.

"Perhaps the ladies would care to go upstairs and wash," came the polite enquiry of our intriguing host from the doorway again. "You will, I know, pardon my own *déshabillé.* My clothes, they are damp, and I have," he hesitated a moment, "a weakness of the lung."

I crimsoned in weak embarrassment.

Bobby gave us a push, in the suggested direction, and whispered in my ear as he did so that it was all right—Uncle Bobby would look after us.

We walked slowly up to the pale young man in the old coat. With a slight bow, he handed Aunt Sophie a white crockery candlestick and lit the tall candle in it.

"The grease," he said, "I do not think it will fall to hurt. The door is immediately at the top of the stairs, *Mesdames*. I will bring you a can of hot water in but a moment."

We heard him go into the back quarters. We knew that Bobby and Pugg watched us from their own open door as we ascended the stairs. But our progress was not rapid. In the first place, we were used to a straightforward staircase with a handrail and balustrading at the side. This one had two curious little landings on it, but no handrail at all. In the second place, the steps were not many, but steep to our tired legs. In the third place—

When we arrived at the door at the top the candle flickered and nearly went out. The first thing Aunt Sophie did once we had fumbled our way into the room was to look under the big, four-poster bed. The effort was, thank goodness, unproductive, other than that my aunt sneezed vigorously.

Noting that the black-out was some complicated arrangement of boards that I dared not touch, I snatched the candlestick from her shaking hand, and yearned unreasonably for electric light. Electric light would, I felt, have cleared up some of our mental as well as physical shadows.

Feet were coming slowly up the stairs now. Our host with the hot water? Poor man, he was moving slowly, as one deadly tired, or one heavily burdened.

"Your hot water, *Mesdames,*" came his voice outside. He was breathing hard, as if the exertion had been more than his strength at present allowed. I felt a faint glow of remorse at allowing him to wait on us like this.

"Oh, thank you very much," I said.

"A pleasure, *Mademoiselle*," he called back, and there was a faint laugh in his voice. We heard him go away.

I stared at my reflection in the mirror, a small mirror on a dressing table with a frilled white cotton valance to match the bed. I stared hard. Candles are always stimulating to the imagination.

Add to the candles a curious, intermittent knocking sound. Then a series of creakings, followed by a long drawn-out sigh. A sigh that seemed to come from the depths of Nothingness and creep back into the space behind the four-poster.

I watched the hot water steam comfortably round Aunt Sophie's head as she bent to it. I turned back to the room. It had a solid, peasant respectability and cleanliness. The sounds I heard were the normal contractions of old woodwork; nothing to be afraid of. Besides, deep in this kind of country, everything sounded different . . . I opened the door a crack. Below, I could hear Bobby and Pugg talking pleasantly together. They had purposely left their door open. There was nothing wrong there—as yet.

We did full justice to the bacon and eggs when we met them some ten minutes later. Aunt Sophie, indeed, with the housewife's vision of an empty larder facing the poor man on our departure, felt she had to apologise for us.

The young host bowed charmingly again.

"Not at all, *Madame.* Who knows in these days when one may eat again? We know only the past, not what comes after. That is well understood."

It was a curious little speech, spoken quite casually. I saw Bobby's eyes narrow . . . The young man smiled, conscious, perhaps, that he had gripped our attention. I saw that he had a dimple in his pale cheek. Now that I was fed, I refused to be melodramatic. He was probably a *poseur,* evacuated out of his element, working off a little temperament on this unexpected audience of strangers. I spooned up the sugar remaining at the bottom of my last cup of coffee, and felt both satisfied and languid. If there was any worrying to be done, Bobby and Pugg could have the exclusive rights.

The seat allocated to Bobby was a rocking-chair. His movement in it lulled me. He looked, in spite of the wear and tear of his calling, like a large, well-behaved schoolboy. It was comforting to know that, behind the scene, his brain was working at mature, steady pressure. I could rely on Bobby.

And on Pugg, too. Only Pugg was different.

I saw that he was offering our current mystery man a cigarette. To my surprise, the young man's hand trembled a little as he took one.

"Staying here long?" asked Pugg conversationally.

"No, I don't think so. In fact, M'sieur Walnutt" (for the amiable Pugg had not thought it necessary to hide his name), "it is almost certain that I shall be leaving quite soon."

"Nice bit of country, but I should imagine it gets a bit lonely sometimes."

"Yes. There are times when one feels the loneliness very much."

It was an ordinary enough conversation, but I was to remember every inflection of it later. The young man stood a little behind us. With one hand he hugged the coat closer to him. The cigarettes glowed like tiny braziers in front of the three men's faces. The Dictator's double (whom, after one or two sneezes at Skuteszky, Pugg had formally christened "Stinks") sat immediately on Aunt Sophie's right, drawing with long, placid puffs on a particularly strong pipe. Aunt Sophie was nodding.

The young man cleared the table, refused our offers of help, and quietly withdrew.

His footsteps died away. Bobby leapt from his rocking-chair. He made no sound. He just made for the patchwork curtain.

I stared uncertainly from him to it. One or two pieces of velvet gleamed on it, dotted here and there like precious dreams, but mostly it was made of neat squares of heavy serge and cotton. Outside the cottage a dog yelped.

Inside, it was very quiet. What was in the other part of the room?

Bobby's hand was outraised to grip the curtain . . .

The silence inside seemed to close down on us. Pugg and I were now on our feet. Aunt Sophie and Stinks nodded side by side at the table.

Bobby softly lifted the curtain. After all, if we were caught unwarrantably in the act, we could always explain that we were admiring it.

The portion of the room into which we stared was small. We could reach out our hands and touch the chair which was its only piece of furniture. The daylight smudged in from a window immediately facing us.

In the chair sat an old man. His boots had on them the mud of the farm. One work-worn hand hung over the edge of the chair, his greying head lay on his chest.

He was quite dead.

In the window was a lighted candle.

The window was tiny, high-pointed and uncurtained, like —like a church . . . It was this light which had brought us here.

We turned back to the room where we had breakfasted. The oil lamp threw a bright circle of light on to the white tablecloth. Aunt Sophie's eyes were shut. Stinks was still puffing gently at his pipe. The rocking-chair still oscillated feebly.

In the doorway stood the tall young man in the shapeless old coat, with a gun in his hand.

"Yes, I killed him," he said.

CHAPTER XXII

AUNT SOPHIE USES THE POKER

THERE WERE OTHER NOISES now in and around that lonely cottage. Hell itself seemed to be breaking through its pie-crust of earth. Filling our ears came the drone of aeroplane engines. Second by second, they seemed to be bearing straight down on us, and we felt important enough to be their target. Then the fires they had started already far behind, spit curses into the sky after them; the glare burst through the tiny, church-like cottage window, settled on the dead figure of the old Frenchman, passed on to his killer . . .

C'était la guerre. And, once again, a reminder that bigger issues than our personal safety lay in our hands. At all costs, the British Government must be informed that the man assumed to be Leopold Rosbad was not Leopold Rosbad. That Leopold Rosbad was still, as Bobby would put it, "floating spare" somewhere in Germanised Europe. But the young man with the gun had clearly killed that day. And maybe he was not alone.

"You are not a Frenchman?" asked Bobby sharply.

"No." He clicked his heels slightly as he spoke, and I noticed again the dimple in his cheek. "Draw the curtain of the other window!"

With one half of my mind I registered the fact that the bombers had passed over us.

"Do as he says," ordered Bobby, his own eyes never leaving those of the young man in the old coat.

They were unwieldy curtains, on rusty hooks, but I drew them wide at last.

My eyes smarting with excitement, I saw straddled across the garden, a black, twisted shape. Wisps of smoke licked about it and then merged into the strengthening daylight. I stared at a great black cross. It was the first time I had seen the wreckage of a German bomber.

"My brother and my best friends are inside it," came the voice of the man with the gun behind me. "Dead." I swung round, placing myself squarely in the window, some idea at the back of my mind that on no account must he see again the smoking, twisted pyre.

"Dead," repeated the man who was our enemy, his glance taking in all of us, "as he." A slight gesture insensibly lingered on the old Frenchman in the chair. There was a thin, ruthless line to the German's mouth.

"Now, look here—!" said Bobby, and, with leaping horror, I saw the urgent determination in his eyes. I tried to shriek a warning. Danger, imminent danger, was about to strike us through Bobby, and my mouth became too dry to utter a sound. War was again edged with personal, primitive mastery. War was around us, in us. We were steeped in war. *C'était la guerre . . .*

On Bobby's lips, too, words died. . . .

The gun in the young German's hand wavered. He appeared to straighten up; then, with a soft sigh, he crumpled to the floor.

As he crumpled, I saw that, from the neck downwards, the whole of his back was sweating blood.

"*Auf Wiedersehen!*" he whispered.

He was dead when we reached him.

~ ~ ~ ~ ~

I think I must have fainted. The next thing I heard was Bobby telling Pugg very decisively that something was too dangerous. But somehow I knew that once more Pugg was winning.

I groaned. Four alarmed faces immediately hove into my vision. Figuratively speaking, I patted each one on the head. Four very different faces, but the best friends I should ever know. Perhaps if war brought this satisfying sense of comradeship, it was not such a bad thing after all. Then I remembered the German whose own friends had died by his side. The German who, himself so badly wounded as to be near death, had staggered to the cottage and killed the old Frenchman. The candle he had lit for the repose of the Frenchman's soul. The queer conceit there must have been in him as he had waited on us! As he had waited for death!

The light was stronger now. Cold, grey, and accusing, it lit up splashes of red on the floor where blood had dripped from him and we had not noticed. Voraciously, it travelled beyond, to the young, crumpled body. He had deliberately killed a man, a man who should have been a friend of ours. Perhaps, just as deliberately, he had intended to kill us. Somehow, I preferred to remember his heavy, lagging footsteps up the steep stairs with the can of hot water, the dimple in his cheek. *C'était la guerre.*

Aunt Sophie was fussing over me.

"Out of the way, Bobby, you great gump!" she was saying with grim determination. "Of course, with you as Commanding Officer, I might have known something like this would happen! Enough to give the child a shock for life!"

Pugg and Bobby tripped over themselves in mutual haste to drop the patchwork curtain back into place, and then stood shoulder to shoulder before the dead German. I laughed at their stiff, serious faces, because, after all, they were accentuating the horror, rather than hiding it. Aunt Sophie thought I was having hysterics, and shook me until I slumped helplessly.

Some instinct, however, must have told them eventually that they were doing the wrong thing. Aunt Sophie hugged me so tightly I could see nothing, but I heard Bobby and Pugg pairing up the dead German with the dead Frenchman behind the patchwork curtain,

In her own interest in the proceedings. Aunt Sophie's grip on me loosened. I raised my head quietly. They were behind the curtain. Two dead men. Two live men.

Pugg came out. Then Bobby.

The curtain stuck on the rod above. Bobby tugged it. It still stuck. Pugg catapulted back to his aid. Their preternatural solemnity was awful. They looked like a couple of amateur villains. I nearly screamed out to them to stop this play-acting on my behalf, that I knew what was behind the curtain, and that, in any case, what I might see was no worse than what I could imagine. My breath hurt like a knife at my throat.

The curtain dropped neatly into place. With a sigh of relief, the executives turned expectantly in my direction. Just in time, I re-hid my face on Aunt Sophie's shoulder. It was nice to feel that I was so ruthlessly protected. For all the world I would not let them see that what I suddenly wanted to do most of all was to creep morbidly behind that patchwork curtain and stare my fill.

No serious demonstration occurred, however. From outside came the rattle of a horse and cart.

Aunt Sophie dropped me and reached for her poker.

Suet Pudding? Was this a trap after all? My chin went up. This time we were warned and armed with their own guns, and Bobby and Pugg, at any rate, knew how to make the best use of them. In their hands at this moment they looked malignantly at home.

I took out my own gun and pointed it firmly at the door. It was most unlikely I should hit anyone, but noise, I had seen it stated, was Hitler's secret weapon in this war. Screaming bombs, roaring tanks, a catapult of noise from which there was no escape. Well, at that moment I felt intensely patriotic and capable of roaring and screaming with any bomb. Was I not rendering my quota of national service in the far-flung outposts of the line? We were desperate, hunted creatures. Death had soaked into that cottage over-night. And whoever stood on the threshold had with him sorely-needed transport. The door slowly opened.

A vaporous sunlight shone round the figure of the man who stood framed in it. It was Stinks.

But Aunt Sophie had already hit him on the head with her poker.

CHAPTER XXIII

THE TERROR ON THE ROAD

STINKS WAS STILL UNCONSCIOUS in the bottom of the cart. Bobby was driving, with Aunt Sophie on the front seat beside him, and gleams of sunshine in his hair. Pugg and I were in the back of the cart with Stinks, and still in shadow.

"What I vote," said Pugg," is that we take the shortest cut back to the Château."

There was a ghastly, incredulous silence. "But don't you see," pursued Pugg, "Suet Pudding won't dream of looking for us at our starting-point again. He's far too good a German for that."

Curiously enough, it was from Aunt Sophie that the first spoken criticism came. Aunt Sophie was in adventurous mood.

"Do you mean to tell me that I've been running round all this time in a circle, like a cat with a tin can tied to its tail? I never heard such rubbish in all my life!"

Bobby, as C. in C. of the Tin Can Brigade, looked so hurt that I galloped to his assistance.

"But, Aunt Sophie, we're the gainers, not the losers, through our efforts! At least," trying to be honest, "to some extent anyway."

"Oh? And what, pray, have we gained?"

"Experience," I said profoundly.

Aunt Sophie eyed me with suspicion of the deepest dye. "Experience which is most undesirable for a young girl." Bobby cut off my legitimate retort with a whoop of brave animal spirits.

"We'll do it!" he cried, flicking the horse into a surprised canter. "Oddsbodikins, little apples, and suffering catfish! We'll do it! Home, James, and don't spare the horses!"

Aunt Sophie looked as if she were about to forbid something or other, but was undecided in her choice.

"The carriage, it waits!" said Stinks suddenly and very distinctly, sitting up.

Pugg and I hurriedly laid him back.

"No, it doesn't, old man," said Pugg soothingly. "You've missed an active quarter of an hour or so."

"Eh? Humph!" said poor Stinks, still mistakenly endeavouring to assert himself. With a stiffness that was purely physical (for the night air on the mountains had given her twinges of her old enemy, rheumatism), my aunt turned and bestowed on him a gracious smile. She had evidently decided that home didn't sound such a bad place, after all.

"I think we really ought to thank Mr.—Mr.—er—Stinks—for the able manner in which he provided transport out of that horrible cottage."

"Er—yes, yes, of course!" murmured Bobby and Pugg together, stung into action. Then, a little sheepishly to Stinks: "Thanks—er—thanks, old man!"

Stinks peered at them with his shrewd, tired eyes, and drew a deep breath.

"A pleasure, *Madame*," he said, but his eyes finally rested on me. "Then—everything is—all right?"

"Everything's fine and dandy!" I assured him, patting his hand.

Thoughtful silence ensued until Stinks got cramp.

~ ~ ~ ~ ~

For some while, we were able to keep to the secondary tracks, but at last we had to touch one of the great main roads. And along that thrusting artery we saw them. Women and children mostly, and old men, with panic galloping at their heels, their scanty belongings bundled on their backs, on the backs of ponies, on prams and bicycles and grinding cars. Last night, the voice of an old man had announced to them the fate of France. All train services were suspended and civilian movement prohibited. Yet still they came . . .

"My God!" said Pugg, "if this should ever happen in England!"

"From what I know of your country, it never would." Stinks was standing very erect in the cart, shading his puckered grey eyes with his hands, his tough grey hair blown up straight from his head.

"What makes you say that?" There was a new respect in Aunt Sophie's voice.

Stinks turned and regarded her directly.

"Where would they go?" he asked simply. "Besides, do they not say that the English never know when they are beaten? Since I have met my present company, I have realised they speak but truth. There are difficulties. Somehow we shall win through."

He beamed, and sat down in the cart suddenly, equably, as though he had made an after-dinner speech.

"Well—er—we hope so." Under this unsolicited testimonial, Bobby and Pugg looked as embarrassed as two schoolboys.

After some manoeuvring on Bobby's part, we joined the refugees. Their rough bandages made a grim, grey pattern in the sunlight. For the most part a tired silence lapped at them. Some had endured right across France.

Still we did not know the terror that dogged them.

We saw the plane dive out of the clouds . . .

Mothers, babies, men, horses, carts, the great chain of misery, scattered to the ditches.

From ahead, machine-gunning . . . little pock-marks of earth and smoke . . .

"For God's sake, keep flat at the bottom of the cart!" shouted Bobby.

With one sweeping gesture, Pugg had evacuated Aunt Sophie from her front seat and placed her flat in the bottom of the cart with the rest of us. Alone on the front seat, Bobby was still trying to control the frightened horse.

A muttered curse.

A muttered prayer.

The plane so low that a well-aimed rifle shot could have brought it crashing beside us. No one had a rifle. All they had was the panic of the helpless, and here and there a roll of soiled blankets.

Rat-tat-tat-tat.

"Oh, the devils!" sobbed Aunt Sophie. It was the only time we ever heard her break down.

With a little quirk of its tail, the plane zoomed upwards.

"Wait!" said Bobby tensely. He was apparently still unhurt. "Way back, perhaps a quarter-of-a-mile, the road is jammed solid with people."

The bombs fell. I saw them coming. I heard them coming. We all saw and heard them coming. They struck where the road was jammed solid with people.

"Always it is so," said an old man beside us, wiping the dust from his stubble of beard. "The dirty pigs they come; they go." Almost apathetically, those of us who were whole sorted ourselves out and got moving again. The old man's voice droned on. No one listened to it except us. "Rat-tat-tat-tat . . . zoom . . . cr-rump, cr-rump. Not a sign of our planes, not one, these five days." His blood-shot eyes searched the empty sky with an indescribably weary patience.

"Nor of the dirty English, who expect us to fight their dirty battles for them!" croaked a haggard streak of a girl by his side.

A vicious, snake-like hiss came from the throats around us. I saw the lines tighten round Pugg's sensitive mouth. This was the first encounter with anti-British feeling among the people. It was deliberately fostered, of course, but it was significant.

From force of habit, we had been speaking in French, the French of the district. I held my breath until it was almost an agony, as though in some way this self-control would save us. If this panic-soaked crowd guessed that here, right at hand, were some of the "dirty English," we could expect but short shrift. Had we escaped Suet Pudding, only to be trampled to death by his indirect victims?

It was, I maintain, the *bon Dieu* who sent the car stridently demanding passage at that moment. The crowd had been through too much to deal with more than one thing at a time. As they squeezed themselves nearer again to the ditches, they eyed the car like wolves. It was a luxurious limousine, stained with mud and fresh blood. An old man with grey hair was leaning back in it, his eyes closed. A small occasional table, an expensive, graceful relic of another age, was tied to a roll of bedding on the roof. On the expensive table was one thing: a woman's head with the eyes still open. The fair curls were blowing in the wind.

The dealers-of-death came again at noon.

We reached the Château des Roches as the sun was setting.

~ ~ ~ ~ ~

Whether Bobby expected to be challenged here I had no means of telling. Aunt Sophie volubly anticipated an angel with a flaming sword in the form of a company of German soldiers. For some reason, I could not rid myself of a sinister vision of M'sieur Labourd, the man from the *Sûreté.* Yet, one glimpse of the old turreted pile wiped my misgivings off the slate. Here, if anywhere, war had not touched; the cloistered arches were serene and smiling. For some hours, perhaps, Suet Pudding had cast his evil shadow over it. Now that questing shadow had passed on. Behind those shuttered windows, those great barred doors, we should be safe again. A white-bearded sanctity was spread out over us.

I prepared to march up to the great front door with a metaphorical band playing our signature tune, *"Rule, Britannia!"* A horrible doubt came to me. It would be just like Bobby to have forgotten to take the key with him, and make us crawl in through a more or less convenient window. Then I forced myself to relax. Front door or window—what did it really matter? Neither was beyond our powers; neither would take more than a few minutes.

Bobby swung the car away from the Château, and once more trod on the accelerator. Pugg, explained that we were making a detour so that we could (on foot, of course) climb up the gorge-face on the other side, and make our entrance via the evil-mouthed cave and the dark, secret tunnel.

"I," said Bobby, disregarding our exclamations of horror, "will assist Aunt Sophie, and Pugg will do the same for you."

"And please, what about me?" entreated Stinks.

Bobby smiled on him paternally.

"You will trot along in the middle, solo, with an eye skinned for any emergency, before and behind."

"Thank you," said Stinks, in a rather subdued kind of voice.

"And since when have we become mountain goats?" queried my aunt frigidly.

"But Bobby," I gave tongue even more explicitly, "you're mad! Nobody has ever climbed that gorge-face! It's unclimbable!"

"So you think, my angel. So we all thought. Until Suet Pudding showed us we were wrong."

"Suet Pudding?" Something flickered at the back of my mind. "You'd better translate this, my lad! It seems to me I'm a chapter or two behind."

"It's perfectly safe once you know the way, Lorrie," soothed Pugg. "We'll make it easily."

My aunt breathed heavily.

"Good gracious!" Then, recovering ground, as it were: "Look here, you two-faced reprobates, if I die, I want somebody to bury me decently. You take a note of that."

"Cheer up, Lady Methuselah! As Pugg says, there is absolutely no danger. Where Suet Pudding did it in the dark, surely we can do it in broad daylight?"

"When," I asked with gentle patience, "did Suet Pudding do it in the dark, Bobby?"

"Why, when he escaped from the cave, of course, you gump!"

I half-grinned, So I was right! Suet Pudding had *escaped* from the cave that night he had surprised me and Stinks under the bed!

"You know, you want an awfully good memory for the Secret Service, don't you?" I said sweetly.

Bobby grunted at me in vague suspicion, but he had obviously forgotten his earlier edition of the story.

"It is the prerogative of the fair to be merciful," whispered Pugg.

Bobby wanted to know what the hell we were giggling at.

Closer inspection of the gorge sobered me up considerably. Surely no sane person would attempt to climb up that? If ever Nature flatly refused to co-operate, it did here. It did more. It challenged. And the stakes were Death.

Moreover, the strain of avoiding being seen by curious eyes was ever with us. Even an innocently roving child might report our presence. In spite of these drawbacks, Bobby's spirits—to Aunt Sophie's disgust—rose higher and higher. He had come back to his beloved Château. I gathered it was going to be another thousand years before Suet Pudding found us this time.

As time wore on, however, there must have been something infectious about his optimism. For the first time, as we threaded our way along the bottom of the gorge, I felt suddenly confident that we were a match for Suet Pudding. So long as we stuck together, we were invincible. Had not Stinks said the English were unbeatable?

Although it had been a crushing blow at the time, and its repercussions were certainly not yet over, our discovery that Stinks was not the all-important Dictator of Troubania did, I felt, simplify matters for us. From the first, I had hated Bobby being loaded with all that responsibility. Of course, poor Stinks was important too, but it was a different kind of importance. A personal importance and not a national one. Moreover, it would so sock Suet Pudding in the eye when he found out that he had been taking all this trouble over an ersatz product.

A little sigh escaped me. If only we knew where the real Dictator was! If only we had been able to stand at a safe distance with a magnetic pointer, and say: "Here is your Leopold Rosbad, the real Dictator of Troubania!" And then magnanimously leave it to some other Britisher to collect him. Rather abruptly, I decided to confine myself to gratitude that we had not got him on our hands.

Bobby was right about the climb up the gorge to the cave. Once on the right track, footholds sprang up almost miraculously in front of one's eyes. Neither Aunt Sophie nor I could have done it alone, but Bobby and Pugg seemed atavistically at home on a mountain-side. On the other hand, Bobby made one fatal mistake.

In the cave, there was a man waiting for us.

CHAPTER XXIV

TOO MANY DICTATORS . . .

I WANT TO FORGET that fight at the mouth of the cave. Bobby, who was leading, with Aunt Sophie practically strangling him, got the brunt of the attack.

With a superhuman effort, he tossed Aunt Sophie clear. She landed, thump, on her hands and knees, and screamed. The two men locked in deadly grip in front of her. On that treacherously smooth lip, it was a matter of seconds.

Their feet slipped . . .

Feverishly, I clung to the face of the gorge. It was as if the heavens above me had opened . . . as if the very rock itself had split into a million pieces. Bobby's clawing feet halted just above my head. There was another pair of feet not six inches away, presumably those of the man who had been waiting in the cave. They, too, had found a foothold. I saw a dark, moving hump skirting round them; Stinks was gamely continuing the journey on all fours.

When I looked again, the two pairs of feet above me were also once more in motion. A blast of wind hurled itself from side to side of the gorge. It licked at us like an exploring tongue from hell . . . but we all arrived at the lip of the cave together.

Aunt Sophie, still on her hands and knees, was peering out for our corpses. Panting, a little incredulous about our own safety, but very much alive, we stared at each other.

The stranger was dead, caught between two jagged rocks, when Bobby climbed down after him. Aunt Sophie looked shocked but satisfied.

The boulder at the entrance to the tunnel was open. For some reason, Pugg closed it behind us.

"*En avant!*" yelled Stinks.

Both he and Aunt Sophie got stuck in the narrow bottleneck of the tunnel, and had another moment of panic. Bobby, either through loss of weight, or increased skill, squeezed through without trouble.

But our nerves were strained to breaking-point. A harsh word would have set us foaming at the mouth. We were coming home, but who was to say what we should find here? The slimy, guarded mouth of the cave behind us was grim enough warning. Yet we had come too far to turn back.

"I feel as if I were being pulled out on a string," mumbled Aunt Sophie suddenly in front of me.

"Shouldn't we be nearly there, Bobby?" I whispered ahead, over her shoulder.

"I wish to God we were!" flared back his impatient reply.

"Won't be long now," said Pugg soothingly at my elbow.

Our forebodings were justified. When we reached the secret panel into the Château, the opening mechanism was jammed, and the auxiliary leather noose gone. The Château was closed to us. Perhaps because she, too, felt apprehensive pins and needles all over her, my aunt chose this moment to be humorous.

"Love Locked Out!" she made sepulchral announcement.

My brain was so stunned that it took me several seconds to sort out and correlate the remark to the oil painting reproduction hanging in our drawing-room of a regulation Cupid beating in vain at a locked door. With an inappropriate vision of Cupid's rosy little posterior, I giggled. Pugg maintained an almost too discreet silence. Bobby cursed fluently, but mostly under his breath. He was, he justifiably felt, being tried beyond his strength.

Then, out of the darkness, silence fell on us. A grisly silence, almost uncanny in its intensity.

"The damn' thing's *got* to open!" thundered Bobby, hurling himself forward on it.

"Of all the muddle-headed nit-wits!" Aunt Sophie pushed him aside. "Here, let me try with my poker."

They both tried with the poker.

"You know," superimposed Pugg's Rolls Royce voice, "you blokes don't seem to know the rudiments of your own Secret Service."

"Huh?" grunted Bobby, dropping the poker, probably from sheer exhaustion.

"Rule WXYZ/777/RUR/2," said Pugg, stepping forward without a tremor. "OPEN SESAME to all doors. Sub-heading: The Secret Knock. One long tap, like this—"

Before anyone could stop him, he rapped his knuckles sharply on the panel. "Followed by three snappy ones, like so—"

Again he demonstrated, leaning negligently against the panel.

"It is recognised by the person on the other side, and—*Good God!*"

The panel slid open, and he tumbled out head first.

"Well, that's opened it, anyway," observed my aunt.

Outside, a man put his foot on Pugg's chest.

"Come right out, all of you!" There was a crispness in his voice which untactfully emphasised that we had no alternative. True, we were armed; so also, my newly-awakened professional instinct noted, was the man who challenged us.

As it happened, Aunt Sophie had been standing next to Pugg, so she went first. As if I were six years old, she grabbed my hand and pulled me willy-nilly after her. Aunt Sophie was having no more nonsense if she could help it. Possibly she, as well as I, knew that, having returned to the home ground, Bobby was going to shoot this out . . .

A crawling sensation down my back, I was pulled with the whole force of Aunt Sophie's determination over Pugg's prone body. The man's heavy boot was still battened on Pugg's chest.

I stole my first glance at the man. It was not, as I had half feared, Suet Pudding, or any of his men that I knew.

"Bobby!" I screamed, "don't shoot!"

For it was—no, it was not Stinks! Stinks was peering out of the tunnel behind Bobby's shoulder, like an agitated hen.

To Aunt Sophie's amazement, I wrenched myself free. At all costs Bobby must be prevented from starting his shooting match. With a loud yell I bolted back to the panel and stood squarely in it, facing the man in the room. Bobby could not shoot through me! Behind Bobby still stood Stinks.

"Who are you, please?" I asked the man in the room.

His reply came without hesitation.

"I am Leopold Rosbad, Dictator of Troubania," he said.

~ ~ ~ ~ ~

Now we had two of them, the Real and the Substitute. Two of the most wanted men in all Europe. After a second's cataclysmic reflection, my forebodings disappeared like smoke. I felt thrilled to the marrow.

How our unique position had arisen, I did not know. Routine details of this Adventure were not, in any case, my business. Mine just to wallow before all the shifting facets of accomplishment.

Bobby, with a praiseworthy example of British phlegm, looked a little red in the face but completely master of the situation. The mutual greetings of the two Dictators left him little chance of doing anything more practical. At first sight, they gasped, embraced, and were indisputably surprised to see each other still alive. For the first time we heard Skuteszky pronounced as it should be pronounced by a third party. It was with a great shout of appreciation that the Real Dictator learnt that we had shortened it to *Stinks.* Life and hilarity seemed to be flowing about us once more.

I stared gloatingly from our old Dictator to our new one. There were minor differences, of course, but I would hardly have believed such resemblance possible. *And we had them both!* In the innocence that was apparently just another word for "Service" guile, we had drawn Suet Pudding after the Ersatz so that the Real could walk in to the place of assignation without opposition! A few locked doors and windows had been petty hindrances, of course, but modern Dictators obviously have to be versatile. Most of them, in any case, spring from useful artisan stock.

Not that the Real Dictator of Troubania showed any embarrassing evidence of humble origin. He carried himself, in fact, better than Stinks. My eyes travelled over him in solo assessment. The same sturdy, sloping-shouldered build. His hands were large, but well shaped and well kept. The same direct gaze, in repose a little grim, the same best feature: the mouth, firm but curiously generous . . . Suet Pudding and Nazi preparedness must not triumph over us all. He must not!

If only Dickie Tampler would come snooping round that door again with his "damned instructions." Surely Bobby would not wait any longer now? With a curious sensation, I looked round, almost as if someone were at my elbow.

It was a stupid fancy. There couldn't be anyone there.

"You knew M'sieur Richard Tampler, of course?" asked the Real Dictator . . . and it seemed to me that his eyes followed mine to the door.

"Knew?" asked Bobby sharply, his blue eyes suddenly hard with anticipation.

"He helped me through Lyons with all the skill and daring that I expect from an Englishman."

Bobby's shoulders went back.

"They got him there?"

"To my grief, yes."

I felt myself go limp. Even I had understood. I stared horribly at the closed door. *Dickie Tampler was dead.* Only his ghost could walk through that door now.

They had killed him for helping this important personality who now stood in our charge. As, if they got the chance, they would kill us.

I saw by the very impassivity of Bobby's face that he had received confirmation of his worst fears. Dickie Tampler was his best friend, but something more than a brave man's life had been lost in Lyons that day . . .

"Do you think," came Pugg's plaintive voice from the floor, "that I could have a cushion?"

We all started violently. Pugg was still sprawled on the carpet, with the Real Dictator's foot planted on his chest. We had all forgotten him. On his face was a look of saint-like resignation.

I saw the corners of the Real Dictator's mouth twitch.

"This," said Bobby, "is Mr. Jonathan Walnutt, commonly known as Pugg."

"For doubtless good reasons," smiled the Real Dictator. He removed his foot. "Rise, Sir Pugg!"

Pugg scrambled to his feet like a puppy, and finally stood before the Real Dictator with downcast head, beating his breast with his hands.

"Unworthy as I am, Oh King," he mouthed gravely, "I thank you. No boot so heavy has ever stayed on this poor chest of mine. Nor one so large!"

Bobby chuckled, but, knowing him as I did, I realised that his glance at the Dictator was a faintly apprehensive one. How did Real Dictators stand up to this sort of freemasonry?

"The fool of the family," he grinned. "You must forgive him, for he means well."

"I think Mr. Walnutt and I are going to get on famously," said the Real Dictator, shaking Pugg by the hand. Both, thank goodness, were satisfactorily accepting each other as good fellows. It was a man's assessment, carried out under somewhat unusual conditions.

Aunt Sophie, clutching her back, suddenly shrieked.

In a flash, there were guns in the Dictator's and Bobby's hands; guns in Pugg's hand and in Stinks'. I began to feel myself despicably slow on the draw.

My aunt, with wide-open eyes, was facing the window.

"What is it?" asked Bobby hoarsely.

"My rheumatism," said my aunt.

CHAPTER XXV

CANDIDATES FOR HEAVEN

THE DICTATOR WAS PACING up and down the room with unfeigned impatience when Bobby came back from a reconnaissance of local conditions. To my dismay, there was a spurious air of gaiety about our returned host.

"All snug and comfortable, folks?" he greeted jovially. "Any complaints to the management, or anything like that?"

"The accommodation is excellent, M'sieur Treslin. But when do we leave?"

I caught my breath. After all, we had only just come.

"For heaven's sake, Bobby," said my aunt sternly, "don't stand there flapping that greatcoat like a fifth-rate Mephistopheles. Sit down. You look whacked to the wide."

Bobby looked hurt, and then, with a naïve sigh of relief, obediently flopped down into a chair.

"I am rather tired. The whole country's gone bats, or something. Unless there arises a genius at the controls, there'll be murder on one side of the street when Jerry comes, and the fatted calf on the other."

"Somebody else let you down, Bobby?" I hazarded gently.

He nodded.

"At the moment, I wouldn't trust St. Peter himself, even if he had his identity papers and ration card with him."

"When do we leave, M'sieur Treslin?" The Dictator was trying to get one thing settled at a time. Then, as Bobby hesitated to give the good news—

"You have asked me to put myself blindly in your hands,' he went on, raising his own clenched fists heavenwards. "Very good. But," with ponderous sarcasm, "surely your

Government's instructions for you to remain here are now null and void?"

"Government instructions, sir, are never null and void. But," eyeing him squarely, "I think your arrival here renders them a little—shall we say?—defunct."

"Excellent! You should have been a Troubanian, M'sieur Treslin. What is your plan?"

Bobby got to his feet.

"To-morrow we slip across the frontier with a gang of professional smugglers. That's the best I can do. They're a sturdy set of lads and are, moreover, in my debt for a service I once did them. It'll be a hard journey for the ladies, I'm afraid, and," frowning miserably, "a poor substitute for the Fleet."

Smugglers! Real, tough-bearded smugglers, with reputations as black as night! Why, it was almost as good as the Fleet! But how would Aunt Sophie take it?

Aunt Sophie did not turn a hair. Perhaps, like me, she was only too grateful Bobby didn't want us to start out again that night.

"And what is the usual line of these ruffian friends of yours?" she asked calmly.

"Mostly silks and tobaccos," grinned Bobby.

"Silks . . . Now, I wonder if they've a length of something nice for Loreley's birthday?"

"Aunt Sophie! You're a darling!" I hugged her. "Bobby, do you think they would?"

"We can but try. Now, there are hard times ahead, and I suggest that everybody gets to bed and gets a few hours' sleep. So far as I can see, we are at least a jump ahead of Suet Pudding anyhow."

~ ~ ~ ~ ~

It seemed that I had hardly dropped off when Bobby woke me. To my surprise, I found it was morning, and he was holding in his hands a cup of tea.

"Pugg's gone," he said solemnly.

For a second, I did not take it in.

"Pugg's gone?" I repeated idly, stirring the tea. Then, the tea forgotten, so that only a miracle saved it, I leapt up.

Gone? Gone where? What did it mean? What *could* it mean? Why, that Suet Pudding had found us, of course! That our overnight sanctuary, with its shuttered and bolted windows and doors, was just a big draped cage from which we should all, like Pugg, be picked one by one! And each time the cloth lifted, I should see Suet Pudding's ruthless, deep-set eyes, smell crushed violets . . .

Bobby caught me by the shoulders.

"Snap out of it, wench!" he said urgently. "I wish you hadn't such a beastly imagination. Pugg's not been kidnapped, or anything like that."

Now that Bobby was our C.-in-C., was I not to believe my own ears and eyes? I was so surprised I snapped.

"If it's not a rude question, is this another of the traditional accomplishments of the 'Service'? Or is he just sleep-walking?"

Bobby fiddled with his tie. Unless I was very much mistaken, he wasn't a bit surprised at Pugg's disappearance. A breath of discovery came to me . . .

"Oh—he—he's just gone," mumbled Bobby.

But that meant—! But it couldn't! The ostensible explanation that Pugg had ratted on us was not possible. Men like Jonathan Walnutt have been bred to go down with their ship. He was a born jester, with a flair for finding the easiest way of handling high explosives; but he would never let a pal down. I had to grin as I remembered the gladiatorial boot of the Real Dictator on his chest yesterday afternoon. That was so typical of Jonathan Walnutt. You just had to laugh at him and wring his hand. Jonathan Walnutt, Esquire. Yes, it suited him. Pugg . . .

And Bobby had the audacity to tell me I had a "beastly imagination"! Mechanically, I handed him the empty cup. I was beginning to see why Pugg had gone. He was trying to establish official contact for us again. Perhaps he and Bobby had got cold feet over the smugglers? Perhaps something else had happened? Whatever the reason, words to describe his errand failed me. It was as if icy fingers had closed my throat. The idiot! It was incredible. It was great. It was just like Pugg. And he and Dickie Tampler would soon be warmly shaking hands in heaven.

I gnawed my underlip until I felt the skin giving, and gloried in the pain of it. In all probability this was the plan Pugg had been urging on Bobby at the farm. Why, then, had Bobby changed his mind? Pugg was used to getting his own way in the end, of course, but then, so was Bobby—And the smugglers had been a grand idea! Why had we changed it?

"Because, my dear," replied Bobby very gently, in response to my enquiry, "there aren't going to be any smugglers. They've decided the trip's too dangerous, and called it off."

I clapped my hands to my aching throat. Tough-bearded smugglers had called off a trip which we just had to make! It was as if already the barbed wire of the concentration camp was closing about us. Bobby's underground service had, I knew, broken down. Very soon, he expected it to be working again, probably stronger than before; but it was the next twenty-four hours that were vital for us. We were up against a personal as well as a political hatred. While he lived, Suet Pudding would leave no stone unturned. And, God, the number of stones he was capable of handling!

Dickie Tampler, the professional, had crashed. How could Pugg, the amateur, succeed? He had entered a world in which Velasquez, and Rembrandt, and even Cezanne, could help him not at all. One might as well send a child of three out into the black-out. With sudden ghastly intensity, as though by supreme effort I could stop the universe in its motion, I prayed that the death which awaited him would be quick and merciful. Thought of him caged in some filthy Franco-German prison was torture to every nerve in me. But they would never break his spirit, that I knew. One day he would be led out into the sunshine, head still up, the inevitable jest on his lips, in his eyes . . . and very soon, he would be lying cold and still for ever! The words came from me before I could stop them:

"*Why* did you send him? *Why* did it have to be—" I clapped my hand over my mouth as I realised the enormity of my accusation.

"Why did it have to be him instead of me?" Bobby quietly finished the sentence for me. "Well, you see, I couldn't find an alternative. He starts with the advantage of being comparatively unknown; but I can assure you I'm not enjoying myself much either."

I stared at him blankly, not knowing what to say. I knew I was the worst kind of pig that ever breathed. I knew it; but it didn't help me, or him, or anybody else. I would have walked over red-hot coals if it could have been any use. It wasn't. Now I had hurt Bobby abominably just when, with two Dictators on his hands, I should have been straining every nerve to help him.

"Bobby!" I cried; "I'm sorry! I didn't mean anything, really I didn't!"

Hands in pockets, he moved across the room.

"I know you didn't, Brown Eyes." He stopped, facing the window. The strong, clean lines of his shoulders were silhouetted against the light. "I know this isn't the time or place to discuss our love-lives, but you've fallen for Pugg, haven't you?"

As he stopped speaking, there was a silence in the room in which I felt you could have heard the breathing of a sparrow. I could not now have said a word to save my life. I just stood there, staring at his broad back. I suddenly realised how stiffly he was holding it. Like a soldier. And that didn't help me either.

"If you have," went on his voice, coming in queerly disembodied fashion from that rigid back, "it's all right. Only I thought I—well, you and me—"

Once more, words tailed off, but this time he swung round. I was shocked by the dark strain on his face. It was as if, in endeavouring to score all emotion from it, he had drained himself of vitality in the same way as—I shivered—

that young German airman had been drained of blood. Yet I felt his steady, pleading eyes compelling mine, the eyes of a man who knows he has lost everything. I met them for a fraction of a second, and then, although I felt myself looking away, looking anywhere but in his direction, I moved to him.

Moved until I stood close, dumbly, like a desert slave.

"Bobby—!" I gulped.

And then his arm went round me, as it had always gone round me when things went wrong, since I was a little girl.

"Bobby, I'm so miserable," I sobbed, as I had sobbed before on dozens of occasions.

And, as on dozens of occasions before, he tilted my chin, and made me blow into a clean handkerchief, and through a mist of tears I saw the old wide smile back on his face, merged, however, with a new kind of gentleness.

"It's all right, Lorrie," he said again. "His is the sort of job that has to be done swiftly or not at all. He'll come back by dinner-time. You take my word for it."

I was not saying anything. I couldn't. I was not analysing that promise. I knew I dare not. Its comfort was too precious.

"And even if, in the course of *anno domini,* I marry a hundred wives," went on Bobby, "I shall always wear next my heart the memory of a little girl with great brown eyes and a heart of gold, who played with me and laughed with me a hundred times, even when she was miserable." There was a deep vibrating note in his voice which made me feel as if I were being drawn out to it like the strings of a violin. Briskly, he repocketed his handkerchief with one hand, and with the other he tilted my chin and gave me a little sock on it.

"Chin up, wench?" he teased.

"Chin up, Bobby!" I somehow laughed.

Only as we reached the door did he put his hands again on my shoulder.

"I want you to be very happy, little Brown Eyes," he said. "And Pugg's a damn' good fellow."

"Thanks, Bobby," I said tremulously. With an effort that made me feel like a drunken codfish, I turned my face to him. "Do you really think he'll come back, then?"

Bobby's eyes and mine met this time, a long, steady regard that was like a searchlight between us. Then Bobby spoke almost brusquely.

"I'm going to tell you the truth, wench, because I think you can take it. We shall make a fight for it, of course, but there's been another ghastly blunder somewhere. If Pugg doesn't come back—well, it's a 100-1 that we go out. But he'll come back. Pugg's like that."

A shadow fell on us.

"Your pardon, but have I your permission to continue my experiments with my great explosive, yes?"

CHAPTER XXVI

THE GREAT EXPLOSIVE

STINKS' FACE WAS PUCKERED EARNESTLY; his hands were buried in his trouser pockets with a would-be casualness that deceived nobody.

"Explosive?" echoed Bobby, still clinging to me. "*Your* explosive?"—as if the possessive in some way added to the dynamics of the word. We were becoming so accustomed to shocks, and, withal, Stinks was so gently apologetic, that it did not occur to us to protest in any way.

"Yes. My explosive bomb. My explosive bomb which, when perfected, will be the agent of destruction the most powerful in the world!"

Hadn't we enough on our hands? I stole a glance at Bobby. Was one of Stinks' "bad turns" coming on? Ever since Aunt Sophie had hit him on the head with her poker, he had not given us a moment's trouble. And now, there was a hell-for-leather ring in his voice that closely resembled that of the Real Dictator's. To my anxious eyes, Stinks did not appear currently mad. A little over-enthusiastic, perhaps. I remembered that he was a scientist.

I saw Bobby shake his head almost imperceptibly at me. To my surprise, Stinks smiled with a dignified sort of secret triumph.

"You, too, do not believe me," he added. "Yet permit me this favour, and in twenty-four hours, perhaps in forty-eight hours, perhaps before dinner, you shall have proof! And then," his voice thrilled and swelled like the notes of an organ, "then you will come to me and say,"—he smacked his hands; he almost executed a little dance—"Yusef Skuteszky is no Dictator. He is the scientist the greatest the world has ever seen! I, Yusef Skuteszky, to you it promise!" He stood suddenly, rigidly, to attention.

"And this power so great, so urgent to-day, shall be given to two people only. Two people and two nations shall unite in its mighty strength against the oppressor. Leopold Rosbad, Dictator of Troubania, and you, my friend! Troubania and England!"

I do not know if Bobby thrilled. I did not even know if there was really anything to thrill at. All I knew was that I felt suddenly monkey-glanded with pride. Pride at Stinks. Pride at Bobby, who apparently stood for England. Pride even at myself.

Bobby was busy pouring out drinks. They raised and clinked their glasses. With a flourish, Stinks drank: with an ever greater flourish, he threw his glass over his shoulder into the fireplace. It shattered with a tinkle that made me jump. Without moving a muscle of his face, Bobby as grandiloquently followed his smashing example.

I jumped again. It was a display of manners to which I was unaccustomed.

"It rests with you, my friend," said Stinks, with a calm that was so exact it could almost be measured. "With your permission, it goes forward. Without your permission, nothing! I am as a man blind, a man deaf, to all the beauties of my dream!"

Well, what could Bobby do? Of course, how even the greatest scientist the world has ever known could evolve a super-explosive out of Bobby's Château and apparent air was more than I could see. Although perhaps he did not know it, the time factor was also against him. I told myself that I was even yet a novice and, as such, could hardly be expected to cope with the higher problems.

To my satisfaction, Bobby also seemed doubtful.

"Everything I require," replied Stinks, "I with me brought when I first came to this Château. When I it left, I it hid again, with my snakes-and-ladders."

The interest in my face stiffened at the mention of his confounded English game. Drat the man, why must he bring that up?

I saw Bobby's lips move slightly, whether in prayer or curse I never knew; but he had my equally silent sympathy. Much had been explained, but there remained a certain unknown quality about our ersatz Dictator which, in the present circumstances, was more than invigorating.

His broad shoulders hunched, his eyes gleaming with enthusiasm, he lurched towards Bobby. He spoke quietly, but his voice shook. The same build, the same features, as Leopold Rosbad; but not the same eyes. It was then for the first time I grasped the essential difference between the two men. In Stinks' eyes, behind their steady, honest greyness, like a poor relation lived Fear. The Real Dictator, the man for whom Destiny stood waiting, arms outstretched, had, I felt convinced, never known Fear in his life.

"All these months," said Stinks, "they have kept me away from my experiments. I beg of you—"

Bobby's wholesome smile flashed out. What was one more explosive among so many?

"All right, old man! Come along, and we'll see if we can fit you up with a laboratory."

~ ~ ~ ~ ~

Hitler and Mussolini had met to gloat over Pétain's surrender. From our side, M. Baudouin was wildly bleating that France would only accept honourable terms of peace. There was as yet no remission of hostilities.

Had Paris been taken? How far was England behind France in the peace negotiations?

I was surprised to find that I still had a healthy appetite. Perhaps appearances were deceptive, but Bobby seemed capable of sustaining life on excitement alone. At any rate, he disappeared again with no mention of breakfast.

Getting hungrier and hungrier, I wandered down to the kitchen.

Inside the door, I stopped dead.

I realised, of course, that another shock was more or less due; I hadn't had one for at least five minutes. But the last thing I expected to find was the Dictator of Troubania getting a meal ready for us.

Moreover, there was a broad, scientific technique about him. He had taken off his coat; one bright blue brace sagged negligently over his shoulder, while the other upheld law and order with soldierly exactness. He had not yet seen me, and I didn't quite know whether to arrive or depart.

The etiquette of meeting Dictators had from first to last been somewhat muddled up for me. First, there had been Stinks, with his snakes-and-ladders board under the bed. All one did there, apparently, was to make sure one wasn't strangled out of hand. Since then, of course, I had grown to like Stinks enormously; only he wasn't a real Dictator.

The man now getting our breakfast was. As a matter of fact, up to this moment, I had even found time to be more than a little awed by him. He was so obviously the real thing. Pulling out a gun and shooting off an offending nose or ear would be no trouble at all to him.

Bracing myself, I took a step forward. Accommodating important personages was nothing new for the Château. I just had to prove myself equal to it too. If only I didn't feel so entirely hands and feet!

He looked up . . . and watched my entry in silence.

"Good morning," I said brightly.

To my relief, he smiled.

"*Mademoiselle* looks as fair as a flower in spring."

I dropped him a curtsey. After all, meeting Dictators wasn't so bad. The first half-dozen were the worst.

"A flower that's come along to do a little work!" I rashly promised.

With a smile of approval, he pulled his braces into alignment, shrugged himself into his coat as if I were royalty, and stood awaiting my orders.

"The Queen has come into her own."

I began to feel a little perturbed again. Of course, every woman knows that she is indispensable in the kitchen, but apparently we are either too stupid or too sensible to be told so nowadays. Unfortunately, my culinary experience was almost as slight as his. He had retired from the field with dignity. I could not. But I managed. He opened the tins. I made an appetising display of their contents. So engrossed were we in our intricate tasks that our conversation was practically monosyllabic, but without social or political embarrassment.

"The lady your aunt?"

"Oh, she won't get up yet."

"A tray later?"

"I think so."

"You like peaches or grapefruit?"

"Peaches."

I was startled by a congratulatory grunt from Bobby in the doorway. I glanced up at him from above the white apron which the Real Dictator had tied about me, and I thought I interpreted rightly the twinkle in his eye. I set him to work to toast the stale bread I had found in the bin.

Finally, we sat down. The space between each one of us at the table was enormous, but we bridged it with a happy sense of personal achievement.

And, once more, I allowed myself to look ahead.

Bobby afterwards told me that on three separate occasions he looked up and caught me with my mouth full of burnt toast, staring at Leopold Rosbad, Dictator of Troubania, with a look of such grim determination that he blanched. He may be right about the determination. He was certainly right about the burnt toast. He had made it himself.

Troubania might be small, but its strategic importance was undeniable. And we had here the dynamic, rallying focus which the United Nations needed. We had to get him to England! We just had to! We were pledged to it as if we had sworn the most solemn oath. It would be agony to fail now! We could not! We would not!

My courage was due to be tested sooner than I thought.

Even as we sat there, Evil sprang out. A sudden, devastating shock of noise and horror that left us stunned and quivering. I could not tell what the Evil about us was; but the blood in me went cold . . .

I saw the Dictator's blazing eyes. Bobby's fair hair had once more flopped in curls over his forehead. His face for a second showed unspeakable horror; then his eyes were glinting too . . . Good, they were going to make a fight for it!

I groaned in spirit as I remembered the gun they had given me, now lying ineffectively under my pillow upstairs. Perhaps THEY would find it . . . My skin crawled with combined terror and self-disgust.

Bobby crept across the stone floor to the door, opened it slowly, left it open . . .

Footsteps . . .!

A man was coming up the dark stone passage that led to the kitchen. He was a strangely sombre blur, unrecognisable; but it was not, I thought, the stalking figure of Suet Pudding. It seemed to be moving towards us with an uncanny, fixed stare . . .

Bobby drew me back out of the line of fire. Then they took up their positions, one on either side of the door.

In spite of their precautions, it was I who saw the man's face first. Some sort of strangled sound escaped me. Then everything happened at once.

A hoarse voice started to speak. A hoarse voice that was cut off abruptly, because Bobby had him by the throat, and then, almost simultaneously, released him.

"Gugg, gug, gug," said a smoke-blackened Stinks.

With our permission, he had continued his experiments of his great explosive. The noise we had heard was his success. I wiped the salt beads of perspiration off my upper lip, and went upstairs to reassure Aunt Sophie that all was well.

There was no reply as I knocked on the door of her room. That was strange. This sudden hell must have awakened her.

Full of fresh foreboding, I pushed open the door.

The room was empty, and more untidy than I had ever imagined any room of Aunt Sophie's could be. That foreboding was clear-cut enough now. It was only the fear of looking a fool before the two Dictators that prevented me from rushing back to Bobby and dragging him up to see what I saw.

Setting my teeth, my eyes feeling as if they were popping out of my head with fright, I searched every place in the Château where Aunt Sophie could possibly be. Not until I was absolutely sure did I hurtle down to break the news.

The cloth of the cage had really been lifted this time and, with characteristic devilry, the victim Suet Pudding had selected was Aunt Sophie.

CHAPTER XXVII

PURELY MEDICINAL

BOBBY AND THE TWO DICTATORS were in heated argument. My heart gave a great thud of relief. By some miraculous secret code, they knew already!

I crossed hurriedly and ranged myself alongside them. We were all in on this. I must show them that I could keep a grip on myself.

"But it's *incredible!*" said Bobby; and, once again, I thanked God for the brave determination in his eyes. Aunt Sophie, at any rate, would be gallantly avenged. "*Marvellous!*" he ended.

I blinked. Marvellous?

"You are sure," Bobby tapped his breast pocket, "that there can be no mistake?" Stinks smiled broadly.

"No more can anything go wrong! I, Yusef Skuteszky, command, and up she goes! You, my young friend, command, and up she goes! You, Leopold Rosbad, Dictator of my country, command, and up she goes!"

Had they *all* gone mad? I held my ground beside them with difficulty.

"But Bobby," I said, "they might have killed her!"

"Huh?" said Bobby.

The two Dictators apparently noticed me for the first time.

"*Up she goes!*" I shouted, almost sobbing, "and you three great men stand around arguing how marvellous it is, when ah the time poor Aunt Sophie may be lying dead and mauled—"

Bobby took me by the arm. His face had turned a sudden bright red. Well, serve him right. I held my head up and faced him sternly.

"To my untutored mind, there seems to be a bit of glory going here," he said, with a wink, an actual wink, at the Real Dictator.

"*Vive la Gloire!* That is fine!" replied the Real Dictator with what was uncommonly like an answering wink.

I gaped at them, the moisture of sheer misery beginning to creep out on my brow. What was wrong with them? What had happened?

"Now," said Bobby smugly, "suppose you tell us all about it?"

Almost beside myself, I pounded on the table with my clenched fists. Wasn't every moment lost now doubly precious? Couldn't they see that? Didn't they *want* to see it?

Marvellous indeed! My poor Aunt Sophie . . .!

"Well, what about Aunt Sophie?" queried Bobby, with the gentleness one applies to a child of six.

"She's gone," I answered sullenly. "Gone! Vanished! Disappeared! Up she's gone!"

Bobby retreated a pace.

"Well, don't split the eardrums, darling! This is the only set I'll have."

I hardly heard him. Could there be any connection between Pugg's disappearance and Aunt Sophie's? It meant that Pugg had gone not of his own brave free will, as Bobby had suggested. It meant . . .

"Listen, my sweet," said Bobby, handing round cigarettes with an air, "that explosive of Stinks' is the goods. As I've told him, I'm no expert, but I know enough to be able to say that it will revolutionise the war! It's amazing, really amazing!"

The Real Dictator bent towards me earnestly.

"Nothing like it in the world, *Mademoiselle*; it is colossal! An Air Force equipped with these beautiful bombs could—*poof!*—flatten the world!"

"You see," Bobby butted in excitedly, "T.N.T. is explosive enough, but you've only got to sneeze at it, and *voila,* you get a nice tombstone! This bomb of Stinks' has all the bite, and is to a large extent shock-resisting."

"Troubania will be proud of Yusef Skuteszky." The Real Dictator patted his double affectionately on the back. "Is that not so, M'sieur Treslin?"

They started applauding each other again.

"Oh, good!" I said politely, my fingers twitching. "But what about Aunt Sophie?"

"Aunt Sophie?" repeated Bobby interrogatively. There was no mistaking his lack of interest.

"And Pugg, too!" I persisted, with what I intended to be heavy warning.

"Pugg, yes. But he's different." He suddenly hesitated. I saw that he was breathing a little more quickly, although otherwise he appeared unmoved. "Her bed's been slept in, hasn't it?"

"Yes."

"Well, then!" Triumph was once more in his eyes. "Look here, darling, one almighty jerk to my nervous system per ackemma is as much as I can take. At least till dinner-time, I am immune to any further shocks."

I made one more effort.

"But, Bobby—!"

"You're not suggesting, are you, that Pugg's kidnapped her?"

"No, but—"

"Then the old lady will turn up in a few minutes, don't you worry. She can't have left the premises. Look here, I'll tell you what I'll do," he went on with absurd masculine superiority. "A two-pound box of chocolates—even in these days, mark you!—to a postage stamp, that she'll have shown in"—he looked at his watch ponderously—"twenty minutes."

They were laughing at me, all of them.

"You go along and play something harmless. Like—like—"

"Snakes-and-ladders," suggested Stinks artlessly, and with obvious intent to help. I saw from the gleam in the Real Dictator's eyes that he, too, had been told the screamingly funny joke of my first meeting with Stinks under the bed.

Stamping my feet all the way, I marched out. I was so angry I could have cried—and nearly did. Feverishly, I prayed that I might never have to depend on any of them again. I bit my lip furiously. I would show them! Somehow—I didn't know how yet—I would find Aunt Sophie, and even if I could not bring her back, even if she were already dead, they would never be able to poke fun at me again.

Go and play something harmless, indeed! While they talked, talked, mark you! of their fine new whatever it was that would do more damage than anybody had ever thought of before. That was all men were fit for; to blow things up like children, and then blow them down again!

I felt feverish with anxiety. Aunt Sophie's room! That should be my starting-point. All detectives first searched rooms and beds and things. My hand on the knob of the door, I found myself standing stock-still, thinking like a steam engine.

Slowly, I entered the room. There was nothing here which flattened my theory. Methodically I noted the pair of Bobby's pyjamas temporarily consecrated to Aunt Sophie's use (and how funny she must have looked in them!) abandoned in a heap on the floor. The man-size slippers appeared to have been discarded with even less dignity: one sprawled on the bed, the other coiled shyly round the wash-stand. As for the bed itself, there was no doubt that it had been slept in. It had not only been slept in; it looked as if it had been wrestled with.

As I looked at it, I nodded my head, feeling exceedingly wise and somewhere round about the age of fifty. I didn't need a man to tell me where Aunt Sophie had gone. Moreover, I knew, as clearly as if it had been written down for me, why she had gone.

Bobby had been right in that she had not been forcibly removed from us. That took a slight edge off my triumph, but I didn't really mind.

She had gone home to get her rheumatism liniment.

Very well, I would march in her footsteps. If Aunt Sophie could go home, so could I. If—if anything went wrong . . .

well, it was Bobby's fault! According to his superior knowledge, Aunt Sophie had not left his all-embracing Château. Well, I would go out, find her, and bring her back! Even *he* was not going to laugh at me before those two grinning Dictators!

I squeezed out through a small window just above groundfloor level. Good heavens, how had Aunt Sophie got out? That was my first bad moment. I learned afterwards that she had, with Olympian calm, walked out of the heavy, church-like back door, locked it again, and taken the key with her.

It was a bright, clear morning, with a suspicion of the mid-day heat to come. I wobbled between the ages of fifteen and fifty as I made my way down the familiar road: fifteen when the spirit of freedom and the sense of retouching familiar things bubbled up inside me; forty-nine at least when an unnoticed stick cracked under my heel; somewhere between the two as, walking carefully on the lawn instead of the path, I approached our own front porch.

There was a shadow across it, almost as there had been that day when the man had lain dead in it. Dead. I hastily pushed the thought from me; also the fact that he had been "Cyclops," one of Bobby's fellow-agents. As was Dickie Tampler—who also was dead . . . We were living through desperate moments, but war and international intrigue still seemed alien in our village.

I skirted the front porch and made for the back door.

I had to pass the sitting-room window . . .

What drew me to it, silently, as cautiously as if I were a mouse approaching a piece of cheese, was the fact that it was half open . . .

It was a french-window. One had only to step inside . . . Inside the window, facing it, was an armchair. It had always faced the window ever since I could remember. It had always, at what she considered the proper times for it, held Aunt Sophie.

It held Aunt Sophie now.

An Aunt Sophie who was as drunk as a lord.

And was rapidly becoming more and more drunk, assisted, in his most benign and luscious manner, by my waking and dreaming nightmare, Suet Pudding.

I must have made some exclamation, for he turned. But something had warned me in time. I ducked back behind a laurel bush—and how friendly that laurel bush seemed!

I smelt the crushed violet scent as he came nearer.

I heard him push open the window.

Then I heard him go away, apparently satisfied.

"Hic," said my aunt distinctly.

"Another glass of this excellent cognac," said Suet Pudding fulsomely. "Purely medicinal, of course."

So it was cognac with which he was dosing the poor old soul. I squirmed back to the window, my curiosity deeper than my fear. Why?

"I think . . . I—will," said my aunt, enunciating each word with earnest distinction. "Just a small portion, if you don't mind."

I heard the hulking, sunken-eyed man who was hunting us pour out the "medicine." I wanted to rush forward, but I dare not. What could I do? And what was Suet Pudding's object? To dope her into insensibility before he tortured her was plain nonsense. And not the kind of nonsense in which Suet Pudding would indulge.

I held my breath until I felt my eyes beginning to pop out of my head.

"And when you see your friend, Mr. Robert Treslin, and his guest again—" said Suet Pudding . . .

That, I think, was the worst moment of all. I saw his plan now—a plan so craftily typical of the man—as if it had been handed to me on a salver, and my knees nearly gave beneath me. Merciful heavens! had Aunt Sophie in her doped state already told him that Bobby was at the Château with the Dictator? If so, Bobby must be warned at once!

For all that, something rooted me to the spot. I told myself it was no use once again storming back with half a yarn. Besides, I could not leave Aunt Sophie there, helpless and alone!

"Never liked that man," I heard my aunt muttering between her teeth. Possibly—only too probably—she was referring to Stinks.

"No," cooed Suet Pudding, "a woman like you wouldn't. By the way, where is Mr. Treslin at the moment?"

So she hadn't told him! Not yet—But I could do nothing!

Nothing could stop the steam-roller success of Suet Pudding! Everything depended on Aunt Sophie now—and Aunt Sophie was drunker than a lord!

CHAPTER XXVIII

THE MAN WITH THE BANDAGE

AUNT SOPHIE STARTED SINGING to herself. I went suddenly rigid. It must be just coincidence that she had chosen *"Rule, Britannia!"* Aunt Sophie could not possibly know of our old signal.

Suet Pudding, when he spoke again, had evidently lost his first coating of patience.

"What are they doing now? You know, don't you?"

"*—shall be slaves!*" completed Aunt Sophie triumphantly.

"I can't say I know, but—" I craned my neck round the window. Safe or not, I must see what was happening. Suet Pudding, his back towards me, was standing over her. She was waggling her head skittishly at him. "But—*hic*—I can tell you what—I—think."

I prayed that he would hustle her, and put her off her stroke. But the sunken-eyed monstrosity was too crafty for that. He waited with the patience of a serpent.

"I think," pursued my aunt, "that they have formed a Su-i-cide" (she divided the word into syllables and so managed it) "Club with all the bes' people in Germany, an' that they are arrangin' tha' the day tha' man Hitler rides into Paris will be his last!"

Some form of insect made a snack lunch off my neck, but I hardly noticed it.

"Bobby Treslin's heart—hic—was always in the right place," wound up my aunt.

I leaned back against the wall, panting. We didn't stand a dog's chance now. Assassination of Hitler! Why, the whole Gestapo and probably half the Army would be loosed on us!

I took a step forward, and then a step backward. What was I to do?

"You're sure of that?" It was Suet Pudding's voice, with a new edge to it. Like a jack-in-the-box, without conscious thought, my head went round the window again.

He was half turned to me, but peering into Aunt Sophie's face. Aunt Sophie was blinking up at him like a trusting spaniel.

"You know, young man," she said suddenly, solemnly, "I don't think I like your face."

I saw his mouth and the muscles in his face tighten as he reached out his podgy hands and shook her.

"Are you telling me the truth, woman?" I heard the sting in his voice like that before. My eyes, as I peered forward, felt swollen with terror.

"I resent those remarks," said my aunt sturdily but tipsily. "I am not a woman. I am a respectable lady. And will you please take off your hat when you are talkin' to me." She put out an aimless hand and with it flicked his hat dexterously from his out-thrust head.

Tense as both I and the situation were, I almost giggled.

"That," she said, relaxing back into her well-worn, familiar chair, "is better. Much better. But," she paused, considered him, suddenly prodded him in the chest, "the fact that you doubt my word shows that you are no gentleman. Hic."

I saw Suet Pudding draw a deep breath. Now it was coming . . . Wait for it!

"Mr. Treslin has two guests, hasn't he? Those two gentlemen who are so very much alike?" His voice had an insistence in it like a knife sharpening.

So he did know! Or, at any rate, he suspected! This was awful!

"Funny you noticed it, too," said my aunt. " 'Stror'nary alike. Two of them. Or is it three?" She prodded a little at the air.

"Three?" said Suet Pudding sharply.

"No." Aunt Sophie shook her head stubbornly. "At the

moment, there are only two of you. Just two. One and one.

"And I must say, young man"—the words came out with appalling distinctness—"that I don't like either of you."

"I'll get you another drink," said Suet Pudding, more helpless than I had ever known him. He walked, too, a little stiffly. I remembered that his ribs were probably strapped up. It was while he lingered to pour out a drink for himself that it happened. Once again, I was powerless to prevent or aid. The slightest sound from the window would have swung Suet Pudding round . . .

Aunt Sophie got to her feet. There was something long and shiny in her right hand. She staggered as she walked. With a little frown, she hesitated, transferred her grip on the long, shiny thing and doggedly used it as a walking-stick. My eyes glued to it. It was the heavy brass poker from the grate.

It connected with Suet Pudding's head as he threw it back to drink.

I had seen it coming, of course. I had seen Aunt Sophie cross the entire width of the carpet that separated them. I had seen the intense concentration with which she had taken her own weight off her weapon. Practically disembodied with excitement, I had seen her raise it with both hands . . .

Suet Pudding had slumped to the floor almost in two sections. First his knees had given, then his great torso, to fold up over them. It was impressive, and in some way deadly.

I burst into the room in time to stop Aunt Sophie from settling down to sleep beside him.

I took the poker from her, and diverted her towards the chair. Half-way, I reconsidered. Once in that chair, she would be asleep in a second. How long before Suet Pudding recovered consciousness? Under the same treatment, Stinks had taken approximately a quarter of an hour. In any event, Suet Pudding's lapse would obviously be of much shorter duration than Aunt Sophie's brandied stupor.

We had to get back to the Château—with as long a start on Suet Pudding as possible.

Aunt Sophie was already a dead weight on my arm. I

carefully propped her against the bookcase, and tore off the curtain cords for use on Suet Pudding's arms and legs. The very thought of contact with his flesh turned me queasy, but, as I knew very well, my life depended on my efficiency now.

Even so, I could not bring myself to prise open those great yellow teeth and force a gag between them . . .

When I was ready, Aunt Sophie came like a lady. In her right hand, she clutched a bottle of rheumatism liniment.

~ ~ ~ ~ ~

Fortunately, as it proved once again, we had no neighbours to take an interest in our affairs. Our progress was erratic but stubborn. If only every minute had not counted, if only the way back to the Château had been about a quarter of what it was, I should have appreciated its undoubted humour. The necessity of getting back to Bobby, of warning him of the new "spot" in which Aunt Sophie had placed him, bit into me like—well, like one of the acids that went to make up Stinks' explosive. I felt I too might explode at any moment.

I nearly did when a young man apparently materialised out of the hedge around a bend, and raised his hat.

"I beg your pardon. You are Miss Vance?"

"Y-yes," I said.

My aunt teetered and dug him in the ribs.

"I think you are makin' a mistake, young man. We do not know you. In any case," she spoke with sudden authority, "that is not Miss Vance."

The young man turned to me.

"You said—" he rebuked in a sort of helpless distress.

His face was vaguely familiar to me. Surely I had seen those dark eyes, that rather well-shaped mouth before? True, one of the eyes was now obliterated by a bandage, and there was a piece of sticking-plaster across his lower lip. Such was my state of mind that these appendages did not strike me as being in the least unusual; I just noticed them—that's all.

"I—hic—" said my aunt, "am Miss Vance." And made a low, bobbing curtsey.

I helped her up, and clung closely to her. I found that the young man on the other side of her was also clinging closely. There was a twinkle in his eye which made me suddenly like him.

"I am Miss Loreley Vance," I said.

He raised his hat again, and we smiled across Aunt Sophie at each other.

"*Rule, Britannia/ Britannia rules the waves!*" piped up my aunt suddenly. I giggled. There must be some obsession for that tune in the family.

"*Britons never, never, never shall be slaves!*" She was now plunging onwards. We perforce had to go with her.

The quicker the better, of course, from my point of view; but what about the young man from the hedge?

"Whea-ups," he said, as my aunt made a particularly bold lurch. "Funny we've never met before," he went on in a normal tone of regret. "My name's George Ramsbotham. Excuse the disguise, by the way," he motioned airily to his set of bandages, "but Dickie Tampler and I got into a bit of a scrap, as you may have heard. That was when poor old Dickie got his. I tried to back him up, of course; but it's a bit out of my line of country, I found."

He had been with Dickie Tampler . . .! My mind gave a leap.

"Anyway, you got away," I said. We were talking of big, heroic things in the same casual manner that was normally given to the weather. That, I thrilled, was the current language among the people in the "Service," people who *did* things. I felt as if I had been admitted to a freemasonry of speech and thought of a race apart.

"Yes, I got away," he said. "And that's the point." His bright, unbandaged eye met mine confidentially over the top of Aunt Sophie's bobbing head. "At the moment my problem is to get in touch with Bobby Treslin." He spread his free hand, shrugged his shoulders in an absurdly Gallic manner. "A message for young Bobby Treslin of the most importance I have." In spite of the plaster on his lip, he grinned broadly. "Miss Vance, I ask you, what am I to do? I have been to the jolly old Château. Locked and shuttered. Old Dickie didn't have time to give me any further information. I am desolate. And then I see you and your aunt, and to my eyes you look like a combination of manna and milk and honey."

"How extraordinary!" I said feebly.

He grinned, and became suddenly that odd, mysterious half-age between fifteen and fifty which I had felt in myself during this excursion.

"But seriously, can you help me, Miss Vance? It really is frightfully important that I get in touch with the old bird."

His eye fixed on me appealingly. "More important than you know."

But I did know. That was the fun and the thrill of it! This was the miracle for which we had given up hope. And if I had not gone out to get Aunt Sophie, we should have missed it. And those "damned instructions" on which our lives depended might have fallen into the hands of Suet Pudding! I reflected severely that this George Ramsbotham was evidently not a professional, or he would have known how to get hold of Bobby without knocking at the Château door.

Bobby couldn't be cross with me *now,* however much he disapproved of my leaving his Château. How wrong it was not to take any risks! If I had just crawled into my shell and "played something harmless," if dear old Aunt Sophie had not wanted her rheumatism liniment so badly, what a mess we should still have been in!

~ ~ ~ ~ ~

I proudly led him into Bobby's presence.

"Bobby, this is George Ramsbotham. He has the message from Dickie Tampler—" I felt as if I were announcing a minor royalty.

Something I saw in Bobby's eyes halted me.

At the same instant, a hand gripped my shoulder like a vice.

"Hands up, Treslin! And you, Rosbad!" snapped the voice of the man I had brought.

CHAPTER XXIX

DEVIL'S BRIDE

EVEN THEN BOBBY WOULD HAVE MADE a fight for it but for me.

"You're beaten, Treslin," came the bark in my ear. "If you want further proof, I shoot the girl first." His gun was pressing into, seemed already to be scarring, my ribs.

"Don't mind me, Bobby!" I shrieked, bracing myself for the tear of the bullet. Almost, I faced round to the man I had brought to beg him not to make his puncture hurt too much. I set my teeth hard. Bobby must do something! He must!

His hands went up.

I honestly do not know which was greater: my relief or my exasperation.

But Bobby would have had no chance. I saw that in a flash. The same flash that allowed two other gunmen to squeeze by us and pound their way confidently into the sanctuary which I had betrayed.

Wise in their generation, they did not go within measurable distance of Bobby's fists. From that safe, gun-trained distance, they ordered right-about-turn. Still at safe distance, they marched Bobby and Stinks out of the opposite door. They disappeared. That was all.

I was left with—

Merciful heavens!

"Don't you worry, my dear," said Suet Pudding. "We shall not make *you* drunk. We have other plans for you." Looming over me, he chuckled, and exchanged a glance with the treacherous "George Ramsbotham." A glance so full of meaning that instinctively for a few seconds I kicked and struggled.

"Loreley, where are your—hic—manners?" said my aunt.

She was beaming beatifically against the background of the empty room that had held Bobby. A Bobby whose face as he had been tricked away would live with me to my dying day. I blinked back the tears from my eyes. I had betrayed Bobby and ruined us all. I wished I were dead.

"Which is her room?" Suet Pudding was frowning at Aunt Sophie.

A gleam of hope came to me.

"I—I'll take her up," I said.

"I have no doubt," he replied with cold venom; "but you have already given me so much trouble that I think—"

And then, I suppose it was the reaction from the unfinished threat, but I felt myself trembling more at its quiet ending than at the threat itself. "We will all take her up."

And we did. That was what I was beginning to fear and hate most of all about Suet Pudding. What he said he would do, he did—in the end. It was an intangible thing to fear when there was so much of him from which to choose.

Dinner-time came. I clung violently to the one threadbare consolation that so far Leopold Rosbad, Dictator of Troubania, did not appear to be in his toils. What had happened to him? Had he uncannily sensed danger in time? Nor was there any sign of Pugg. That meant, of course, that he, too, had failed; but I was thankful for it. To triumph so far, and then to walk straight back to Suet Pudding's venom-dripping clutches would be the worst kind of hell for him and for us all.

Even now I sometimes wake in the night thinking of that meal which no one but Suet Pudding would have taken the trouble to stage. Probably in that lay its final sting—for him as well as us. For that the loaded Treslin banqueting table was intended as a bitter mockery there was no doubt . . .

"Don't want any dinner," I had snarled, sitting firm and feeling incredibly forlorn and childish when he had come to collect me.

He had laughed, wrenched me to my feet, and, horror of horrors, holding my arms, had drawn me close to him.

"Of course you do," he said.

His face was close to mine. I nearly fainted, and he dropped me like a red-hot coal.

Sedately, arm in arm, we went down to the big dining-room, with its tapestry, its smoke-blackened carvings which all had a niche in the history of the country he hated. The Château seemed derelict and aggrieved. I could feel the soft warmth of Suet Pudding's flesh as we made our farcical entry into the stately room. It was the feel of his arm and his body close to mine, and the emptiness of the atmosphere, that strained me almost to breaking-point.

Suet Pudding placed me at his right hand. Bobby, when he was escorted down, looked paler than I had ever seen him. Stinks was the same as usual. Mind and body, for too long had he been the tool of fate to show any signs of cataclysm now. He eyed the loaded table with calm, almost academic interest; it was as though he were assessing its protein value for meeting the stresses that lay ahead.

Stiffly, in a silence that almost dimmed the familiar outlines of the room, we sat . . . and sat . . . Neither Bobby nor Stinks made a move; neither looked anywhere but straight in front of him. Like watching sphinxes, a guard stood behind each chair.

"Well, do we eat?" I asked, with an inane giggle.

"By all means," said Suet Pudding. "All good Englishmen like to die on a full stomach."

In dry-mouthed, stinging-eyed desperation, I helped myself to *hors-d'oeuvres.* Even if Suet Pudding had added poisoning to his other accomplishments, we might as well get it over. I passed the dishes to Stinks as my best hope. Suet Pudding was watching us both like a cat with a mouse.

I saw Bobby itching to sweep the whole lot to the floor. I knew that sullen look on his face. And he was quite capable of doing it, too. I prayed that he wouldn't. I realised, feeling in my wisdom about sixty, that this was just what Suet Pudding was waiting for. It was so necessary to his sneering, bombastic make-up that his adversary in his defeat should feel and look small. And, behind the bombast, there was something else, something very alert and cunning.

Stinks helped himself so generously to food that, to my delight, Suet Pudding's eyebrows went up.

My hand trembling, I passed to Bobby. Bobby put out a hand.

"Arsenic or cyanide?" he queried, raising the most lazy-looking, quizzical eyes I had ever seen.

"Neither," said Suet Pudding. "I am afraid—that is to say, I hope from your point of view—that you will end against a wall."

Bobby nodded his head gravely.

"Excellent tinned *hors-d'oeuvres,"* he declared. "Always thought they would come in useful at a time of crisis. But," he threw down his fork with a gesture so sudden that Suet Pudding actually jumped and one of the sphinxes took a fear-some step forward, "my dear fellow, you yourself aren't eating! How remiss of me!"

It was a remissness for which he made amends. His face ingenuous, his eyes at their very laziest, to my delight and terror he proceeded to plaster Suet Pudding with his own hospitality.

"Do have a little of this," came his pressing reiteration. Or—

"You must try this!" Or—

"This really is delicious!"

He kept Stinks imperturbably passing and repassing unwanted dishes. But for this, Stinks settled down to his meal with his usual admirable tenacity. I provided an admiring audience.

Finally, Suet Pudding could stand it no longer.

"I don't want anything! I don't want any of your blasted food!" he almost screamed at last, pounding his fists on the table.

Bobby had won.

Trembling now that the end had come, I realised that Suet Pudding knew it; and the knowledge hit him where it hurt most: his self-conceit.

~ ~ ~ ~ ~

The man was a born devil. After dinner they separated us again, and I was put into a mysterious closet—a sort of French priest-hole—on the top floor. Watching his large, flexible hands unseal yet another of the old Château's secrets unknown to Bobby, I began to wonder if there was anybody in the world who could finally best him. With quivering thoroughness, I prayed that I did not let Bobby down again.

Suet Pudding left me without saying a word. The devil knew the value of silence. And he was in no hurry. He was waiting for something. In my mouth his gag was a mere refinement of torture; ropes bound my wrists and ankles tightly to the chair in which I had been roughly pushed. They, too, were a touch of parade-ground brutality. I had no idea of the secret mechanism which unlocked the door; even if he had left me free, I could not have escaped from this secret walled closet. Nor would Bobby—even a free Bobby—have been in better case . . . unless he heroically pulled the walls down brick by brick. Under my gag, my stiff, instinctive smile failed to keep up my courage. Suet Pudding win, Suet Pudding lose, he had boxed me up like a Mistletoe Bough Bride.

Surely Suet Pudding or . . . someone . . . would come back. Surely Suet Pudding or . . . someone . . . would come, *if only to taunt me.* As the empty hours went by, the temptation to hurl myself and the chair to which I was so cruelly fastened, against this new secret wall that was in Bobby's Château, to bang the chair and myself against it until the chair was broken and myself numb, grew unbearable, unbearable, unbearable! Soon, I should resist it no longer, and that way lay madness.

The only light came from a vent shaft in the ceiling. Soon, that light would be failing. I should be alone—in the dark, in a ghost-ridden secret closet!

The conviction that Suet Pudding did not intend me to leave this diabolic prison alive drummed into me . . . thud . . . thud . . . like something hammering into my bruising flesh.

This couldn't—*couldn't!*—be happening to me! I grasped at my courage like a drowning man to a straw, and it felt of much the same constituency. My bitter fury against my own stupidity still did not help me at all.

Surely Suet Pudding would come back . . .

When he had completed his plans . . .

Bobby stood accused now of a plot to murder the Fuehrer. I shuddered away from the thought of what might be happening to him at this minute. God, no! I must not think of that! I remembered too that he had in his pocket the complete formula of Stinks' life-work; of bombs which would flatten the world, bombs which were vital to England. In every way, to whichever angle we turned, Suet Pudding had won. The rubber truncheon and death would finish the story.

Mercy? I gave a high laugh. No! we neither expected nor asked for mercy! Quivering, I pulled myself together. This was what Suet Pudding was aiming at. To crack our nerves so that we blabbed, and he could turn our brains inside out . . .

I stared dully at the blank wall, thinking steadfastly on laughing-eyed Pugg who had also failed. But he, I felt certain, had been able to make some sort of fight for life and freedom. Even if the odds were stupendous, there was a certain exhilaration in leaping forward in a last grand challenge! For a moment my breath seemed to suffocate me. Something inside me was sick and whimpering for Pugg.

Jonathan Walnutt, Esquire. Pugg . . .

In turn, I wiped that vision from my mind. This was no time for lowering my resistance to Suet Pudding by whining over what was past. Our puny party had tried to halt for a moment the giant of madness that was sweeping Europe. Pugg had jettisoned himself to save us; but his little candle had been snuffed out gloriously. Defeat and death were inevitable for all of us.

Late in the evening, Suet Pudding came. I knew that he had calculated to the last instant those hours of tortured isolation and suspense. Now, according to him, my morale must be comfortably broken. Triumph oozed before him as he entered my prison. It was like the slimy track of a snail behind him.

But he had made one mistake. He had left me too long. I had suffered so much, both mentally and physically, that I was numb.

Padding silently forward, he tore the gag from my mouth. His bloated, gloating face unexpectedly brought me to boiling point.

"You're horribly sure you're going to win, aren't you?" I blazed hoarsely.

He gave me a curious look, a look I was to remember afterwards.

"Yes," he said.

"But you won't, you know," I went on, with new-born, stiff calmness, and every word I spoke seemed to ram home our helplessness.

"No? Why?"

I flung back my head.

"Haven't you heard that the English never know when they're beaten? And this time you're up against Englishmen!"

Morale cracked? Not on your life! Stinks could stand up to him. So could I!

"Quite comfortable here?" he enquired, sneering round, anti-climax fashion.

"Very snug," I agreed, with what I hoped was a sarcastic lilt to my hoarse voice.

His sunken, codfish eyes bored into me.

"I don't care," he said, "to be jostled by one of your sex. It is time little girls who did that grew up. Had some education whipped into them."

"Some people could also do with an education in manners," I flared.

Underneath his cords, I clenched my hands. If only Bobby or Pugg could walk in at that door! But I must not think of them—not now. Pugg was probably dead, and Bobby was as helpless and in even worse danger than myself. I was in Suet Pudding's hands. I looked at them, white and podgy, and yet inflexible as iron in their grip. I began to feel less calm. I was a fool, of course, to stand up to him. I ought, if only because I was a woman, in enemy hands, to simulate some form of humility. But I couldn't! I just couldn't! He smiled, and turned to go.

"By the way," his too-curved lips were smiling horribly as he stood by the secret door, " 'Mr. Ramsbotham' is showing quite a flattering interest in you. I hope you are suitably honoured."

He was not joking. He, one of the *Herrenvolk,* really meant that I should be honoured. The skin on the back of my scalp began to creep.

"I think possibly," went on Suet Pudding, "he had better explain one or two things to you. I will send him in."

Suet Pudding had come.

Suet Pudding had gone . . . and I knew no more than before . . .

I glued my eyes to the secret door. It quivered a little and, as it opened, the man who had duped me so easily stood promptly revealed to me. There was the same twinkle in his eye that had attracted me before, but I realised now that it was a calculating, sadistic glitter, natural to the man. He had taken off his property bandage, and there was a white mark across his lip where he had torn off the piece of sticking-plaster. He entered lightly on the balls of his feet. Somehow he was like a boxer stripped for action.

"Hullo?" he said. It was the same intonation that Bobby often used. But, oh, the difference between this man and Bobby! And what mincemeat Bobby would have made of him! And then, somehow, it was as though Bobby knew what I was up against, and was with me, bless him! in spirit.

"Chin up, my wench!" he seemed to whisper right in my ear. And I almost smiled at the man who had tricked me as he swaggered across and sat on the arm of my chair. I recognised him now, too; he was one of the men who had been in the cave.

"You're looking pretty bobbish, considerin'," he said. "What about a little kiss?" And he took it.

Although I felt cold inside, I continued to smile.

CHAPTER XXX

THE GATES OF HELL

"WHAT ABOUT A LITTLE EXPLANATION, Mr.—er—Ramsbotham?" I countered.

"My name is Kurt Herwigler," he said stiffly.

I started. Here, then, was the man who had "scooped up" Dickie Tampler "on a plate" right at the beginning.

"I shall just call you Earwig," I said. I think he perceived my biological train of thought, but whether from force of circumstances or personal agreement, he made no protest.

I jogged my brain into real action. This time I must get myself a little information—and how I needed . . . and feared it! It was no use asking for Bobby—not yet; the Earwig would deliberately take my heart in his hands and squeeze every drop of blood from it.

"You appear to make yourselves very much at home in other people's houses," I suggested with a grimness which I hoped hid the fact that my mouth was pinched with fear.

The Earwig appeared to take the remark as a personal compliment.

"Herr Vipoering and I have our methods," he minced.

"I don't see why," I grunted.

"See here," he said, "little girls should be seen and not heard. But I will tell you this: if, in her day, the illustrious Comtesse Treslin's great-grandmother had not—shall we say?—lost the plans of the Château des Roches, you would certainly not be here now. So you can comfortably say your prayers tonight to an amorous little ghost in a Louis XVI gown."

Yes, I remembered a somewhat scandalous story about the lost plans. So, with the usual Nazi preparedness, Suet Pudding had them! No wonder the old Château had betrayed Bobby!

So completely desperate had I become that even this tiny excursion into the realm of explanation keyed me up. To some extent, I began to feel that Suet Pudding was efficient, but after all *human.*

"Haven't given you anything to eat or drink since dinner, have they?" asked the Earwig.

"N-no." Come to think of it, they hadn't. I began to wish, too, that I had foreseen this period of "diet," and had partaken more heavily of the feast while I had the chance.

"No. And they won't."

He allowed time for that to sink in.

"But," he added kindly, "if you wish, things could considerably improve for you."

"What do you mean?" I had to ask it. After all, diet was one thing, starvation another.

"Well, this plot of Treslin's for destroying our Fuehrer; we are, of course, obtaining details from that misguided young man himself. But, if you searched your memory—" He paused suggestively.

It was fortunate that my hands were tied, or I should have hit him on the nose. Curse their dark, bitter souls! I had to buy my way out by selling Bobby! I saw the Earwig preening himself on his suasive charm, obviously mistaking my ferocious silence for consideration. I did not disabuse him. I saw something else: he could not quite hide the wolf-like anxiety with which he waited for my answer. This thing was so important to him and Suet Pudding . . .

"If," I said slowly, "there is such a plan to destroy the Fuehrer, and if I knew any details of that plan, how would it help me?"

"Herr Vipoering would be prepared to let you go—on certain conditions, of course."

"And my aunt?"

"Your aunt is still in a drunken stupor. When she wakes —" he shrugged his shoulders—"I do not know. Herr Vipoering has a bump on the head from her poker. He is quite justifiably annoyed. But . . ." his arm slid round my neck, "possibly," pulling my ear, "it could be arranged, *hein?*"

My head was swimming; my own words, I decided, must give me courage.

"It sounds fine," I heard myself saying, and I was relieved to hear that my voice sounded fairly normal. "But, to my extreme regret, there is, so far as I know, no plan to destroy the Fuehrer, and therefore no details."

He sprang off the arm of my chair.

"But you admitted—"

"I admitted nothing," I contradicted stoutly. "I said, *if* there were such a plan. There isn't."

He slapped me across the face. And stood over me. As I forced myself to meet the glare in his eyes, an electric bell whirred. It sounded like an uncanny visitation.

"Excuse me," he said, with laborious elegance. The hand which rubbed the deep cleft in his chin trembled a little, I saw.

To my surprise, he pressed a switch in the wall.

"Observe," he said, nodding to just above his head.

I strained my eyes. What was going to happen now? I saw a picture gradually gaining clarity and luminosity. With a little gasp, I recognised it. It was a picture of the room next door!

"It is the room next door," said the Earwig. "Look!"

In the picture there was a man standing near the barred window. My heart leapt. *Stinks!*

"This screen," said the Earwig, "is a species of second sight used fairly extensively in certain circles in the United States, but which Herr Vipoering has also found exceedingly useful from time to time. What you see on that screen is actually taking place NOW in the room to which the instrument is connected. Herr Vipoering, solicitous as always for your comfort, *Fraulein,* has decided that in this case you shall be the privileged looker-in." He smirked. "I understand you have made quite an impression on a man who is very particular over his women. My congratulations, *Fraulein!*"

I goggled at him, feeling like a performing seal, waiting for the fish.

He dropped me a kiss.

"*Auf Wiedersehen, Fraulein.* The play is about to commence . . . By the way, it may interest you to know that our victorious armies are now at the outskirts of Nantes."

Now he was gone. First they came, and then they went. Was this some new barrage on my nerves? I supposed so. It—it was pretty horrible. And Nantes wasn't very far away . . .

"My apologies," said Suet Pudding. "I had to leave you."

I stared round wildly. I had not seen him come in.

Still I could not see him! I felt the sweat coming out on me. Had he come again. *Where?* Had he now the cloak of invisibility? Anything, *anything,* I felt was possible with him. I would not scream. I would not, I would not! Almost at the limit of my endurance, I saw the room in the screen again, and realised I was hearing the voice through some unrevealed loudspeaker. Suet Pudding was not with me in his gross fleshiness. He was in the other room.

Why had I been chosen as the eyes and ears for his play?

I sat stiffly, helplessly, in my chair, a well-guarded understudy to destruction becoming more and more scared every minute.

Oh, they were cunning, those devils! But what could I do? I supposed they regarded me as the weakest link in our party. Which, of course, I was. I gritted my teeth, but I didn't feel any more stable. The steely menace that underlay everything, every word they spoke, every well-planned action, was ruthlessly closing!

Yet it was not of steel that Suet Pudding spoke. His mind had gone back to the gutter, to the cunning wolfdom from which he had sprung. He was going to have poor Stinks flogged!

"I have found a most suitable whip in the riding stables, Yusef Skuteszky," he sneered to a finish. He stood there, stiffly on account of the ribs Stinks had busted for him, a concentration of brain and brute terrorism. I struggled in my chair until the cords bit and drew blood, struggled under yet another catastrophe,

Suet Pudding had addressed Stinks by his own name! Obviously, then, he now knew that this was only an ersatz Dictator. Which, in its turn, meant—what? My head was aching so horribly I could hardly think. God, I prayed, stop this awful torture, stop it! Neither Stinks nor I could stand much more.

Of our great-hearted party, there remained only the real Leopold Rosbad. Had they found him? God in heaven! had they found him?

In dreadful fascination, I watched the screen which portrayed the drama in that room. In tight-fisted, impotent hate that was like a canker right inside me, I watched the suet-pudding face and sunken eyes of Carl Vipoering. Compared with him, the Earwig was just a—a loathsome tame insect!

"Your meaning is as clear as it is characteristic," said Stinks levelly.

Well done, Stinks! Suet Pudding's hand worked, but his face remained motionless.

"You degrade the wrong man; you put the wrong man in your torture camps," went on Stinks, "and, when that man escapes, you chase him half over Europe, always with the same admirable efficiency, losing him at the crucial moment."

Was Slinks working to a plan? I found myself shaking my head wisely. Like us all, Stinks was just—well, clinging to his own self-respect while he could. I applauded and trembled alternately. To Suet Pudding, Yusef Skuteszky, with awful experience behind him and courageously-bottled fear in his soul, was a very different opponent from the insolent-eyed though equally helpless Bobby. But perhaps Bobby was not so insolent-eyed now . . .?

"Yet to-day I have found you," said Suet Pudding, his eyes hard and unwinking.

"To-day you have found me." The dignity of which Stinks was the natural sovereign had fallen on him like a shroud. "And still the wrong man!"

I held my breath. Suet Pudding put a hand to his lips, stroked them . . .

He raised his voice to someone at the back of the room.

"Fetch your prisoner, Herwigler!"

I knew then, of course. Knew before the Earwig could parade Leopold Rosbad, Dictator of Troubania, that we had no cards left. We were beaten finally to our knees.

I saw understanding, too, in Stinks' eyes. Understanding, and something that made my temples throb madly.

"Information has come to me that the English never know when they are beaten," said Suet Pudding conversationally. "Well, our mutual English friends, and a certain stinking scientist, shall be taught." He chuckled throatily, devilishly. "Oh, yes, they shall be taught."

"The value of bombs, I believe, is also being pressed home to the English intellect." Stinks spoke now softly, a little pedantically, for all the world as if he were giving a lecture to a circle of students. "The room to which you have brought me was, curiously enough, to have been an extension of my laboratory. Perhaps I can interest you in my first—no," he corrected himself, "my second bomb."

I gasped. Was he going to sell out to Suet Pudding?

"Not, of course," continued Stinks, with infinite patience, "the kind of bomb to which you are accustomed."

Suet Pudding's glaring face lightened in intelligent understanding.

"A home-made bombshell, in fact. Excellent, my dear pig of a scientist." He evidently did not see the storm signals in Stinks' tired grey eyes, or, if he saw, contemptuously ignored. That meant—and a faint hope laboriously flickered up in me again—that he did not yet know of the formula for which his country would have given so much. His tank-conscious Teuton mind had concentrated too much on one thing: the finding of Leopold Rosbad, and, flanking this, as it were, the plot against his Fuehrer.

There was time for him to have stopped the play. But he continued to ignore. For the first time since I had known him, Stinks laughed. And it was not a laugh good to hear.

No, I was no longer afraid he would sell out. Stinks would not sell out.

"You are very foolish, Carl Vipoering." His voice was still quiet. "You believe I am dangerous when all I want is to live in peace. You believe my explosive harmless when it is the most powerful destructive force in the world!" And again he laughed, possessed of a spirit stronger than himself.

I saw Suet Pudding glance impatiently at the door; the Earwig must be due back with the Real Dictator. My head was throbbing so that I could hardly see the screen. What would Stinks do then?

Suet Pudding said something. I missed it. I saw Stinks draw himself up to his full height. And his eyes were a hot grey with bloodshot streaks.

A sudden familiar phrase buzzed like a saw in my brain.

"In thirty seconds, *up she goes!*" said Stinks placidly.

Suet Pudding stood there, unwinking, completely master of himself and of the situation.

"Twenty seconds . . ."

But then, it would not enter Suet Pudding's mind that a man, even an ersatz Dictator, would blow himself and his friends to pieces. As he glanced at Stinks there was a look of half-enjoyment, half appreciation round his too-curved lips. To him, Stinks was putting on a better act than he had dared hope; he was coldly calculating how long it would be before he cracked.

But I knew that poor Stinks was not bluffing. Stinks had once more slipped over the borderline of ordinary men's sanity.

"Fifteen seconds . . ."

In fifteen more seconds he would explode the tearing, smashing "bomb" that was the crown of his life. Nothing Suet Pudding could do now could stop him. I filled my lungs, filled them with terror, with horror, with anticipation. There was no escape for anyone. The old Château and everything and everybody in it was doomed. There was really nothing more to see. I closed my eyes, and I think I began to pray.

I heard nothing, but I felt hands over me!

Gasping and shivering, I opened my eyes. This must be an illusion. Perhaps my brain also had gone!

I put my hands tentatively towards the figure that was looming over me.

My hands were free!

It was Bobby!

All my life I shall never forget my revulsion of relief; and two other things: the blood stain that was on Bobby's face, and the berserker rage that was in his eyes.

"Ten seconds," came the monotonous voice from the other room.

"Oh, wait!" I croaked . . . "*Wait!*"

Bobby had now slashed me right from the chair, had me tight in his arms. I clutched weakly at the lapels of his coat. It was better to die like this . . .

I found that we were out of the secret closet. His arms feeling like iron bands around me, Bobby was racing for the main staircase. There was no sound, but I felt suddenly as if I were being hurtled down, down .. . *bump!* Bobby had slid down the banisters with me. The old house was very quiet . . . waiting . . .

"Bobby!" I gasped; "back there—!"

"I know!" he said sharply.

It happened. The force of the explosion wrenched open the great front door, picked us up and whirled us through it like pancakes from the pan. Noise and crashing masonry tumbled about us. Scooping me up again, Bobby ran until I could feel his heart pounding. There was another cut on his chin. The coat lapel to which I had been clinging was torn away.

He laid me very gently on a corner of the lawn. Slowly, with an agony of physical effort, I scrambled to my feet. The Château, which was part of history, Suet Pudding, Stinks, Aunt Sophie, Leopold Rosbad, everybody who was still helping to make history in it, had been smashed out of being. We stared, stupefied, as it settled, stone by stone, in great clanging sweeps. As we watched, a single tongue of flame leapt up from the far corner. . . . Alone, Bobby and I stood outside the ring of destruction, two small, tired and battered figures.

I felt Bobby's arm tighten about me. At that moment, although neither of us knew it, France, obeying the voice of her new master, appointed her plenipotentiaries for the degradation ceremony.

Bobby stirred.

"Aunt Sophie is out in what remains of the rose garden with Leopold Rosbad," said Bobby, with what, but for a deep sadness at the back of his eyes, was one of his old, lazy winks. "We've won, my sweet! We've won!"

I swayed drunkenly against him, and pretended it was just a bit of debris in my eye.

"Then Stinks," I whispered hoarsely, "is the only one of us . . .?"

Bobby nodded, and led me gently to the rose garden. Almost with a gesture of salute, his hand touched the breast pocket in which he had placed Stinks' formula. I met his eyes, and again words seemed paltry and insignificant. Somewhere around us, I felt Stinks must be smiling his gentle, almost child-like smile. Stinks had completed his formula, and it was safe.

We found Leopold Rosbad, Dictator of Troubania, standing like a soldier at the salute, facing the burning pyre.

"The *bon Dieu* has taken from us a great and true friend," he said simply. "And the *diable* a great enemy."

We could start again almost from scratch. Aunt Sophie looked a little rakish, but was practically sober.

I took her hand.

"Some day," she said, nodding solemnly, "somebody will get hurt in a fire like that."

"But how," I asked shakily, "did you three escape?"

Bobby looked more deceptively lazy than ever.

"That fellow Herwigler was a little careless when he came to collect us," he smiled.

The Real Dictator, too, was smiling. I laughed hysterically. So long as we kept Leopold Rosbad, Dictator of Troubania, safe for the destiny of mankind, Stinks had been glad to die, the Château had gladly died. Back to the soil of France had gone its delicate traceries, its playful turrets, its sweeping arches and gleaming steps. As I stared, to my dry-eyed fancy the crumbling stones still breathed life. A new life of accomplishment.

I knew it was not going to be easy, but with Suet Pudding out of the way, our future did seem to clear miraculously. We had to move quickly and stealthily in getting Leopold Rosbad to England, of course; but it would be rather fun now that there was no sunken-eyed bulk of Suet Pudding to bar our way.

I saw Bobby staring down the path. He made a quick grab at me. But he was too late. We were suddenly a feeble little party surrounded by *gendarmerie,* headed by M'sieur Labourd from the *Sûreté* in person. There was a feeling of satisfaction in M'sieur Labourd's eyes as they met Bobby's.

They clamped handcuffs on us—on Leopold Rosbad, on Bobby, on Aunt Sophie, on myself—and led us to a long black car waiting by the side of the road.

CHAPTER XXXI

ORANGE BLOSSOMS FROM HEAVEN

THE FALL OF THE BLOW was so sudden that it was some seconds before I summoned even enough courage to look at Bobby. It seemed like eavesdropping on something private and almost sacred. To my relief, his face was calm, calm as a rock.

The Dictator's head was sunk a little on his chest; his step was as confident as usual, but he appeared to be deep in thought. Both of them were walking like French aristocrats towards the black-nosed tumbril that waited for us. For the first time, I realised that we had collectively, as well as singly, accepted defeat. There was nothing we, or anybody else, could do about it. Suet Pudding might be dead, but his efficiency reached out beyond him. Almost with a groan of despair, the old Château settled down into its death ruins behind us. Our triumph had been so pitifully short-lived.

As though to add point to our destruction, a great black aeroplane droned up and hovered about us like a vulture. With an anticipatory tilt of its wings, it landed in the field close by.

An officer in the uniform of the German Air Force elegantly stepped out, and came towards us. No, there was no escape whichever way we turned. I stumbled on bitterly, my eyes aching with tears. After all, I preferred the car to the aeroplane. It was slower in reaching its destination. There might even be an accident on the way . . .

But the German was already almost upon us. Something impelled me to look at Bobby. His face was so utterly without expression that my heart missed a beat. It was the way he had looked when he had first decided that his home was no longer safe for us. It meant that he was about to try something desperate.

"Bobby!" I gulped—

He turned to me blue eyes that were actually sparkling. Then the blank mask dropped again. I could do nothing, nothing! In a minute, Bobby would be dead, or dying. But I no longer had difficulty in keeping the tears back. My eyes were dry and smarting as a desert. And I was proud; awfully proud. It was better to end fighting than to be led, like any animal, to the slaughter-house.

There was a gun in the German's hand.

I saw the grim, dark face as he saluted.

I saw that it was Pugg.

"I have instructions," said Pugg, "to take the prisoners straight to Paris by plane."

I saw Aunt Sophie turn slowly, saw her mouth open . . . Then she shut it.

"If you will be good enough to provide your escort," Pugg was saying. He was precise, arrogantly courteous. The man from the *Sûreté* frowned, but did not question that crisp German air of authority. Jonathan Walnutt, Esquire, had not failed. I had known he had courage, but never did I imagine he could show such cool artistry as this—or what must have gone before.

We commenced to walk towards the field.

Every hummock of rough earth over which we stumbled prodded at me with warning, with triumph. Pugg, who had not failed—Pugg, who was not dead, regulated our pace, casually, the gun glistening in his hand.

Inevitably, we were approaching the plane . . . Pugg was not dead . . .

Pugg, with the papers and uniform of the young German airman who had died in the lonely French cottage on the mountainside, had bluffed the authorities into letting him have a plane.

Now we were grouped round it.

Still with that air of authority, Pugg pushed us inside. Followed us.

The propeller whirred.

~ ~ ~ ~ ~

I married Pugg, of course.

Aunt Sophie is still confidently expecting the worst.

THE END

RAMBLE HOUSE's

HARRY STEPHEN KEELER WEBWORK MYSTERIES

(RH) indicates the title is available ONLY in the **RAMBLE HOUSE** edition

The Ace of Spades Murder
The Affair of the Bottled Deuce (RH)
The Amazing Web
The Barking Clock
Behind That Mask
The Book with the Orange Leaves
The Bottle with the Green Wax Seal
The Box from Japan
The Case of the Canny Killer
The Case of the Crazy Corpse (RH)
The Case of the Flying Hands (RH)
The Case of the Ivory Arrow
The Case of the Jeweled Ragpicker
The Case of the Lavender Gripsack
The Case of the Mysterious Moll
The Case of the 16 Beans
The Case of the Transparent Nude (RH)
The Case of the Transposed Legs
The Case of the Two-Headed Idiot (RH)
The Case of the Two Strange Ladies
The Circus Stealers (RH)
Cleopatra's Tears
A Copy of Beowulf (RH)
The Crimson Cube (RH)
The Face of the Man From Saturn
Find the Clock
The Five Silver Buddhas
The 4th King
The Gallows Waits, My Lord! (RH)
The Green Jade Hand
Finger! Finger!
Hangman's Nights (RH)
I, Chameleon (RH)
I Killed Lincoln at 10:13! (RH)
The Iron Ring
The Man Who Changed His Skin (RH)
The Man with the Crimson Box
The Man with the Magic Eardrums
The Man with the Wooden Spectacles
The Marceau Case
The Matilda Hunter Murder
The Monocled Monster
The Murder of London Lew
The Murdered Mathematician
The Mysterious Card (RH)
The Mysterious Ivory Ball of Wong Shing Li (RH)
The Mystery of the Fiddling Cracksman
The Peacock Fan
The Photo of Lady X (RH)
The Portrait of Jirjohn Cobb
Report on Vanessa Hewstone (RH)
Riddle of the Travelling Skull
Riddle of the Wooden Parrakeet (RH)
The Scarlet Mummy (RH)
The Search for X-Y-Z
The Sharkskin Book
Sing Sing Nights
The Six From Nowhere (RH)
The Skull of the Waltzing Clown
The Spectacles of Mr. Cagliostro
Stand By—London Calling!
The Steeltown Strangler
The Stolen Gravestone (RH)
Strange Journey (RH)
The Strange Will
The Straw Hat Murders (RH)
The Street of 1000 Eyes (RH)
Thieves' Nights
Three Novellos (RH)
The Tiger Snake
The Trap (RH)
Vagabond Nights (Defrauded Yeggman)
Vagabond Nights 2 (10 Hours)
The Vanishing Gold Truck
The Voice of the Seven Sparrows
The Washington Square Enigma
When Thief Meets Thief
The White Circle (RH)
The Wonderful Scheme of Mr. Christopher Thorne
X. Jones—of Scotland Yard
Y. Cheung, Business Detective

Keeler Related Works

A To Izzard: A Harry Stephen Keeler Companion by Fender Tucker — Articles and stories about Harry, by Harry, and in his style. Included is a compleat bibliography.

Wild About Harry: Reviews of Keeler Novels — Edited by Richard Polt & Fender Tucker — 22 reviews of works by Harry Stephen Keeler from *Keeler News.* A perfect introduction to the author.

The Keeler Keyhole Collection: Annotated newsletter rants from Harry Stephen Keeler, edited by Francis M. Nevins. Over 400 pages of incredibly personal Keeleriana.

Fakealoo — Pastiches of the style of Harry Stephen Keeler by selected demented members of the HSK Society. Updated every year with the new winner.

Strands of the Web: Short Stories of Harry Stephen Keeler — 29 stories, just about all that Keeler wrote, are edited and introduced by Fred Cleaver.

RAMBLE HOUSE's LOON SANCTUARY

A Clear Path to Cross — Sharon Knowles short mystery stories by Ed Lynskey.
A Jimmy Starr Omnibus — Three 40s novels by Jimmy Starr.
A Roland Daniel Double: The Signal and The Return of Wu Fang — Classic thrillers from the 30s.
A Shot Rang Out — Three decades of reviews and articles by today's Anthony Boucher, Jon Breen. An essential book for any mystery lover's library.
A Smell of Smoke — A 1951 English countryside thriller by Miles Burton.
A Snark Selection — Lewis Carroll's *The Hunting of the Snark* with two Snarkian chapters by Harry Stephen Keeler — Illustrated by Gavin L. O'Keefe.
A Young Man's Heart — A forgotten early classic by Cornell Woolrich.
Alexander Laing Novels — *The Motives of Nicholas Holtz* and *Dr. Scarlett*, stories of medical mayhem and intrigue from the 30s.
An Angel in the Street — Modern hardboiled noir by Peter Genovese.
Automaton — Brilliant treatise on robotics: 1928-style! By H. Stafford Hatfield.
Beast or Man? — A 1930 novel of racism and horror by Sean M'Guire. Introduced by John Pelan.
Black Hogan Strikes Again — Australia's Peter Renwick pens a tale of the 30s outback.
Black River Falls — Suspense from the master, Ed Gorman.
Blondy's Boy Friend — A snappy 1930 story by Philip Wylie, writing as Leatrice Homesley.
Blood in a Snap — The *Finnegan's Wake* of the 21st century, by Jim Weiler.
Blood Moon — The first of the Robert Payne series by Ed Gorman.
Chelsea Quinn Yarbro Novels featuring Charlie Moon — *Ogilvie, Tallant and Moon, Music When the Sweet Voice Dies, Poisonous Fruit* and *Dead Mice.* An Ojibwa detective in SF.
Cornucopia of Crime — Francis M. Nevins assembled this huge collection of his writings about crime literature and the people who write it. Essential for any serious mystery library.
Crimson Clown Novels — By Johnston McCulley, author of the Zorro novels, *The Crimson Clown* and *The Crimson Clown Again.*
Dago Red — 22 tales of dark suspense by Bill Pronzini.
David Hume Novels — *Corpses Never Argue, Cemetery First Stop, Make Way for the Mourners, Eternity Here I Come*. 1930s British hardboiled fiction with an attitude.
Dead Man Talks Too Much — Hollywood boozer by Weed Dickenson.
Death Leaves No Card — One of the most unusual murdered-in-the-tub mysteries you'll ever read. By Miles Burton.
Death March of the Dancing Dolls and Other Stories — Volume Three in the Day Keene in the Detective Pulps series. Introduced by Bill Crider.
Deep Space and other Stories — A collection of SF gems by Richard A. Lupoff.
Detective Duff Unravels It — Episodic mysteries by Harvey O'Higgins.
Dime Novels: Ramble House's 10-Cent Books — *Knife in the Dark* by Robert Leslie Bellem, *Hot Lead* and *Song of Death* by Ed Earl Repp, *A Hashish House in New York* by H.H. Kane, and five more.
Don Diablo: Book of a Lost Film — Two-volume treatment of a western by Paul Landres, with diagrams. Intro by Francis M. Nevins.
Dope and Swastikas — Two strange novels from 1922 by Edmund Snell
Dope Tales #1 — Two dope-riddled classics; *Dope Runners* by Gerald Grantham and *Death Takes the Joystick* by Phillip Condé.
Dope Tales #2 — Two more narco-classics; *The Invisible Hand* by Rex Dark and *The Smokers of Hashish* by Norman Berrow.
Dope Tales #3 — Two enchanting novels of opium by the master, Sax Rohmer. *Dope* and *The Yellow Claw.*
Double Hot — Two 60s softcore sex novels by Morris Hershman.
Dr. Odin — Douglas Newton's 1933 racial potboiler comes back to life.
Evidence in Blue — 1938 mystery by E. Charles Vivian.
Fatal Accident — Murder by automobile, a 1936 mystery by Cecil M. Wills.
Finger-prints Never Lie — A 1939 classic detective novel by John G. Brandon.

Freaks and Fantasies — Eerie tales by Tod Robbins, collaborator of Tod Browning on the film FREAKS.

Gadsby — A lipogram (a novel without the letter E). Ernest Vincent Wright's last work, published in 1939 right before his death.

Gelett Burgess Novels — *The Master of Mysteries, The White Cat, Two O'Clock Courage, Ladies in Boxes, Find the Woman, The Heart Line, The Picaroons* and *Lady Mechante*. All are introduced by Richard A. Lupoff who is singlehandedly bringing Burgess back to life.

Geronimo — S. M. Barrett's 1905 autobiography of a noble American.

Hake Talbot Novels — *Rim of the Pit, The Hangman's Handyman.* Classic locked room mysteries, with mapback covers by Gavin O'Keefe.

Hollywood Dreams — A novel of Tinsel Town and the Depression by Richard O'Brien.

I Stole $16,000,000 — A true story by cracksman Herbert E. Wilson.

Inclination to Murder — 1966 thriller by New Zealand's Harriet Hunter.

Invaders from the Dark — Classic werewolf tale from Greye La Spina.

J. Poindexter, Colored — Classic satirical black novel by Irvin S. Cobb.

Jack Mann Novels — Strange murder in the English countryside. *Gees' First Case, Nightmare Farm, Grey Shapes, The Ninth Life, The Glass Too Many.*

Jake Hardy — A lusty western tale from Wesley Tallant.

Jim Harmon Double Novels — *Vixen Hollow/Celluloid Scandal, The Man Who Made Maniacs/Silent Siren, Ape Rape/Wanton Witch, Sex Burns Like Fire/Twist Session, Sudden Lust/Passion Strip, Sin Unlimited/Harlot Master, Twilight Girls/Sex Institution.* Written in the early 60s and never reprinted until now.

Joel Townsley Rogers Novels and Short Stories — By the author of *The Red Right Hand: Once In a Red Moon, Lady With the Dice, The Stopped Clock, Never Leave My Bed.* Also two short story collections: *Night of Horror* and *Killing Time.*

Joseph Shallit Novels — *The Case of the Billion Dollar Body, Lady Don't Die on My Doorstep, Kiss the Killer, Yell Bloody Murder, Take Your Last Look.* One of America's best 50's authors and a favorite of author Bill Pronzini.

Keller Memento — 45 short stories of the amazing and weird by Dr. David Keller.

Killer's Caress — Cary Moran's 1936 hardboiled thriller.

League of the Grateful Dead and Other Stories — Volume One in the Day Keene in the Detective Pulps series. In the introduction John Pelan outlines his plans for republishing all of Day Keene's short stories from the pulps.

Man Out of Hell and Other Stories — Volume II of the John H. Knox weird pulps collection.

Marblehead: A Novel of H.P. Lovecraft — A long-lost masterpiece from Richard A. Lupoff. This is the "director's cut", the long version that has never been published before.

Master of Souls — Mark Hansom's 1937 shocker is introduced by weirdologist John Pelan.

Max Afford Novels — *Owl of Darkness, Death's Mannikins, Blood on His Hands, The Dead Are Blind, The Sheep and the Wolves, Sinners in Paradise* and *Two Locked Room Mysteries and a Ripping Yarn* by one of Australia's finest mystery novelists.

More Secret Adventures of Sherlock Holmes — Gary Lovisi's second collection of tales about the unknown sides of the great detective.

Muddled Mind: Complete Works of Ed Wood, Jr. — David Hayes and Hayden Davis deconstruct the life and works of the mad, but canny, genius.

Murder among the Nudists — A mystery from 1934 by Peter Hunt, featuring a naked Detective-Inspector going undercover in a nudist colony.

Murder in Black and White — 1931 classic tennis whodunit by Evelyn Elder.

Murder in Shawnee — Two novels of the Alleghenies by John Douglas: *Shawnee Alley Fire* and *Haunts.*

Murder in Silk — A 1937 Yellow Peril novel of the silk trade by Ralph Trevor.

My Deadly Angel — 1955 Cold War drama by John Chelton.

My First Time: The One Experience You Never Forget — Michael Birchwood — 64 true first-person narratives of how they lost it.

Mysterious Martin, the Master of Murder — Two versions of a strange 1912 novel by Tod Robbins about a man who writes books that can kill.

Norman Berrow Novels — *The Bishop's Sword, Ghost House, Don't Go Out After Dark, Claws of the Cougar, The Smokers of Hashish, The Secret Dancer, Don't Jump Mr. Boland!, The Footprints of Satan, Fingers for Ransom, The Three Tiers of Fantasy, The Spaniard's Thumb, The Eleventh Plague, Words Have Wings, One Thrilling Night, The Lady's in Danger, It Howls at Night, The Terror in the Fog, Oil Under the Window, Murder in the Melody, The Singing Room.* This is the complete Norman Berrow library of classic locked-room mysteries, several of which are masterpieces.

Old Times' Sake — Short stories by James Reasoner from Mike Shayne Magazine.

Perfect .38 — Two early Timothy Dane novels by William Ard. More to come.

Prose Bowl — Futuristic satire of a world where hack writing has replaced football as our national obsession, by Bill Pronzini and Barry N. Malzberg.

Red Light — The history of legal prostitution in Shreveport Louisiana by Eric Brock. Includes wonderful photos of the houses and the ladies.

Researching American-Made Toy Soldiers — A 276-page collection of a lifetime of articles by toy soldier expert Richard O'Brien.

Reunion in Hell — Volume One of the John H. Knox series of weird stories from the pulps. Introduced by horror expert John Pelan.

Ripped from the Headlines! — The Jack the Ripper story as told in the newspaper articles in the *New York* and *London Times.*

Robert Randisi Novels — *No Exit to Brooklyn* and *The Dead of Brooklyn*. The first two Nick Delvecchio novels.

Rough Cut & New, Improved Murder — Ed Gorman's first two novels.

Ruled By Radio — 1925 futuristic novel by Robert L. Hadfield & Frank E. Farncombe.

Rupert Penny Novels — *Policeman's Holiday, Policeman's Evidence, Lucky Policeman, Policeman in Armour, Sealed Room Murder, Sweet Poison, The Talkative Policeman, She had to Have Gas* and *Cut and Run* (by Martin Tanner.) Rupert Penny is the pseudonym of Australian Charles Thornett, a master of the locked room, impossible crime plot.

Sand's Game — Spectacular hard-boiled noir from Ennis Willie, edited by Lynn Myers and Stephen Mertz, with contributions from Max Allan Collins, Bill Crider, Wayne Dundee, Bill Pronzini, Gary Lovisi and James Reasoner.

Satan's Den Exposed — True crime in Truth or Consequences New Mexico — Award-winning journalism by the *Desert Journal.*

Gelett Burgess Novels — *The Master of Mysteries, The White Cat, Two O'Clock Courage, Ladies in Boxes, Find the Woman, The Heart Line, The Picaroons* and *Lady Mechante*. All are edited and introduced by Richard A. Lupoff.

Sam McCain Novels — Ed Gorman's terrific series includes *The Day the Music Died, Wake Up Little Susie* and *Will You Still Love Me Tomorrow?*

Sex Slave — Potboiler of lust in the days of Cleopatra by Dion Leclerq, 1966.

Shadows' Edge — Two early novels by Wade Wright: *Shadows Don't Bleed* and *The Sharp Edge.*

Sideslip — 1968 SF masterpiece by Ted White and Dave Van Arnam.

Slammer Days — Two full-length prison memoirs: *Men into Beasts* (1952) by George Sylvester Viereck and *Home Away From Home* (1962) by Jack Woodford.

Sorcerer's Chessmen — John Pelan introduces this 1939 classic by Mark Hansom.

Star Griffin — Michael Kurland's 1987 masterpiece of SF drollery is back.

Stakeout on Millennium Drive — Award-winning Indianapolis Noir by Ian Woollen.

Strands of the Web: Short Stories of Harry Stephen Keeler — Edited and Introduced by Fred Cleaver.

Suzy — A collection of comic strips by Richard O'Brien and Bob Vojtko from 1970.

Tales of the Macabre and Ordinary — Modern twisted horror by Chris Mikul, author of the *Bizarrism* series.

Tenebrae — Ernest G. Henham's 1898 horror tale brought back.

The Amorous Intrigues & Adventures of Aaron Burr — by Anonymous. Hot historical action about the man who almost became Emperor of Mexico.

The Anthony Boucher Chronicles — edited by Francis M. Nevins. Book reviews by Anthony Boucher written for the *San Francisco Chronicle,* 1942 – 1947. Essential and fascinating reading by the best book reviewer there ever was.

The Best of 10-Story Book — edited by Chris Mikul, over 35 stories from the literary magazine Harry Stephen Keeler edited.

The Black Dark Murders — Vintage 50s college murder yarn by Milt Ozaki, writing as Robert O. Saber.
The Book of Time — The classic novel by H.G. Wells is joined by sequels by Wells himself and three timely stories by Richard A. Lupoff. Lavishly illustrated by Gavin L. O'Keefe.
The Case of the Little Green Men — Mack Reynolds wrote this love song to sci-fi fans back in 1951 and it's now back in print.
The Case of the Withered Hand — 1936 potboiler by John G. Brandon.
The Charlie Chaplin Murder Mystery — A 2004 tribute by film scholar, Wes D. Gehring.
The Chinese Jar Mystery — Murder in the manor by John Stephen Strange, 1934.
The Compleat Calhoon — All of Fender Tucker's works: Includes *Totah Six-Pack, Weed, Women and Song* and *Tales from the Tower,* plus a CD of all of his songs.
The Compleat Ova Hamlet — Parodies of SF authors by Richard A. Lupoff. This is a brand new edition with more stories and more illustrations by Trina Robbins.
The Contested Earth and Other SF Stories — A never-before published space opera and seven short stories by Jim Harmon.
The Crimson Query — A 1929 thriller from Arlton Eadie. A perfect way to get introduced.
The Curse of Cantire — A classic 1939 novel of a family curse by Walter S. Masterman.
The Devil Drives — An odd prison and lost treasure novel from 1932 by Virgil Markham.
The Devil's Mistress — A 1915 Scottish gothic tale by J. W. Brodie-Innes, a member of Aleister Crowley's Golden Dawn.
The Dumpling — Political murder from 1907 by Coulson Kernahan.
The End of It All and Other Stories — Ed Gorman selected his favorite short stories for this huge collection.
The Fangs of Suet Pudding — A 1944 novel of the German invasion by Adams Farr
The Ghost of Gaston Revere — From 1935, a novel of life and beyond by Mark Hansom, introduced by John Pelan.
The Gold Star Line — Seaboard adventure from L.T. Reade and Robert Eustace.
The Golden Dagger — 1951 Scotland Yard yarn by E. R. Punshon.
The Hairbreadth Escapes of Major Mendax — Francis Blake Crofton's 1889 boys' book.
The House of the Vampire — 1907 poetic thriller by George S. Viereck.
The Incredible Adventures of Rowland Hern — Intriguing 1928 impossible crimes by Nicholas Olde.
The Julius Caesar Murder Case — A classic 1935 re-telling of the assassination by Wallace Irwin that's much more fun than the Shakespeare version.
The Koky Comics — A collection of all of the 1978-1981 Sunday and daily comic strips by Richard O'Brien and Mort Gerberg, in two volumes.
The Lady of the Terraces — 1925 missing race adventure by E. Charles Vivian.
The Lord of Terror — 1925 mystery with master-criminal, Fantômas.
The N. R. De Mexico Novels — Robert Bragg, the real N.R. de Mexico, presents *Marijuana Girl, Madman on a Drum, Private Chauffeur* in one volume.
The Night Remembers — A 1991 Jack Walsh mystery from Ed Gorman.
The One After Snelling — Kickass modern noir from Richard O'Brien.
The Organ Reader — A huge compilation of just about everything published in the 1971-1972 radical bay-area newspaper, *THE ORGAN*. A coffee table book that points out the shallowness of the coffee table mindset.
The Poker Club — Three in one! Ed Gorman's ground-breaking novel, the short story it was based upon, and the screenplay of the film made from it.
The Private Journal & Diary of John H. Surratt — The memoirs of the man who conspired to assassinate President Lincoln.
The Secret Adventures of Sherlock Holmes — Three Sherlockian pastiches by the Brooklyn author/publisher, Gary Lovisi.
The Shadow on the House — Mark Hansom's 1934 masterpiece of horror is introduced by John Pelan.
The Sign of the Scorpion — A 1935 Edmund Snell tale of oriental evil.

The Singular Problem of the Stygian House-Boat — Two classic tales by John Kendrick Bangs about the denizens of Hades.
The Smiling Corpse — Philip Wylie and Bernard Bergman's odd 1935 novel.
The Stench of Death: An Odoriferous Omnibus by Jack Moskovitz — Two complete novels and two novellas from 60's sleaze author, Jack Moskovitz.
The Time Armada — Fox B. Holden's 1953 SF gem.
The Tongueless Horror and Other Stories — Volume One of the series of short stories from the weird pulps by Wyatt Blassingame.
The Tracer of Lost Persons — From 1906, an episodic novel that became a hit radio series in the 30s. Introduced by Richard A. Lupoff.
The Trail of the Cloven Hoof — Diabolical horror from 1935 by Arlton Eadie. Introduced by John Pelan.
The Triune Man — Mindscrambling science fiction from Richard A. Lupoff.
The Universal Holmes — Richard A. Lupoff's 2007 collection of five Holmesian pastiches and a recipe for giant rat stew.
The Werewolf vs the Vampire Woman — Hard to believe ultraviolence by either Arthur M. Scarm or Arthur M. Scram.
The Whistling Ancestors — A 1936 classic of weirdness by Richard E. Goddard and introduced by John Pelan.
The White Peril in the Far East — Sidney Lewis Gulick's 1905 indictment of the West and assurance that Japan would never attack the U.S.
The Wizard of Berner's Abbey — A 1935 horror gem written by Mark Hansom and introduced by John Pelan.
Wade Wright Novels — *Echo of Fear, Death At Nostalgia Street*, *It Leads to Murder* and *Shadows' Edge*, a double book featuring *Shadows Don't Bleed* and *The Sharp Edge*.
Welsh Rarebit Tales — Charming stories from 1902 by Harle Oren Cummins
Through the Looking Glass — Lewis Carroll wrote it; Gavin L. O'Keefe illustrated it.
Time Line — Ramble House artist Gavin O'Keefe selects his most evocative art inspired by the twisted literature he reads and designs.
Tiresias — Psychotic modern horror novel by Jonathan M. Sweet.
Totah Six-Pack — Just Fender Tucker's six tales about Farmington in one sleek volume.
Trail of the Spirit Warrior — Roger Haley's historical saga of life in the Indian Territories.
Ultra-Boiled — 23 gut-wrenching tales by our Man in Brooklyn, Gary Lovisi.
Up Front From Behind — A 2011 satire of Wall Street by James B. Kobak.
Victims & Villains — Intriguing Sherlockiana from Derham Groves.
Walter S. Masterman Novels — *The Green Toad, The Flying Beast, The Yellow Mistletoe, The Wrong Verdict, The Perjured Alibi, The Border Line* and *The Curse of Cantire.* Masterman wrote horror and mystery, some introduced by John Pelan.
We Are the Dead and Other Stories — Volume Two in the Day Keene in the Detective Pulps series, introduced by Ed Gorman. When done, there may be as many as 11 in the series.
West Texas War and Other Western Stories — by Gary Lovisi.
Whip Dodge: Man Hunter — Wesley Tallant's saga of a bounty hunter of the old West.
You'll Die Laughing — Bruce Elliott's 1945 novel of murder at a practical joker's English countryside manor.

RAMBLE HOUSE
Fender Tucker, Prop. Gavin L. O'Keefe, Graphics
www.ramblehouse.com fender@ramblehouse.com
228-826-1783 10329 Sheephead Drive, Vancleave MS 39565

Made in the USA
Middletown, DE
21 July 2020